S0-CFR-164

Cold Spring

A Novel

BY

Scott Griffith

Cold Spring

© 2012 by Scott Griffith

ISBN 9781480097773
Library of Congress Control Number: 2012953429

All rights reserved. No part of this book may be reproduced or transmitted in any form or by any means, electronic or mechanical, including photocopying, recording or by any information storage or retrieval system without written permission from the author, except for inclusions of brief quotations in a review.

Printed in the United States of America
Cover and interior pages designed by SeaGrove Press
Edited by Ronald Thomas Rollet

SeaGrove Press
638 Sunset Blvd.
Cape May, NJ 08204

THIS BOOK IS DEDICATED TO THE MEMORY OF MY DECEASED WIFE, MARGARET EMILY CARR GRIFFITH, WHO NEEDLED ME EVERY DAY FROM THE MOMENT I PASSED THE BAR EXAMINATION TO GET BACK TO WRITING.

ACKNOWLEDGEMENTS

For the time he invested, for the editing, the encouragement and the professional technique he passed on, I want to thank Ronald Rollet, author of *Autumn Travels* and numerous other creative works in stage, film and print, and leader of our writers workshop group. The input of other group members, Richmond Shreve and Blair Seitz, was also critical, especially since they write in different genres and offer a fresh perspective. Richmond also provided the technical support I needed for working on my home computer.

John Sharp, retired FBI agent, provided background, especially on aeronautics. Finally, I must mention my college classmate Nancy Cahill, author of *Carpool*, who first told me how critical it was to join a writers group.

CHAPTER ONE

The driver knew the place.

He drove the limousine up the exit ramp, through the tollbooth, and turned south. The two-lane road wound along the bottom of a steep-banked valley. Hardwood trees flanked the shoulders in the colors of the season. Hunting season.

After a few miles, he turned onto an unpaved private road into the woods. The tires crunched on milled stone, and a regular rolling volley of gunfire echoed in the air a short distance ahead.

The driver had seen it all before, but his passenger in the back seat drew in a quick breath. He watched through the rear view mirror as the man scanned across the mountain landscape out the side window. He looked middle-aged, like most of the passengers on this trip, but seemed different—more over-weight, with a shrunken face, deep bags under the eyes, and red blood lines across his cheeks and nose. The face did not go with the large potbelly. And this guy had stepped right out of the airport already in camouflage and an orange safety vest. It was now almost noon. The driver figured his flight must have left Memphis pretty early. This guy was new; definitely different from most of the clients he brought out here. More polite, maybe—and with that Southern accent.

The passenger reached his hand into the camouflage jacket and pulled out a shiny metal flask. He took a short swig, grimaced, and replaced it.

"Ever been here before?" the driver asked.

"No. Heard a lot about it, though."

"Well, if you're invited here, you've arrived. Very private. You're sure to like it."

After a bend in the path, the lodge appeared in front of them, two-storied and half-timbered, with Tyrolean verge board under the eaves. The limousine pulled up in front and stopped.

The passenger got out. In the open, the gunshots rang out sharper and the air itself smelled of cordite. He inhaled, looked at the roof line of the lodge, and walked up the timber steps to the porch and through a pair of massive oak doors.

The driver popped open the trunk, removed a leather gun case, and followed his passenger into the lodge.

The registration desk spread across half the interior wall, some thirty feet from the door, and left of a wide two-landing staircase. Inside, the lodge breathed elegant silence, disturbed only by the gunfire outside and the passenger and driver shuffling across the floor. The driver dropped the case in front of the desk and stepped aside. The desk clerk looked up.

"Dennis Fancher," the passenger announced, a bit too loudly with his accent. He looked away from the desk clerk and surveyed the interior of the lodge. "Guest of Tom Gould," he added.

"Yes, Mr. Fancher. Mr. Gould is expecting you. He asked you to kindly wait for him in the lounge." The clerk motioned toward his right to the large open dining room with a cocktail bar on one end.

Fancher reached down for his gun case, but the clerk stopped him.

"We'll see to that," he said. He made a shooing gesture at the driver. "Mr. Gould said for you to wait in there."

The driver nodded and walked into a room behind the staircase.

Fancher went over to the bar. He took in the smell of fresh varnish and looked around. The ceiling vaulted two stories, with thick oak trellises. The walls were white pine—maybe local, Fancher thought—but the floor, he noticed, was red Georgia pine. The cocktail bar stretched across half the interior wall. The whole length of the lounge's outer wall was clear leaded glass from floor to ceiling, facing out to the firing range. The only other person in the lounge was the bartender.

Fancher took a stool and the bartender placed a paper napkin in front of him.

"Bourbon, rocks," Fancher said. The bartender filled a tumbler full of deep copper colored liquid and withdrew. Fancher took the glass and spun on the stool to take in the rest of the lounge. Heads of local game, deer and bear, hung on the walls. At the far end, by another interior wall, blue flames danced over iron logs in a walk-in fireplace.

Two men in boots and camouflage pants approached from across the room. One, wearing a wool sweater, Fancher recognized. Tom Gould. He was younger than Fancher, his hair still dark. The other, in a khaki shirt and taller than Gould, was a stranger. As he got close he seemed about Fancher's age, but lean, with graying hair and dark eyes.

Gould extended his hand.

"Dennis," he said. "So glad you could make it."

Fancher laid down his whiskey glass, slipped off the stool and wiped his palm on his pant leg.

"Wouldn't miss a chance to see this place, Tom." He looked at the other man and they shook hands in turn. "Dennis Fancher," he said.

"Bob Ingram. Glad to meet you." Fancher felt the man's hand. It was dry and hard and held his for several extra seconds, before releasing it. His dark eyes locked into Fancher's. Fancher jerked his own eyes up toward the ceiling.

"Quite a place, Tom. Think you get your money's worth, though?"

"I'm sure old man Bennett has," Gould said. "Picked it up after the war. Black money, you know. His son, George, will probably sell it off after the old man dies. Lot of capital tied up."

"I expect so." Fancher reached back for his drink. "What're you guys having?"

"Whatever you're having is fine with me. How about you, Bob?" Ingram nodded, keeping his eyes on Fancher who threw the last of his bourbon to the back of his throat and signaled the bartender for three more.

The other two men took up their glasses, sipped, and slid them away.

"So, Dennis," Gould said, "you want to talk business now or get in some shooting first?"

Fancher took a gulp and hitched up his pants. "Hell with business, Tom. Let's get in some shooting."

Gould signaled the desk clerk, who motioned to someone else, out of sight. "They'll bring our guns to the range for us," he said.

Outside, the three of them stepped up to the firing line, a white wooden fence with attached boxes holding loose 12-gauge shells. It faced a mountain wall covered with red and orange foliage. Gould and Ingram picked up streamlined camouflage shotguns and fed in the shells while Fancher watched.

"Sheeze, Tom, where'd you guys get those things?"

"Bob got them. Down in Virginia, right, Bob?"

"Yeah," Ingram said. "There's an outlet I use down there. I'll give you the number if you want, Dennis."

It sounded to Fancher that Ingram spoke with some accent he had not heard before, but, with the gunfire, he could not be sure. "Thanks," he said. "After lunch, okay?"

"You want to try one of these?" Ingram asked.

"Nah. I'll just stick with my old Winchester." Fancher started loading his own gun.

"We have guns here in the lodge you could have used, Dennis," Gould said. "Must have been hell getting that thing through the airport these days."

"Yeah, especially Pittsburgh. What're we shooting today?"

"Grouse. Raise them here."

Eight other shooters were already firing. The three men adjusted their ear protectors and, when they all finished loading, Gould waved at the blind, a seven-foot high earth embankment covered with brown grass. Three birds wobbled into the air from behind it. Fancher, Gould, and Ingram all fired. The birds exploded into clouds of feathers and fell to the ground. Three more fluttered up. The men fired again.

Behind the blind, teen-aged boys formed into teams in front of stacks of cages. The boys next to the cages opened them up and handed the grouse to the boys next to the embankment. At a signal from the firing line, they tossed the birds into the air, overhead, like footballs. Behind the cages, a stone service road curved along the mountainside and disappeared into the woods.

In the cages, the grouse fed on dried, drugged apples so the guests could make their quotas. Even so, many of the shots missed, and the grouse, unable to fly more than a few feet, plopped to the ground to be blasted into flinders by concentrated volley fire. Some dropped behind the blind and the boys picked them up and threw them back into the air. They tossed the empty cages aside in piles, while the Allegheny ridge absorbed the shots gone wild.

Fancher, Gould, and Ingram continued shooting after the others stopped. Standing amid a pile of spent shells, in little more than a half-hour they had bagged the lodge's daily limit. They emptied their guns, left them on the fence, and walked back into the lodge.

A command barked from a speaker on the exterior lodge wall. The boys rushed out from behind the blind. A pick-up truck rumbled down the service road and out into the space along the firing line. It stopped. The driver, a large man with a close military haircut, dropped down the gate to the truck bed. He crushed a lit cigarette under his boot and lit another before returning to the cab. Then he drove the truck slowly down the line. The boys followed on foot, picking up the slaughtered birds, wringing the necks of any still alive, and tossing them into the truck bed.

When they got them all, the driver took the truck back out the service road behind a fold in the mountain ridge. He backed the truck against a rusty iron incinerator, jerked it open, and fired it up. From the truck bed, he fed the birds in with a transfer shovel. When he finished, he climbed back down and used a garden hose to flush the feathers, gore, and feces off the truck bed, the shovel, and his boots. Then he drove the pick-up around to the front of the lodge, stopping behind the limousine. He went inside, stood by the reception desk, and looked into the dining lounge.

Gould led the other two men to a table by the fireplace, across the room from the bar where the other guests clustered. He waved at the guests and some waved back. He maneuvered Fancher into a chair with his back to the stone interior wall. He and Ingram took seats facing him, with their backs to the bar and the other guests.

"Have to tell you, Tom," Fancher said. "Say what you want about George's old man, he sure knows how to entertain. How the hell did he get this place past the shareholders and the IRS?"

Gould glanced to his side at Ingram. He leaned forward and spoke in low tones to Fancher. "You can look it up, Dennis. Internet, if you want. The old man's company, Tuscarora, has only one share of voting common, and he owns it. The rest is non-voting preferred. That's all George or anybody else has. And this place was all depreciated away sometime in the Seventies. Statute of limitations, you know? Employees?" he gestured behind him at the bartender, "all carried on the books as assembly line workers somewhere. I don't even know where myself."

"Well, how about the banks?"

"There aren't any banks. Old man doesn't believe in banks. Gave up on 'em. Too nosy. Says the government's his bank. Interest-free financing. Of course, if they did a competent job of auditing, they'd have a shit-fit. But they don't do that if you're sole source. Plus, of course, some of our guests here are generals. Maybe I'm saying too much," he added.

Fancher looked at Ingram who stared back. "So, that's why the paperwork you sent us looked different?" he asked.

A waiter arrived with the menus. They ordered another round of bourbons. Then Ingram got up and said, "I really should leave you guys alone for a bit. Business. Your own, I mean. Order me the New York strip, Tom. You know, Pittsburgh style."

Gould watched Ingram walk out of the lounge to the reception desk. Then he reached into his hip pocket and pulled out a folded sheet of yellow legal pad paper. It had a handwritten list of coded numbers down a column on the left side. He dropped it on the table.

"That's what we need," he said.

Fancher picked it up, scanned down the column, and snarled, "That's it?"

The waiter delivered the drinks and left. Fancher sipped on his and pushed the paper back across the table. "No can do, Tom. We went along before, but that list crosses the line. Those aren't rejects, like before."

The waiter returned with an order pad. "You first," Gould said.

Fancher put the menu down. "Oh, I don't know. What do you recommend, Tom?"

Gould smiled and spoke to the waiter. "Three New York strips, Pittsburgh style. And you better bring another round." He turned to Fancher and said, "You'll like that, Dennis. If it's all right with your heart, that is. I meant to ask, how's it going?"

"Doctor says everything's fine so long as I stay on the medication."

Fancher stared at the yellow paper and then over at the reception desk. He noticed Ingram holding a cell phone against his ear.

"He gave you that?"

"George did. But, yeah, he probably got it from him."

"What the fuck's he gonna do with that stuff?"

"I'm just a messenger boy, Dennis."

Fancher's grip tightened on crystal tumbler. "Look, Tom," he said, "I can't say yes or no to this. Bobby Adair and I never expected anything like this shit." He flicked the yellow paper with a finger and it spun faster. He glanced back at Ingram still at the reception desk. "Sure didn't expect nothing like that."

Gould kept silent for a moment. Then he leaned across the table. "This isn't gratuitous, you know, Dennis. There's a couple of million in it for you and Bobby."

"Couple of million?"

"Five each, actually."

"You put it in writing?"

Gould looked up at the ceiling and counted the cobwebs wafting off the crossbeams. "Right," he said. "And what're you going to do? Sue us? You know this all has to be verbal."

"Well," Fancher said, "I gotta talk to Bobby."

The steaks arrived. Gould picked up the paper and folded it back into his hip pocket. Ingram returned and they concentrated for a while on carving and chewing. Gould finally asked, "Ever had it like that, Dennis? Pittsburgh style?"

"No. Good, though."

After they finished and pushed their plates aside, Ingram asked, "Follow any football down there in Mississippi, Dennis?"

Fancher chuckled to himself—this guy's a fucking Californian or something. "Yeah, Ole Miss."

"How are they doing?"

"Okay. Probably make it to one of the bowls."

"Nothing in Pittsburgh this season," Gould said. "Not Pitt or the Steelers."

"So I hear. How about you?" Fancher asked Ingram. "You're from Washington, right? Follow the Redskins much?"

"No," Ingram said, "Not really."

The waiter came to clear the plates. Ingram's cell phone rang on his belt and he excused himself again.

When they were alone, Gould asked. "So, Dennis, what's the word?"

"I'll talk to Bobby like I said. But I don't like it. This all sounds like there's a lot more than money involved here. Politics. Whatever. And a lot more money than we ever talked about before. And whoever that guy is..."

"Money's all there is on our end," Gould said. "Nothing political. I told you what I know about the money. It all goes through Blue Mountain. You'll see it on the checks."

Fancher gave him a startled look. "Blue Mountain? What's that?"

Gould suddenly remembered Bobby Adair told him to keep some details from Dennis. "Just a separate corporation we set up to handle non-government business. Not your problem. Forget about it."

Fancher shook his head and seemed to let it drop. "But ten million. Shit, Tom, that won't even buy a shotgun if the FBI gets into this."

Gould saw Ingram was now talking to the pick-up truck driver by the reception desk. Ingram turned and they exchanged looks. Then Ingram walked behind the staircase. Fancher watched them both, then tried another sip of his bourbon, but it was gone.

"You angling for more, Dennis?" Gould asked.

"No," Fancher said. "I don't know. Maybe."

"We can show you how to shelter the money. You know, offshore."

"You can do that?"

"Sure."

Fancher twisted in his chair and looked out the window at the firing range and the red and orange leaves up the mountainside. "Well, I still gotta talk to Bobby first," he said.

Gould decided to change his tone and play one more card. "Look at me, Dennis," he said. Fancher did, with eyes starting to show the bourbon.

"You think you and Bobby own that plant down in Corinth, don't you?" He watched the watery eyes try to focus. "You don't own shit, Dennis. You own some pieces of paper that say they're share certificates. George holds the mortgage on that plant. You ever heard of Allegheny Factor?"

"Yeah. I mean, I guess so."

"That's George Bennett, Dennis. He holds liens on all your equipment, your receivables, your inventory, your building. He owns you lock, stock, and barrel. Have you pulled a D&B on yourself, Dennis? Bobby has. He knows. George owns you. He lets the two of you pretend to be entrepreneurs to shut up those assholes in the Defense Department. But he owns you. And you, my friend, are in default. You haven't made a mortgage payment for a year. Bobby tell you that? We can shut you down tomorrow."

Gould turned away from Fancher and saw Ingram reappear from behind the staircase. They nodded at each other.

Fancher's mouth dried up. He reached for his empty glass.

"You need a refill?" Gould asked, and waved two fingers at the bar. Ingram ordered two bourbons. After the bartender went away, he dropped the powder into one of them and shook it clear. He returned to the table and placed one of the glasses in front of Fancher and other by Gould, who left his untouched.

Fancher took a long gulp of the whiskey and said quietly, "Still gotta talk to Bobby first."

Ingram sat back down. "I just spoke to your limo driver, Dennis," he said. "If it's okay with you, I'll hitch a ride with you back to the airport. I have some time, though. Why don't we get our guns and go out in the woods, look for some small game?"

"We can do that here?" Fancher asked.

"Oh, yeah. It's all private," Gould said. "I have some other business, but I can get you a guide if you want."

Ingram got up. "Sounds good to me. Finish your drink, Dennis. Let's go."

Fancher drank the rest of his bourbon. Gould waved at the pick-up truck driver by the reception desk. "Take them out over Trail C," he said.

He watched them leave and trudge out along the mountain path past the blind. Then he took the two whiskey glasses back to the bar and gave them to the bartender. He waited while they dropped into the soapy dishpan under the bar. He greeted the other guests and went up the staircase to his room.

Thomas Gould, CFO, Blue Mountain Industries, waited. His receiver lay in the open attaché case on the second double bed. A fifth of Scotch on the night table was a quarter down. The receiver emitted four short beeps. Gould refilled his whiskey glass and punched on the audio.

"It's done," Ingram said. "Heart attack."

"Okay. Anything else?"

"Colovic made the 911 call after we were sure."

"The pick-up driver?"

"Yes. From my phone, out on the trail."

"And you'll dispose of that, right?"

"Yes. Somewhere between here and Pittsburgh."

"Anything more I need to know?"

"No. Now I'm out of here."

Gould turned it off, picked up the room phone and dialed. The voice on the other end said, "Bennett."

"I got the message. Ingram and his man just closed the deal."

"All right."

"I tried every angle to change his mind, but nothing worked."

"That's why Ingram had to be there with you."

Gould waited. "I didn't buy into anything like this, George. I know I got you into contact with Ingram and the others, the angels, but like I told Fancher, to me this was just about money."

"We'll talk about it when you get back here. Not over the phone."

"Okay, okay. What next?"

"Go down to Corinth. Make it clear to Bobby Adair what is expected of him. He told me he got Fancher to hold off on that letter until he talked to you. Did Dennis say anything about that in your meeting?"

"No. And I didn't ask. So, if he was going to send it, he won't now."

"He was going to turn, Tom. We did what we had to do. So, we bought some time, at least."

"When do I go to Corinth?"

"Tomorrow."

"Okay," Gould sighed.

Bennett waited, and then asked, "Tom, are you all right?"

"No. Of course not. I didn't expect anything like this."

"Had a few drinks?"

"What do you think? That guy Ingram scares the shit out of me."

"Sure. Well, rest up tonight. And hang in there, Tom. Couple more months, okay? Then we liquidate, and we're done with all of them."

Gould sank back down on the bed. Nothing more but to keep moving ahead. Cash out in three months, like George said. Then, head for the Caymans or something. Work on his golf game. Get a boat. Learn to sail. He dropped more ice into his glass and poured more Scotch.

Bennett made the call to Manhattan from his office on a private line he had installed a year ago. The voice answered in low, accented English.

"Milos?" George asked.

"Yes, George."

"We had to close part of our deal today."

"Ingram? Mississippi?"

"Yes."

"Will it cause any delay in delivery?"

"I don't think so. My treasurer is going down there to make sure."

"Thank you for keeping me informed. But, please, you should limit your contacts with Mr. Ingram if at all possible."

"He is out of reach right now. But you are the banker. You're what this is all about, for me."

"Yes. I am the banker. And there are some things I do not need to know."

"Yes, well this is all new to me. You know best. Tell your man in Africa anyway."

"Yes. And thank you, then, for your call."

The dial tone sounded in his ear and Bennett replaced the receiver.

He spun in his desk chair and looked out the window, over the point of land where the Monongahela and the Allegheny join to form the Ohio. The edge of a weather front dropped mist into the valley, over the flanking hills, and blurred the lights along the mountain ridges and riverbanks. But he saw none of this. Three months, he whispered. Three months. Then he'd be through with those angels Gould led him to. And, finally, free of his father and his father's old lawyer, Harlan Moan.

The call from Manhattan went out over the satellite to the old Portuguese fort on the East African Coast. Milos Vrenc conveyed the news. The possible problem with delivery he had reported earlier appeared to have been remedied.

"By Ingram," he said.

The Ossete assured him that the funds were available for transfer to Belgrade when further news arrived.

Ingram climbed into the limousine. The driver asked about his other passenger.

"He had a heart attack, I heard. I think the lodge called for an ambulance. Anyway, he won't be coming with us."

"Too bad," the driver said. "He didn't look too healthy to me."

The limousine pulled out over the stone pathway. They heard the distant wail of the sirens as they drove out onto the highway and back to the Turnpike.

CHAPTER TWO

Harry Bryce shifted and the gray metal chair groaned. He turned another page on the folder of documents on his gray metal desk. The furniture dated from World War II, maybe earlier. There was no other sound but the hum from his desktop computer and the clanking hot water pipes. Aside from him, the offices were empty. His chief, Kauffman, the "Professor" they called him, closed his Section of the Department of Justice at noon since it was the Friday before the Christmas holidays began.

One cardboard document box sat on the floor beside him. Twenty-two others sat sealed and stacked in the file room across the hall, crammed with more documents, he assumed, exactly like the ones on his desk. They arrived a few hours before, Bates-numbered and stamped "Property of Tuscarora Industries." All 23 of them delivered in response to a grand jury subpoena served in Pittsburgh in October and dropped in his office temporarily. Technically, the documents needed indexing by the paralegal, Barbara Shaw, before anyone else should touch them, but Bryce figured she was off partying somewhere along Eleventh Street. He had time so he picked out the box numbered 17 from the top of one of the stacks left by the UPS man, cut it open, and pulled out one of the thickest files. He did not expect to find any "hot" documents, but if they were there the legal defense team would have buried them in the middle of the submission. If they did exist and led to an actual indictment, he would get there following a trail through this mostly irrelevant paperwork now in front of him. It would take an insider, somebody he could turn with blind luck and leverage to lead him down the trail to relevance. It would take a while.

He opened his casebook, a three-ring binder on his desk next to the Tuscarora documents, and flipped past the Dun & Bradstreet report on the company's financial structure to the plastic protector containing the document that started the case: a handwritten, unsigned letter and envelope post-marked from the Memphis airport and sent to the FBI Field Office in Jackson, Mississippi. He read it again.

> I work in a subcontracting firm in Corinth, Mississippi. Our general contractor, Tuscarora Industries, has requested we divert some strategic Air Force equipment we are making to an exporter. I am an Air Force veteran. I think this is against the law, but I can't stop it from happening.

The Jackson Field office checked the Air Force and Defense Departments. They found one firm in Corinth with a record of some defense work but with no outstanding prime contracts. By coincidence they picked up a local obituary of one of its partners who died the same date as the letter's postmark of a heart attack while on a hunting trip in Pennsylvania. The obituary added that he was an Air Force veteran. But there were no recoverable fingerprints or handwriting samples to make a connection.

The Agent in Charge forwarded the file to D.O.D. fraud counsel in Birmingham and she sent it on to main Justice in Washington. When it arrived, Washington was in the middle of its annual budget battles and every section of the Justice Department was told to scramble for statistics. The Professor laid claim to the file, secured grand jury authority, then dumped it on Bryce's desk.

The whole thing was probably worthless, he thought. An anonymous informer like this could have a lot of motives to cost Tuscarora thousands of dollars in legal fees coping with a grand jury investigation. Or he could just be another conspiracy nut. Bryce had seen a lot of both. If the Professor asked Bryce's opinion first, he would have said preliminary investigation at most. But he'd only just arrived in Washington, so he wasn't asked. And now with the whole thing locked up in a grand jury, nobody could say anything for at least eighteen months even if a reporter or Congressman or White House staffer got wind of it.

At least Herrick, the Washington law firm representing Tuscarora in this matter, gathered, copied, stamped, and delivered right on schedule all the corporate documents without any pleadings in court. Bryce would do the same on his end. Follow the rules. Keep the record clean.

He closed his binder and pulled another file, one labeled

"Contracts," out of the document box. The first document was the Solicitation. The second was the Award—of what? He looked for the block on the Defense Department form that said what the contract was about—communication equipment of some kind, specified in military argot. This left him no clue what the contract was actually for, but he decided to copy the award page for his casebook.

Bryce took the document down the hall to the copier room. The corridor was Army green, streaked with old hand prints on the walls and a worn linoleum floor embedded with grime. He switched on the copy machine and waited for it to warm up. It gave off an ozone odor that mingled with the Clorox and rat poison left by the building maintenance staff that morning in quick preparation for the holidays.

Somebody hung a mirror on the wall years ago. He looked at himself. His eyes were clear, not red anymore, but his hairline was still receding. It drove him crazy. Whenever he met partners at big firms like Herrick they had healthy piles of hair even if graying, sometimes half way down to their eyebrows. Seemed like a law of nature.

Finally, the copier beeped. He made the copies and hit them with the three-hole punch. Back in his office, he returned the contract file to the box for Barbara Shaw's official inventory. He put the copies in his casebook, highlighting the contract number and date. Maybe relevant someday, but right now, mute as a stone. At most, circumstantial, but it kept his own record clear.

He sat back down in the complaining chair, breathed deeply, and dialed the number he had been putting off. He hoped he could just leave a message.

"Hello." That familiar voice.

"Maureen. Harry here. Merry Christmas."

"Same to you." Familiar voice. Flat, cold.

"Can I speak to Tess?"

"I'll put her on."

Through the receiver, Bryce heard her call out, "Tess. Come to the phone. It's your father."

Father, not Daddy. He could hear his daughter's running steps.

"Daddy," she said. "Daddy, when are you coming for me?"

"Tomorrow, Gorgeous. Merry Christmas."

"I miss you, Daddy."

He clenched his teeth. "I miss you, too, Baby." He listened to her puffs. "Do you have the Christmas tree up and everything?"

"Yes. I helped decorate it, too. It's beautiful."

"I look forward to seeing it." Bryce took a breath and paused again. "Are you all packed?" He did not want to spend any more time than necessary there with his ex-wife.

"Yes. And I did it all myself. I'll be all ready when you get here."

"Good. Now remember, go to bed early so Santa doesn't miss the house."

"Oh, Daddy, this isn't Christmas Eve. That's tomorrow, remember?"

"Oh, right. Well, then we'll bring your presents to Gramma and Grampa's."

"And be sure we leave cookies for him, Daddy."

"We will. Now remember, I come for you tomorrow and then we go to Gramma and Grampa's."

"I know. I know."

Another pause. "I miss you, Tess. Always remember that."

"I will, Daddy."

Bryce exhaled. "Okay, Gorgeous. See you tomorrow. Can you put your Mommy back on the line?"

"Yes," Maureen said immediately, just as he expected.

"I'll be there by late morning. Elevenish. I'm staying in Washington tonight and it's a good three-hour drive depending on traffic."

"Partying tonight." Still no question. Still flat and cold.

"Working. Errands."

"Sure."

"Eleven at the latest, Maureen. Can you put Tess back on?"

"Daddy?" Immediate again.

"I told your mother I'll be there about eleven."

"Okay."

"So bring your presents, and then we go to Gramma and Grampa's for more presents."

"What did you get me, Daddy?"

The panic hit him. Presents. How many? What? "That's a secret, Tess. You know that. You find out Christmas morning."

His daughter said nothing. He listened to her tiny puffs of breath. "Well," he said. "See you tomorrow morning. Be sure to get to bed early."

"You, too, Daddy."

"Okay. Good-bye, Baby. I love you."

He let the line go dead, then hung up. He sat back, listening to the sound, like industrious honeybees, of the computer. First Christmas away from home. First one with no women around to remind him about family chores like presents and the cards. He had forgotten them, too.

The U.S. Attorney in Philadelphia "suggested" he go into rehab after the second D.U.I. He went to one in Florida for a month. While there he was served with the divorce papers. When he came back he found himself transferred to Washington, to the Professor's unit. His father arranged it. They were old associates, and Bryce knew not to object. But before beginning his new job, his father packed him off to the shore for another month of R&R. Then, while down there on the beach, his father and Professor Kauffman both ordered him to make the divorce case go away. So he settled with Maureen, leaving her the house and Tess, keeping only his seven-year-old Honda, his clothes, and his law books—plus an unsecured loan for all the legal fees. At least Bryce still had a regular government paycheck. His father made sure of that. The only thing he bargained for was visitation rights.

Separation from Tess was the worst part, and he accepted the blame. He loved holding her, reading to her in bed at night and making up stories about Princess Tess. She said she missed that, too, and it was a big part of their visits. She always asked why he didn't live with her and her mother, but he could not talk about it to her. Or anybody else for that matter. Maybe when she was older he would answer her. But for now, he just did not want her to think it was her fault. He wondered what, if anything, Maureen told her, but he never asked, just saw his daughter in strict accordance with the court order, weekends once a month and stipulated holidays. But he did call her every Sunday evening from his apartment in Maryland.

He looked at his watch—three o'clock. He put on his overcoat and ran up the street to the department store. It was decorated for the season, lights and plastic evergreens, with the store speakers ringing out "Jingle Bells." The first floor was filled with confused men just like him.

He ran to the jewelry store first. Three presents: mother, sister, and daughter. Next, to the book department: something to read to Tess. Next, the toy department, education section: chess set with Disney characters. Next, cards. He got enough. Like the other men, he had customer service wrap everything.

He left finally with a large bag full of gifts, reminding himself to stop at a liquor store for some discount wine for his mother. Back in the office, he dropped the presents by the door. Not quite four o'clock. He started gathering the case files littered across his desk to lock up in a drawer.

The telephone rang and he answered.

"Uh, Harry Bryce?" It was a man's voice and Harry could hear ice clinking in a glass through the receiver. The sound still set his nerves on edge. Does that feeling ever go away, he wondered?

"Speaking."

"Department of Justice?"

"Yes. Who is this?"

"Glad I caught you, Mr. Bryce. My name is Harlan Moan. I'm an attorney in Pittsburgh."

"Yes?"

"I have a client I'd like to have speak with you."

"About what?"

"Tuscarora Industries."

Bryce shoved the lose papers aside to clear a legal pad. He wrote, 12-23 @4 P.M. Harlan Moan (ph) re: Tuscarora.

"You on the defense committee?"

"I represent only my client." The voice came through a bit arch.

"I know that, but are you on the defense committee? I mean, talking to Herrick?"

"No. And I am accepting no fee in this matter. This is pro bono."

Bryce waited. He noticed for the first time the voice sounded a bit elderly. Maybe somebody's uncle. Finally, the voice said, "My client will not be debriefed by the Herrick firm, if that's what you are asking, Mr. Bryce."

"Who's your client, then."

"Later. You will learn that if we can agree to a meeting."

"What's he got?"

The ice clinked again in the unseen glass. "Let me put it this way. May I call you Harry?"

"Sure."

"Thank you. Let me put it this way, Harry. My client has information that will, I believe, advance your investigation."

"Information? Or evidence?"

"Well, both, actually. Direct and indirect."

"Documents?"

"Some, yes."

"Admissions?"

"Uh, well, yes. They'll need to be put in context, of course."

"By?"

"Principals in Tuscarora. Officers."

"Any of it recorded? Tape?"

"No, unfortunately. All this happened very quickly. For my client, at least."

Bryce assumed the client had a conflict, maybe was fired, but decided not to open the subject for now. "Okay, what do you want from me?"

"Immunity. Letter immunity would be preferable, under the circumstances, as you will come to appreciate."

So, Moan knew the procedures. "Why?" Bryce asked.

"When you hear the evidence—or, rather, I should say information—when you hear it, I think you will agree it is the best way to proceed for now. I mean not to process a clearance request." Bryce waited and finally Moan added, "I worked for the Department, Harry. Many years ago, of course, and I haven't done much criminal work since then, but some things never change."

Bryce put down his pen and decided, again, not to pursue Moan's opening. "I'll need a proffer before I can give you anything. You must know that."

"First of all, Harry, my client is not in any way personally culpable, to my knowledge. The immunity request is entirely on my advice."

"Well, then, you know I'm in the evidence buying business. Tell me what you've got."

The voice on the telephone line exhaled and the ice cubes chuckled. "Okay. First of all, there were documents called for by your subpoena that were not produced."

Bryce picked up his pen again. "On whose instructions? Herrick's?"

"No."

"Were they removed or destroyed?"

"Removed."

"Then there will be gaps in the Bates numbers. The Herrick firm will have some questions to answer."

"My client can explain how they by-passed the lawyers."

"They?"

"George Bennett and Tom Gould."

Bryce flipped open the case file binder to his list of Cast of Characters. Bennett he knew about, but the name Gould appeared nowhere. "What kind of documents?"

"My client can explain that. Also, offshore contacts. East Africa. Some through New York and other U.S. contacts."

"Private or government?"

"More like tribal, it seems to me. Former Soviet Union stuff."

Another opening too big to pursue this late in the afternoon, Bryce thought. "So, what's your client got to say about all that?"

"Later, in the proffer interview, if we reach an understanding."

"How many documents are you talking about?"

"Red-rope envelope full."

"Originals?"

"Of course."

"What's his position in the company?"

"Let's just say upper management."

Bryce put down his pen. This was the end of note taking for a while.

"So, is immunity in the picture?" Moan asked.

"I'll have to take the proffer interview with your client, in person. Then clear it with my Section Chief, at least."

Moan interrupted, "That's Winston Kauffman?"

"Yes. You know him?"

"Let's just say I know the name. Look, I want to keep this between the two of us for the time being."

"No can do. You just said your client's in upper management. I don't have authority to grant informal immunity to someone in that position."

"That makes it sound like a deal breaker."

"Why?"

"My client and I have fears that there are some leaks in the Department in this case. Also, and this is important in my client's mind, there is a suspicion of murder. I would call it a suspicious heart attack, at most, but it is part of my client's motivation in coming forward. No real proof, but it makes this more than just a matter of job security to my client."

"Who? I mean the heart attack?"

"A subcontractor. My client can tell you about it."

Bryce flipped back to the file from Jackson, Mississippi. "Subcontractor where?"

"I don't have my notes in front of me."

Bryce closed the case file again. "It sounds like, from your client's point of view at least, you took a bit of a risk in contacting me. By phone and all."

"I did some checking, Harry. I know your office is not in Main Justice. I know you are a recent transfer to Washington. And I guess, from my time back there, your office is pretty empty right now. Mine is."

"You guessed right on that." Bryce wondered what else Moan had checked into about him. "Okay, Mr. Moan. You probably know I suspect your client is nuts, but where do we go from here?"

"Yes, Harry. I've dealt with my share of nuts, too, and not just in Washington. But I have good reason to know my client is not one of them. So, what protection can you offer me—I mean, my client?"

"With your conditions, Queen-for-a-Day."

"I think I get it," Moan said, "but it has to be in Pittsburgh. In my law office, not the Federal Courthouse. And we have to do it as soon as possible, not after New Years. You will learn why from my client. And just you. No co-counsel or paralegal."

"Well, obviously we can't do it tomorrow."

"How about Monday. The twenty-sixth?"

"I was planning to take some time off. At least until the first of the year."

"It will only require a couple of hours. It will be worth it, I assure you."

"All right. I'll fly out to Pittsburgh on the twenty-sixth. I'll call you from the airport when I land." Bryce jotted down Moan's address and telephone number. "I'll bring a duces for the documents."

"You won't need it, but okay, good. That'll keep the record clear for both of us, and for my client, of course." Bryce listened to the ice again. "Harry," Moan said at last, after what sounded like a swallow of whiskey, "my gut instinct is that this is not a run-of-the-mill contract fraud case like I handled back there years ago."

"I gathered. But if your client suspects murder, why not just go to the U.S. Attorney out there?"

"Well, Pittsburgh is a small town when it comes to this kind of thing. Everybody knows everybody. Tuscaora is fairly prominent out here. You've got grand jury jurisdiction in Pittsburgh and I thought that's best for my client right now." Moan said nothing more and rang off.

Bryce pulled the subpoena form up on his computer screen, then had another thought. He turned it off and walked out to the typing pool. He got a paper subpoena form, sat at a secretary's desk with a manual typewriter, and typed in the blank space, "All documents relating or referring to Tuscarora Industries, Inc.," with a date for the next scheduled grand jury session, in January. Back in his office, he pulled up the forms for letter recipient and Queen-for-a-Day and hit print, without filling in any of the blanks. He got out a wallet folder and loaded it with the subpoena, the letters, his note pad with the information from Harlan Moan, and the case file ring binder. The subpoena was the first thing he had done off-book since transferring to Washington. It came from his gut, like Moan had said. Then, for the record, he called Professor Kauffman.

"Go home, Harry," the Professor said. "I closed the office five hours ago."

"Something just developed in the Tuscarora case. We need to talk."

"What is it?"

"Informant. Maybe."

"Come on over, then."

Bryce took the wallet folder, went back outside, and walked down to Pennsylvania Avenue. He showed his ID to the guards in Main Justice and took the elevator to the third floor. Like most of the building this afternoon, the corridor to Kauffman's office was empty. The slapping sound from his shoes hitting the marble floor echoed off the marble walls. Half the ceiling lights were off, leaving the hallway pierced in long, angled shadows. No lights shone through the office doors on the way, but one did through the Professor's door. The secretary was gone from the outside alcove. Bryce walked into the inner office and closed the door behind him.

The Professor sat in a high-backed Naugahyde chair, between a scratched mahogany desk in front and a scratched credenza behind him with a desktop computer, with a dead screen. It had National and Department flags on poles on each flank. Kauffman was looking down, writing by hand on a legal pad with a jeweled fountain pen. Behind him was a framed photograph of his wife and a new gift pen set. Since his return to Washington, he had covered the office walls again with framed degrees and awards and prints of eighteenth century naval battles.

Bryce sat in the low-backed chair in front of the desk and looked briefly through the window behind his boss, past the ornamental iron bars to the gray stones of the Second Empire building across the block, until the Professor put down his pen.

He glanced up at Bryce over the top of his half-rimmed glasses.

"Well?" he asked.

"Could be a break. Could be a nut."

Kauffman steepled his index fingers on his upper lip. He arched his thin eyebrows over the glasses.

"Rather early, is it not? You haven't even issued ad tests yet, have you?"

"No. The documents just came in today. But you never know when somebody gets religion."

"Or why."

Kauffman swiveled in his chair and looked away from Bryce

to his print of the Battle of Pondicherry. He assigned the case to Bryce after obtaining grand jury authority and when his transfer to Washington became official. Getting the authority had been a bit difficult. There were discrete inquiries from the State and Defense Departments, from the Pennsylvania Congressional delegation, and from the White House. They all passed through the Deputy Assistant Attorney General, Pickering Thayer, and Thayer ordered Kauffman to keep him current with any developments. In fact, Thayer had repeated the request to him that morning. He waited for Bryce to volunteer more details.

"I just got off the phone with a lawyer in Pittsburgh," Bryce said at last. "He claims to represent somebody in upper management. Wouldn't say who." He opened the folder on his lap and looked down at his notes. "Lawyer's name is Harlan Moan. Claims his client has documents withheld from the grand jury. Claims he can tell us something about Tuscarora's off-shore dealings, like those mentioned in the anonymous note, I guess."

Kauffman stared out his window. "Did he say anything about the Caucasus?"

Bryce referred down to his notes. "He said East Africa, tribalism, and New York."

"How about Cold War, any of that?"

"He mentioned something about the old Soviet Union. His client thinks there are leaks about the case in Justice. I agreed to do a Queen-for-a-Day, so he doesn't have to worry about clearance." Bryce waited for more from Kauffman, but got nothing. "I thought I had to report it to you, anyway. And, like I said, probably just another nut case."

"Yes. Best to keep it out of the system this early. Anything about the source's motive for coming forward now?"

"To avoid possible obstruction charges, I assumed, but he, Moan, I mean, said his client is suspicious about somebody who died of a heart attack recently. Moan didn't sound like he bought that himself, but he indicated it was at least part of the motive for coming forward."

Kauffman finally turned around and relaxed into a slight grin. Bryce returned it. "So, when is your meeting?" he asked.

"Day after Christmas. In Pittsburgh. I'll fly out of Philly. No overnight."

"Pittsburgh?"

"Yeah. He said he wanted to do it in his law office. And just me, he said. Nobody else from the office."

"I see." Kauffman picked up his pen again. "So, we can assume all that talk about Department leaks is at least sincere. Are you optimistic?"

"I've learned never to be."

"Good."

Bryce got up to leave, but the Professor, still looking down and jotting on his pad, waved him back. "Stay just a minute, Harry. I have been directed to report developments in this case to the DAAG. Congress, you know." He hit the speakerphone on his desk.

"Thayer," it answered.

"Hi, Pick. Win Kauffman here. I've got Harry Bryce with me. You know, the lead counsel in the Tuscarora case we spoke about this morning."

"Hello, Harry," the speaker voice said.

"Hello, Mr. Thayer."

"Harry just told me we might have a break in the case." Kauffman spoke louder into the speaker than he did to Bryce, leaning in toward it. "He says he's not optimistic, and I know you don't need to hear all the details. Actually, there isn't much anyway, but you asked me to keep you posted."

"Glad to hear that, Win. What kind of break?"

The Professor peered up at Bryce, but Bryce stayed quiet, his face a bureaucratic cipher. A flurry of air from somewhere inside the building rustled the flags and the water pipes belched a low complaint.

"Harry's been contacted by an informant, or actually, a lawyer claiming to represent one." Kauffman's eyes flicked a question at Bryce, and this time he nodded. "Harry's arranged a meeting."

Nothing came back through the speaker for a moment, but finally Thayer asked, "What's he got to offer?"

"Harry's still in negotiations." Kauffman kept the query in his eyes and Bryce nodded again.

"Anybody we know? The lawyer, I mean."

"Somebody in Pittsburgh. Like I said, Harry doesn't expect much from it."

"Sure," Thayer said. "Well, I understand you have to follow up on all your leads. When are you meeting with them, Harry? Here in Washington, I assume."

Bryce leaned toward the speaker, but Kauffman held up his palm and stopped him. "Those are details we should not get into at this stage, Pick. After Christmas, of course. That's all."

"Yes, of course," Thayer said. "Still mastering all these protocols down here. Well, good luck, Harry. Bring back a scalp. And Win, thanks for keeping me informed."

Kauffman clicked off the line. He bit his lower lip before looking back at Bryce. He extended his hand, but did not rise from his chair. "And good luck to you, Harry. Give my holiday greetings to your father. And to the rest of your family."

Bryce got up, started out, and then stopped at the inner door before opening it. "Can you explain any of that?" he asked.

"Nothing to explain. Pick asked for a briefing this morning, and he just got one."

"That wasn't much of one."

"Sufficient for the purpose, which is to cover all our backsides with the politicians. For the record. But without any record. Except both of us as witnesses."

Bryce knew that was all the answer he would get. "By the way," he said. "That lawyer, Harlan Moan, mentioned that he worked in the Department years ago. Said he remembered your name. You know him by any chance?"

"Does sound familiar. There's a Martindale's in Mrs. Williams' office out there. Take a look."

Bryce did and poked his head back through the door. "He's in there. Pittsburgh all right. Says emeritus."

Kauffman waved a sign of dismissal and Bryce left. When Kauffman heard the footsteps far down the corridor, he ripped the top sheet off his legal pad, wadded it into a ball, and aimed it at the trash can, but stopped. He crammed it into his vest pocket, instead. He checked to make sure the speaker was off and the outside door was closed before he picked up the receiver and dialed a nine-digit number.

"O'Shea," Kauffman said, "are you, what do they call it, texting? Or blogging? Is that it? I can hear you tapping away in the background. You told me it's not secure enough yet. Those targets might pick you up."

O'Shea was only two years from retirement, or at least he hoped so, and the FBI had already confined him to background checks and security clearances when the Professor latched on to him. Kauffman got him transferred to his Section on special assignment and set him up in his home in the suburbs, with all the technology the Professor could get his hands on, tied to the Section by internet, beeper, and fax.

"That's the idea, you told me," O'Shea said. "So I'd look like some teenage hacker to them. What's up?"

"We may have to meet again in Philadelphia. In the Solarium. In a few days."

"Oh?"

"Harry's had a contact with Harlan Moan who claims to represent a possible informant. Assign al-Fasi and Aziz to tail Harry Bryce for the next four days."

"Starting when?"

"Right now. From his office. He's on his way back there now."

"Harry's a bad guy?"

"No, but he might be tailed by one."

"Weapons? Other than official, I mean?"

"Just official. And official ID. No indication of any major security issues so far. Tell them they'll have to follow him to Philadelphia. Then to Pittsburgh. Use that machinery of yours to get his flight schedule."

"Will do."

"After they get back, we'll have a meeting on Spruce Street."

"Been over a year now. You still have that place, huh?"

"Of course."

The call ended. Kauffman cleared the papers and the blank legal pad off his desk, put them in his brief case, and left for the short commute back to Georgetown.

Thayer waited until he reached the grass in front of the National Gallery of Art and stood in the middle of hundreds of tourists before making the call. When he finished, he started back to Main Justice looking for the best place to trash the cell phone on the way.

CHAPTER THREE

Back in his office, Bryce booked a round trip flight from Philadelphia to Pittsburgh and printed out the confirmation. He tried calling the number he had for Harlan Moan to confirm the meeting and time. A taped voice told him to leave a message and Bryce did and hung up. He put the travel documents with his notes and the rest of the file in his briefcase.

He started to draft a memorandum of Moan's call, but stopped with his fingers over the keyboard. He remembered the Professor's comment about being too early to put it in the Department's system. He logged off and shut down the computer. He looked out his office window at the beads of cold dew forming on gray concrete blocks on the building across the street. It was late. He would write it at home. He shut the briefcase, spun the locks and got up to leave.

The lights in the outer corridor snapped back on. He heard footsteps coming down the hall. Barbara Shaw stopped and framed herself in his office door.

"Harry," she said, "what are you still doing here?"

"Just a few last minute things." He took his raincoat off the rack and put it on. "What about you?"

"I just remembered I had to pick up a few things for my trip I left on my desk."

Bryce recognized her winter coat, but otherwise she looked different. Under the coat he could see she wore a knee-length black party dress. She had on large earrings, larger than the ones she wore at work, and heavier mascara, and her hair, always tied back in a bun when on the job, flowed around her shoulders. Before this, in the office, she came across to him as professional, in appearance prim, or maybe handsome. Now, she was actually attractive.

She looked at the box on the floor by his desk . "What's that?" she asked.

"Tuscarora. The documents came this afternoon."

She shot him a disapproving look. "I have to inventory those before you start rooting through it. Hope you kept it all in order."

"You won't get to it until after New Years. You're going—where is it, the Caymans—for a couple of weeks?"

"Yes. So, find anything hot in there?"

"No, but while I was at it, I got a call from a lawyer. Claims to have a client who got religion. I'm meeting them after Christmas."

"Oh. A break, huh? Well, take that box back to the file room before you leave." She walked down the hall to her own office and after a few minutes called out, "Say, Harry, are you leaving now? Can you give me a ride?"

Bryce went into the corridor holding his briefcase. "Sure. Where to?"

She hurried back, closing her coat around her dress. "A party. It's just out Ninth Street about a mile. My car's in the shop."

She maneuvered behind him to flip off the lights in his office, taking a moment to scan his desktop. "The box, remember?" she said.

Bryce took it back across the hall and returned for his briefcase. She looked at it and asked, "What are you doing? Taking work home for the holidays?"

"Oh, it's for that meeting I told you about."

He picked up his bag of Christmas gifts from the reception area on their way out. In the elevator, Barbara thanked him for the ride and held her arms around the coat, keeping it tight over her knees. When they reached the parking lot, Bryce let her into the passenger side of his gray Honda and apologized for the papers and dust on the seat and dash. Shaw watched through the rear view mirror while he dropped the briefcase and gift bag in the trunk.

On Ninth Street Bryce slowed down and stopped in front of a liquor store. He told her he promised his mother he'd pick up some wine, but at the door, he hesitated and turned back. Before getting into the Honda he saw a black Dodge Challenger with heavily tinted windows drive past.

"No wine?" she asked.

"I'd rather try another place," he said. "Better selection."

He kept a block behind the Challenger as they continued out Ninth Street.

After ten or fifteen minutes, Barbara directed him to turn right onto a residential street. Shaw pointed to the party house on the next corner and Bryce stopped. It was the only single house in sight, a three-story brownstone, with the first floor lights shining.

"Why don't you join me?" she asked.

"I don't know if I should. Thanks, anyway."

"Oh, come on, Harry. It's a chance to meet some people. Besides, it's better for me not to be a single all the time. I think they'll all be couples."

"All right. But I can't stay long. Where do I park?"

She guided him around the corner and down Eighth Street. They came back to the house, mounted the front marble steps and Bryce raised the brass doorknocker. The door opened.

"Harry Bryce!" the host said with a wide grin. "Barbara."

"Gideon?" Harry paused and looked questioningly at Barbara, but Gideon Aubrey quickly swept them both inside. They stood in a foyer in front of two equal sized formal rooms. The room to the left had a long table covered with bottles and a bartender behind it. A half-dozen young couples were in there chatting amid low baroque chamber music. The room to the right was empty except for two caterers arranging food on another long table.

"Barbara," Gideon said to them, "how surprising of you to bring Harry." He switched his wine glass to his left hand, wiped his right palm on his pants and extended it to Harry. They shook and Harry found the palm still damp.

"Surprising to me, too, Gideon. She didn't tell me this was your party."

"I wasn't aware you knew each other," Shaw said.

"We were classmates in law school," Bryce said. "First year. You went off into tax, wasn't it, Gideon?"

"Yes. And we had a professional contact a few years ago up in Philly. One of my corporate clients. But no indictment, right, Harry?"

"Right." Bryce scanned the inside of the townhouse. In all three rooms, the floor and ceiling molding had been stripped and stained. The walls and ceilings were painted uniform white with no tint; blue track lights ran along the walls. The oak floor framed Bokhara carpets in the center. The furniture was right-angled, wooden and Scandinavian.

"Nice place, Gideon," he said. "Looks like you had a lot of work done to it."

"Oh, yes. It was a funeral home. Got a good deal on the price, but it took almost two years to gut it all out. Five or six contractors. You cannot imagine what that's like in Washington. I'm not quite ready for Georgetown. Not yet, at least. That over there," he pointed to the room with the caterers, "was where they had the viewings. And that," he pointed at the wine table and bartender, "was the reception area. Let me have your coats." He led them into the room with the wine and took the coats through a door in the back. When he returned, he called for the guests' attention.

"Everybody, this is Harry Bryce. One of my law school classmates, many, many years ago now. Still with Justice, I think. Right, Harry?" Bryce nodded. "And you all know Barbara. She's with Harry. I'll let you introduce yourselves." Gideon turned back to them. "So, Harry, I have to ask. What are you doing in D.C. this time of the year? How do you know Barbara?"

"I got transferred down here last August, officially. I spent most of August on the beach, so I didn't really settle in here until September. Barbara's one of our paralegals."

"I know she works there. It is wonderful that the two of you work together and got to meet. You don't know very many people in town yet, I guess, outside the office."

"That's about it. How about you? Still with the Herrick firm?"

"Oh yes. Same old, same old. Well, in here there're some new people for you to get to know. Just mingle. Drinks are there and the food will be in the old viewing room. Excuse me while I go check on that."

Aubrey left them. The other guests smiled and returned to their own conversations.

"Can I get you a drink?" Bryce asked Barbara.

"Just red wine. Any kind, thanks."

He approached the bartender who asked if pinot noir would be acceptable. Bryce said it would and asked for ginger ale for himself. The bartender said all he had was Perrier and handed him a bottle with a straw. When Bryce returned he found Shaw talking to Aubrey, who excused himself again, went to the wine table and then to the foyer to greet arriving guests. The reception room began to fill up and Aubrey moved back and forth through a back door with their coats.

Bryce handed her the wine glass. "You should have told me this was Gideon's party," he said. "How do you know each other?"

"I used to work at Herrick before moving to Justice. I assumed you knew that. If I'd heard that you and Gideon were old friends, I would have mentioned his name. Would you have come if I had?"

"Of course not. Herrick represents Tuscarora."

"But that's a criminal matter. Gideon does civil, corporate work. They keep a Chinese Wall over there around the criminal stuff. Tuscarora's probably not even one of his clients."

"Yes, I understand there's nothing wrong technically, but I'm new in town and I want to be careful about appearances."

"God, Harry, I'm sorry, but nobody in this town cares about who shows up at Christmas parties. People get together. They all have conflicts at work of some kind, technically. Maybe that's a big deal up in Philly, but in Washington nobody cares. You've got to get used to it now that you're here."

Bryce took the straw out of his Perrier bottle and stuck it in his pocket. He sipped the water from the bottle, and looked around at the other guests filling up the room. Most of the men wore dark suits and ties, probably right out of work. The women, like Shaw, wore dark dresses and large earrings. One man came into the foyer who looked different, taller and older, with thick gray hair and dark eyes that struck Bryce as both inquisitive and menacing. He escorted a woman who also looked different to Bryce, like a silent film actress with a bone-white face, coal black hair and red lip-gloss. The man's hand moved down her back and over her waist as he ushered her toward the wine table, past Bryce and Shaw.

The cell phone rang in the Challenger.

"She thinks what we're after is in the trunk of his car in a briefcase. She did not see anything on his desk. Have you made the car?"

Larson said, "Yeah."

"Can you get in the trunk without damaging it?"

"Yeah."

"Don't take the case. Just get the names and the date and time of the meeting."

"Is the case locked?"

"Probably. I don't know."

"It'll take a little time. Keep them there for a while. Street's pretty empty. I parked a block away."

"Yeah. And she said you're in the damn black Dodge with the tinted windows. Barbara thinks Bryce suspects you're a drug dealer."

"Give it a rest, man." Larson flipped the cell phone shut, picked up the toolbox from the seat, got out and walked around the corner to the gray Honda. It was parked under a street lamp.

Two men in a blue Taurus kept their eyes on the Honda through their rear window as a man in a black leather jacket over a solid, square body, and carrying a toolbox, came down the street. The driver, al-Fasi, turned on the headlights, pulled out and drove around the block, passing Larson once. Larson stopped. They circled the block again. In the passenger seat, Aziz put his service revolver on his lap. When they got back to the Honda, Larson was standing under the street lamp with the toolbox on the curb next to him. al-Fasi punched up the high beams and stopped. Larson froze. Aziz rolled down his window.

"You need some help?" he asked. "Want us to call the police?"

Larson ignored them. He got out of the light and hurried back to the Challenger. He drove down to Dupont Circle to wait for the next call.

The Taurus went around the block one more time and parked within sight of the Honda.

Aubrey rejoined Bryce and Shaw, and said the buffet would be ready soon. Bryce asked who the other guests were.

"Mostly junior associates. And their dates or mates, of course."

"How about that guy?" Bryce said, indicating the tall older man with the silent film starlet. "He doesn't look like a Herrick junior associate."

"That's a new client of mine. I just brought him into the firm the last year or so."

"So now you're a rainmaker, Gideon. Make partner yet?"

Aubrey flicked a wrist. "Senior associate, Harry."

"You'll make partnership too, I'm sure. So, what does that new client do?"

"Import/export. He owns a firm over in Virginia. Look can I refresh your drinks?" Aubrey took Shaw's glass and Bryce's empty Perrier bottle over to the wine table. When he returned, he excused himself again to consult the caterers in the old viewing room..

Barbara stayed with Harry and started talking about the other people at the party she once worked with. The conversation, and laughter, in the old reception room grew louder. He listened for a while, holding the Perrier bottle with a tightening grip but not drinking.

Finally, he interrupted. "Barbara, I think I really have to get going as soon as I can say good-bye to Gideon. It's that drive tomorrow up to Philly. And I really don't feel comfortable here."

She stopped, looked over at the bar, the bartender and around at the other couples, listening as their conversations grew louder. She said, "I understand."

Aubrey reappeared and announced to everyone that the food was ready. He exchanged looks with the man he called his client and signaled toward the rear door, but Bryce stepped between them. He made apologies, explained his morning plans, and said he had to leave. Aubrey said he was glad to renew their acquaintance, and hoped they would stay in touch. He asked Barbara if she was staying.

"Oh, I'm sorry," Bryce said. "I just assumed I would take her home, but if she wants to stay, that's fine."

"I'd appreciate the ride, Harry," she said. "Let me go back there with Gideon and make sure he gets the right coats."

They went back together and when the door to the study closed she whispered, "Everything okay?"

"Shit, no."

"What happened?"

"Client's man says he's being tailed by somebody. He couldn't get into the trunk. He doesn't know who they are. No badges or anything."

Shaw picked their coats up from the pile on one of Gideon's leather chairs in the office. "What's that mean?"

Aubrey shrugged. "No clue. He's going over to your building. Try to get Harry up into your apartment for a while."

"Well, then, you tell him to keep that goddamn Dodge someplace out of sight. I'll try to get him some time."

She left Aubrey behind. Bryce was waiting in the foyer. He asked after Gideon, and she said he was talking to a client. Bryce helped her on with her coat and they left.

Aubrey circulated among his guests, checked the supply of food and wine, and then went into his study. It was the old funeral home office, still paneled in dark mahogany he had not refinished. He crossed to the cabinet and poured himself a tumbler of single malt Scotch. His client came through the door and closed it behind him.

"So?" he asked.

"Larson said he's being followed. He had to break it off."

"Who? FBI?"

"Doesn't know. No badges. Bryce is taking Barbara home. She'll try to get him inside long enough to give Larson another chance."

"Larson's my man. I'll just tell him to button him. Make it look like a drive-by."

Aubrey squeezed around his client. He slugged down half his drink.

"For God's sake, Robert, will you stop that crap? You only need a few more days. Just keep it all quiet."

"All right," Ingram said. "I pay for your advice. It'd better be worth it."

Shaw directed Bryce to her apartment building. It was a flat orange high-rise with aluminum window jalousies pocketed with gray oxide streaking down the walls. The elevator lobby was visible from the street through double glass doors. Bryce parked in the handicap spot right in front when she assured him no handicaps used it.

The blue Taurus passed by the building.

Shaw started to step out, then stopped.

"Would you mind coming upstairs with me, Harry?" she asked. "There's something I'd like to talk to you about."

"Well, that depends on what it is."

"It's one of the apartments across the street. I'll show you from up there."

They rode the elevator to the third floor. Her apartment was an efficiency with a kitchen alcove behind folding doors. She took his coat and dropped both of them on the double bed, then drew open the folding kitchen doors and began boiling water for coffee. Bryce stepped over to the drapes covering the glass patio door facing a small portico outside and pulled them aside. Mold around the aluminum frame stained the plaster walls.

"What am I supposed to be looking for?" he asked.

"Across the street. I don't know if you can see inside now."

"I don't see anything."

"Let me show you." She came next to him while the water heated. She pointed at one of the darkened units several floors above hers. "There," she said. "Well, at night, maybe you can't see it."

Shaw looked down at street level for a moment and saw the black Challenger move past the front of her building and slow to park in the next block, still visible from the portico. The coffee pot whistled. She pulled the drapes shut behind her and went back to the electric range.

"Decaf or regular?" she said.

"Decaf, please." Bryce took a seat in one of the cushion-less single chairs by the dining table. "Well, what's over there you're so worried about?"

She brought over two mugs and handed him one. "There's a small telescope in one of those units. I can see it in the morning." She took a seat on the edge of her bed, holding her mug in both hands.

"Maybe it's an amateur astronomer."

"No. Not that. It's always pointed this way when I see it, not at the sky. And with the city lights, you couldn't see many stars from there anyway."

"So, you're thinking what? Some kind of creep?"

"That. Or some covert operation. Either way, I'm worried. I'm thinking about moving."

"I'll ask Pete, our case agent, to check on it. Wait until we hear from him before making any changes. But, if you can see it, it's not very covert. Not CIA, I mean."

"Where's your place?"

"Out by College Park. A lot like this, but suburban. You wouldn't like it."

Bryce got up, went to the drapes, pulled them aside and looked out again. He saw a black Challenger with tinted windows and exhaust coming out of the tail pipe sitting a half block up from Shaw's apartment building, and he wondered if it was the same one he'd seen earlier.

Shaw drew his attention back inside. "So, what time are you leaving tomorrow?" she asked.

He returned to the chair but left the drapes open. "About six. I hope anyway. And I really need to get going." But he did not move.

"Pretty early."

"Yeah. I have to pick up my daughter first, then go to my parents."

"Where's that?"

"Philly suburbs."

"How long will you be staying?"

Bryce got up and took his mug to the kitchen counter. "Until New Years. That was the plan, anyway, until this afternoon."

"Oh? What happened?"

"Well, after Christmas, I was going to take my daughter to visit an old friend of mine with a mountain cabin in western Maryland. I go every year at this time. Actually, we met in law school. Like me and Gideon. Before the divorce, I thought about getting a place of my own out there. My parents have a house at the shore, so I thought it'd be nice to have one in the mountains for myself. Of course, with the divorce...." Bryce decided to drop it. "Well, all those plans went to hell. So, here I am in Washington, instead."

"But I mean, what happened today?"

"Oh, yeah. Sorry. I wandered, didn't I? Well, like I told you, I got that call from a lawyer and now I've got to go to Pittsburgh after Christmas instead."

Shaw walked over to the kitchen next to him. "Want a refill?" she asked.

"No, thank you. How about you? Any family plans?"

"Just the trip to the Caymans." She refilled her own mug and returned to the edge of her bed.

"Tell me about your daughter, Harry. What's her name?"

"Tess." She heard the croak in his voice. "This visitation stuff is tough, Barbara. Avoid it if you can."

She waited a moment, considering what to say. "I've been through a divorce, too, Harry. It's tough for everybody. Fortunately, there were no kids in my case."

"Caymans for you, huh? Family get together?"

"No, there's really no one anymore. I'm basically an orphan, now."

Bryce knew he had to go. He started to the door, but then spotted a baseball glove on top of the refrigerator. He picked it up.

"You play?"

"Yeah. In a women's softball league around here."

"What position?"

"Third and catch. My Dad got me into it when I was a little girl. He was my team coach. You?"

"Not since high school. Center field for me. Not good enough for infield." He palmed the glove some more and placed it back on the refrigerator.

She set her coffee mug on the floor and brought over Bryce's raincoat. She knew she could not keep him any longer.

"What's your daughter Tess look like?"

He took the coat and put it on. "Blonde, like her mother. But gray eyes, like mine. Not blue, unfortunately."

"Maybe I'll get to meet her one of these days." She pecked him on the cheek and he left.

On the street, he saw a blond man in a black jacket coming toward the building carrying a toolbox. The man stopped and turned back as Bryce got into his Honda. When he drove up the street, the man was standing by the Challenger Bryce saw from Shaw's apartment.

A blue Taurus came around the corner and maintained an eight-car distance behind him.

From her portico, Shaw watched Bryce's Honda pull away and, with relief, the Challenger stay where it was. She forgot to ask Harry if he had a photograph of his daughter. She was sure, now that she thought of it, he had a wallet photo. There were no pictures in his office, but he had just been transferred. Blonde hair, like her mother. Pale gray eyes, like Harry's. But happy eyes. Happy to see her father tomorrow. Barbara would ask to see that photo after the holidays.

Aubrey's party began to thaw quickly as the bartender served more whiskey, gin and vodka, and the caterer switched the music from Pachelbel to rock and roll. He said he had to leave his guests again and take another business call in the study.

"What did you find out?" the voice demanded.

"Nothing. Bryce is being tailed by somebody else."

There was a pause. "We have to teleconference tomorrow morning. Ingram's office."

"Christmas Eve?"

"We've got only four days to closing. Then the deposit clears, and you can take off all the time you want."

"What time?"

"Nine. Tell Ingram. And have that insider of yours there. We need to know all she can tell us about the prosecutor's plans."

"Keep the tail on him?"

"Break it off tonight. Pick it up again tomorrow."

Aubrey opened the door and waved to his client. Ingram left his escort behind and came in. Aubrey passed on the new orders over two fresh tumblers of single malt Scotch.

Shaw took the call from Aubrey lying on her bed. She told him the latest about Larson and the proffer in Pittsburgh. He told her to meet with him tomorrow.

CHAPTER FOUR

Bryce headed out Rhode Island Avenue toward Maryland, but at the D.C. border, he made a quick decision and turned around. In his office, he went right to Barbara's desk, paged through her Rolodex and copied down three numbers—an international one listed under George Town, Grand Cayman, and two under Herrick. One of the Herrick numbers he recognized, but not the other. Before he left he remembered to pick up the staff Christmas card list with the home numbers. The drive back to College Park went quickly through empty streets.

In his apartment, he dropped the briefcase on the littered couch, turned on the television, muted the sound but left on the 1951 film of A Christmas Carol, with Alastair Sim, Jack Warner and Kathleen Harrison. He scooped some ice cream, and then started drafting the memorandum on the Harlan Moan call.

When he woke at six the television was still on, now with images of church services. The ice cream in the bowl on the coffee table had turned liquid. He showered, dressed, took his vitamins and packed. He picked up the Christmas card list and made another call.

"Merry Christmas, Pete," he said. "Sorry to be calling you now."

"Harry? What do you want?"

"I'm going to be on leave until after New Years. I'd like you to check a couple of things while I'm out." Bryce read off the George Town and Herrick numbers.

"All right," O'Shea said. "You want to tell me where you got 'em?"

"Later. And no search warrant."

"This George Town number is probably a singles resort. Cuba Libras and all that."

Bryce decided against asking him to check Barbara Shaw's home line for now, but did pass on the Harlan Moan contact, the meeting in Pittsburgh and his flight information.

"I should have written a memo on it yesterday," Bryce said. "I'll

41

do it over the break, but it won't get into the files until I get back. I did make a verbal report to the Professor and he passed it on to Thayer, so we're covered officially for me to take the proffer."

"These numbers got anything to do with that?" O'Shea asked.

"Just run the check, okay? And one more thing. Yesterday, Barbara Shaw told me something about a telescope in an apartment window across the street from hers. I think it's just some creep, but she has all sorts of ideas—CIA and stuff like that. I told her I'd ask you to check it out."

"You were over at your paralegal's place and that's why you didn't get around to drafting the memo?

"Don't go there, Pete. You know I'd lie about it anyway." He gave O'Shea Barbara's home address. Before hanging up, they cursed final holiday greetings to each other.

Bryce turned off the television, turned down the heat and gathered up his bag and briefcase. He stopped at the door for one last survey: dirty laundry, dirty dishes, paper trash—everything in place.

Kauffman took O'Shea's call in his study.

"It's Harry. He told me about the contact with Harlan and the proffer. I didn't say I knew anything about it." He reported Bryce's telephone and telescope search requests.

"So the telescope did what you hoped it would. Made her nervous."

"Yes, but it sounds like Harry's on to something he won't tell me about. Of course, we can't expect him to say much about Shaw, yet. And no mention of that black Dodge al-Fasi reported."

"Good, he's discreet."

"He gave me his travel info. I'll get seats on the same flight for al-Fasi and Aziz."

"And they'll follow him to Philadelphia?"

"Yes."

Kauffman paused, and then added, "When Harry's father, Durham, called me about the transfer, he did not bring it up. Neither did I."

"He broke that contact almost two years ago, didn't he?"

"Yes. And I've wondered if he told Harry anything about it."

"Harry doesn't act like it."

"No, but he has to be cautious about everything after his mess in Philadelphia."

"Are you going to tell him?"

"Not yet. I've decided to leave that to Durham for now. Perhaps he'll bring it up over the holidays. We don't even know for sure what the stakes are in this matter. Maybe it will all come to nothing. No reason to stir up too much fuss right now. And, maybe, as you suspect, Harry knows more than he says. Go ahead and do what he asked. And make sure al-Fasi stays off that GPS satellite stuff. Somebody could trace it all the way back to us. Tell them to just use paper road maps until you can secure us from those computer hackers. And for God's sake keep working on that."

Bryce got on the Beltway, but when he reached the exit for I-95 he decided to avoid Baltimore. He continued to the Bay Bridge and crossed to the Eastern Shore. The car radio started playing "The Messiah." He should have mentioned that black Dodge Challenger to O'Shea, but the connection seemed too remote and he forgot to jot down the plate number anyway. He figured he told O'Shea enough about last night.

The blue Taurus followed too far back for Bryce to notice it in his rear view.

The Challenger sat on the shoulder where the Beltway merged with I-95. Larson was sure Bryce had to pass this point, but after ten o'clock and no sign of him, he called in.

The taxi left Shaw in front of Aubrey's brownstone at eight. The stale smell of tobacco, beer and whiskey filled the inside. Aubrey's ear was stuck to his cell phone. He motioned her into the kitchen behind the old viewing room. After a few minutes he joined her and poured the coffee.

"Harry's going to his parent's place," she said. "Philly suburbs."

"What else?"

"He told me about that Pittsburgh contact. He's going there on the twenty-sixth for the proffer. He seemed annoyed because he said he had plans to visit a friend in western Maryland, in the mountains, with his daughter. Somebody he knew in law school."

"Oh, yeah, I remember." Aubrey said. "I don't think the guy ever did practice law. Well, visitation. So, he'll take a morning flight out of Philly. No overnight. We'll find out the schedule and maybe they can cover the airport out there. Clients want the tail to try to pick him up on I-95."

"You mean the guy in that black Dodge? Tinted windows? Same guy?"

"Yeah."

"I told you, Bryce spotted it last night. He saw it again outside my apartment. Once more and he'll start connecting some dots."

Aubrey shrugged. "Clients' idea. They pay the fee. I just give advice. Anything more about the informant?"

"Nothing. Just what I said, that it screwed up his plans for time with his daughter. I didn't push it, you understand?"

"Did you notice anybody else tailing you and Bryce last night?"

"Why?"

"Larson said there was somebody else. Know anything about that?"

"No." Barbara refilled her coffee mug without asking permission. "Something's not right about this case, Gideon. I never met any of your clients before. You said the deal would close in a few days. I haven't even started to inventory the documents. It'll be months before Harry starts calling witnesses."

"That's what I told them. But when they heard about this informant yesterday, they got shit fits."

"How did they hear about it? Wasn't me."

"Don't ask, Barbara."

She looked down at her mug, wondering how much Aubrey would not say. "Okay, then tell me this much. Who are your clients? Every corporation in America gets investigated now and then. A lot of them are clients of Herrick, and you guys are grateful for guys like Harry. Hourly fees and all."

"Oh, we are," Aubrey said. "We are. But Tuscarora, as a corporation, is not my clients' concern. It's actually another corporation I represent."

"Yeah. So, what's this really all about, Gideon?"

Aubrey went over to the counter and picked up the coffee pot, but didn't pour. "You'll find out pretty soon, Barbara. But not from me. I can tell you only that they're afraid Harry's going to cost them a lot more money than they first thought."

Shaw put down the mug. When this is over, she'd call the broker Gideon sent her to, the one who set up that account for her father.

Aubrey put a hand on her arm. "Time to go," he said.

George Bennett pushed his chair from the desk and leaned back. He couldn't stop thinking about that call yesterday from Aubrey. The government had a new source.

When the subpoena arrived a few months ago, he and Tom Gould consulted with Aubrey and followed his advice. The weekend before the law firm's crew arrived, they sorted through the files personally and removed all the documents the lawyer said would be incriminating. But the documents called for in the subpoena were not the problem, he thought. The real transaction was almost all verbal. And the subpoena never even mentioned Blue Mountain, just Tuscarora. So, the government didn't have much. Until now.

He got up and paced around the room. He used the breathing exercises the shrink taught him. His heart slowed, but not enough. He decided to try some vodka instead.

The deal with the Ossete and his U.S. contacts would be all over before New Years. Then the money would be in his offshore account. But, if the government learns about Blue Mountain, Aubrey said, they could be shut down in twenty-four hours. He and Tom tried to keep everything about Blue Mountain they could to themselves, certainly from his father and his father's lawyer, Harlan Moan. But any employee might have heard something.

He did not want to make that international call, but he felt he had no other choice. They all told him not to—Aubrey, the Ossete, that banker, Vrenc, in New York, and the subcontractor, Ingram, in Virginia. Dealing with this was different. He hadn't the resources and they did. The satellite he installed at the house was his only secure line.

"I see," the Ossete said. "And how will this affect out arrangements?"

"The prosecutor could shut us down, I am told."

"And you can prevent that?"

"I don't have any way to prevent the prosecutor from making contact here in Pittsburgh with the source."

"Did you speak to Mr. Ingram about this?"

"My lawyer advised me to avoid any direct contact with him or anyone else in your operation in the U.S. while the investigation is open."

"You have to defer to him, of course. Very well. I will contact Mr. Vrenc and have him make some resources available to you. But understand, Mr. Bennett, we have customers, too. They are simple people, generous with friends and pitiless with enemies. That is their history. And if your government aborts our arrangements through lack of—what is your word? Diligence? Due diligence? We will see complete liquidation. Am I clear? Our customers will not want to hear about American court procedures."

Bennett stared out his front window and down the Allegheny River at the skyscrapers across it. "I hear you," he said.

The Ossete walked along the interior corridors of the old stone fort in stocking feet, clawing his toes on the Tabriz carpet. He filled a porcelain cup with green tea from a Tsarist samovar, went back to his work station and sent the message to Manhattan.

Milos Vrenc was in the rear of his shop on Fifth Avenue. Antique Persian carpets hung on the gallery wall. Others, more contemporary, sat in squares on the floor. He liked to claim they were all authentic, woven by Arab nomads and Turkish artisans. The store was closed for the holiday.

His grandfather moved the business to Manhattan from Budapest in 1914, and when Milos took over it had clients that included the White House and the State Department. There were many honors bestowed on the business over the years, but one that he inherited as well was not public—directorship of the Trust, which could be traced to the family's origins in Baku. And one of his duties was to take in certain refugees and put them on the payroll.

Vrenc received the Ossete's email. He gave two of these "employees" cash for the flight from Newark to Pittsburgh and contact information to be used only after arrival, then told them to wait while he took a call.

Ingram motioned Aubrey and Shaw into the steel chairs in front of his desk. He dialed and turned on the speakerphone, introducing the two of them as legal counsel. That disturbed Shaw, but she was disturbed more by Ingram himself. Since leaving Herrick, she never had direct contact with his clients. But even when she was with the firm, she never saw one like Ingram. Last night, at the party, he looked more like a thug to her than a businessman. And now close up, he looked even more dangerous, and more intelligent, than he did then.

"My man was unable to maintain contact," Ingram said into the speaker. "We do know the prosecutor is on his way to Philadelphia."

"Why Philadelphia?" Vrenc asked.

Ingram gestured to Aubrey to answer. "His parents are there," Aubrey said. "He's spending the holidays with them."

"Do you know where they live, exactly?"

"We can find out," Aubrey said. "He's picking up his daughter on the way, so Ingram's man has a little time. We know he's flying to Pittsburgh from Philadelphia probably not overnight."

"When?"

"The twenty-sixth."

"He has a daughter?"

"So we are told." Aubrey looked over at Shaw for confirmation, but she looked away.

"And his last name is Bryce? Same as his father, I presume, that he is visiting?"

"Yes."

"Can you confirm his flight itinerary?"

"Probably," Aubrey said. "It will have to be an early flight."

"This information is from Ms. Shaw? How long has she been on your payroll, Mr. Aubrey?"

"About two years now." Aubrey coughed and waited.

Finally, Vrenc said, "Robert, I need to talk to you privately."

Ingram picked up the receiver and held it to his ear. "Yes," they heard him say. "He is my only available asset right now. Yes, I can communicate with him but security might be a problem. As a back-up, yes. Yes, I agree, legal details are on the back burner right now."

After a long stretch of listening, they heard Ingram say again, "Yes, Bryce. Yes, same name, I know. Father, maybe. Our choices are limited. There are some documents out there we'll have to get, too."

When the conversation was over Aubrey and Shaw got up to leave.

"Is that all?" Aubrey asked.

"Yes, for now. We'll need that legal paperwork in three days. And the other information I mentioned. Any problem?"

"No, I don't think so." Barbara noted the hesitancy in Gideon's reply. This guy seemed to frighten him, too.

"I will let you know when and where to deliver them." Ingram waved them a dismissal. "And one more thing, Gideon. I'll deal with Larson. No more contact."

Vrenc passed the travel information from Ingram on to the men, took them out to Fifth Avenue and paid for their taxi. Back in the shop, he confirmed what he could. The funds had moved through the Trust account, as the Ossete vouched for. The documents arrived that morning, in a sealed diplomatic envelope. He sent some instructions to Pittsburgh, then checked the flight schedules from New York and Baltimore to Grand Turk, then to Maracaibo. Before deciding which airport to use, he had to get to Virginia.

Barbara waited until they were out of sight of Ingram's office.

"Why, Gideon?" she asked. "Why did you take me out there and put me face-to-face with him? You know better than to expose me like that; it puts us both on the hook."

"I needed credibility with them, Barbara."

"Credibility? Now they have me, not just knowledge that you have some source in Justice. And what was all that about Harry's daughter? And his father? You said this was only about the Tuscarora investigation. I was just undercover."

"It's just Tuscarora, as far as I'm concerned. I'm going to drop you off at your office. I want you to get Harry's parents' address."

"There's a security camera there, Gideon. How much more exposure do you want from me?"

"To my knowledge, it's about a contract for export of military rejects. Maybe some technical violation of the regs. That's all."

"The guy on the phone, Gideon. Who was he?"

"Ingram's angel. Investment banker in New York. That's all I know. All either of us need to know."

"Then what are you scared of? You were scared back there. I'm scared, too, and you won't even tell me why I should be."

Aubrey stared straight ahead down the Interstate. He crossed the Potomac and parked near Shaw's office building.

"Just do it, okay?" he said.

When she came back, she handed Aubrey a slip of paper. "There were just two numbers. One is probably his father's law office. Looks like they're both in the same town."

She looked out the side window as they passed the streets to her apartment. "It's all bullshit, Gideon, and you know it." And looking more like dangerous bullshit, she thought.

Aubrey stopped at the building entrance. He turned to her, for the first time since they left Ingram. "Barbara," he said, "Look, I have no actual knowledge of any more than what I told you. I was retained to get export licensing for military rejects. Electrical stuff is all I know. I'll deliver the paperwork to Ingram at the appointed time and place, collect my fee and move on."

She reached the curb when he added, "Then, I'm going to forget all about it. And I advise you to do the same. No questions. Just the money. Okay?"

"Okay, and this is it for me, Gideon," she said. "It's over. Make that last deposit. No more."

She went up to her apartment, filled a large glass with wine and drank half in one swallow. She walked to the portico and looked out at the building across the street. How much longer, she wondered, would all this take? Gideon never answered her other question, why his clients cared about Harry's father and daughter. She couldn't see the telescope, so she closed the drapes and went back to the kitchen for a refill.

Bryce crossed into New Jersey, took the River Road along the bank of the Delaware and turned off into a small development parking in front of one of the split-levels. He hesitated, and then knocked. Maureen opened the door. They gave each other forced smiles after he pulled back from the instinct to embrace her rigid body in his arms. She let him in.

Her parents were in the living room next to the Christmas tree. Tess ran over to him. He lifted her up and hugged her close.

"Merry Christmas, Baby."

"Merry Christmas, Daddy."

She wriggled out of his arms and showed him her presents. He exchanged fresh, polite greetings with Maureen's parents.

At last, Tess finished. Maureen brought out the suitcase and bundled the girl in a coat. On River Road, he noticed a blue Taurus with government-issue license plates driving back the way he had just come.

Bryce re-crossed the Delaware at Washington Crossing and wove south on local roads.

"Tell me a Lady Tess story," his daughter said while still on the bridge.

"Sure, Gorgeous. Which one?"

"Dracula. I love that one."

"Well, once upon a time, a long, long, long, long time ago, Lady Tess and her Daddy were riding their bikes in the mountains."

"Where in the mountains?"

"Oh, you know. Way, way out by Savage River, near Uncle Jack's. I'm hoping we can visit right after Christmas."

"Oh, goody. I love that."

"Okay. Well, they rode into a tiny town in the valley. They were hungry and they decided to stop at the McDonald's. So, they did. They ordered hamburgers and French fries. The people said they were all out. Daddy asked where else they could get some hamburgers. But they wouldn't say and they looked afraid. It was getting dark, so they asked the people in McDonald's if there was a motel nearby. And, still, nobody would talk to them. Daddy went over to an old, old man sitting in a corner eating an ice cream cone and asked him. The old man pointed a long, boney finger up at the top of the mountain to something that looked like a castle. 'Up there,' the old man said."

"Lady Tess asked, 'whose castle is that?'"

"And the old man said, 'Count Dracula's. He takes guests.'"

"Lady Tess and her Daddy had never heard of Count Dracula before."

"Yes, we did," Tess interrupted.

"Well, later they did, but not then. Remember, this was a long, long, long, long time ago. So, they rode their bikes way, way up to the top of the mountain and got there just as it was night. They left their bikes against the castle wall and banged on the big wooden door. Boom, boom, boom. They waited and waited. Finally, the door opened. Creak, creak, creak. And there at the door was Count Dracula in a big, black cape. And he said, 'Vat do you vant?'"

"When he talked like that, they knew he wasn't American, so they spoke very, very slowly. 'We are travelers far, far from home and we need food and lodging for the night.' Dracula said, 'Vy do you not stay in the village?' And they said, 'An old man in the village sent us up here.'"

"Dracula touched each of them on their necks and smiled. 'Very vell,' he said. 'You are velcome to my hospitality. But, please, I take no money. Only that you clean up the dust and dishes and toys.'"

"So they said, 'Okay' and walked into the castle."

By the time the Taurus circled the cul-de-sac and headed back Bryce's car was gone. They returned to the Interstate, exited at the sign for Winchester and found a twenty-four hour convenience store. The handwritten note on the door said it would close in fifteen minutes because of the holiday. They got a local street map and al-Fasi used the pay phone outside to call the Professor for more specifics on the address.

❖ ❖ ❖ ❖ ❖ ❖ ❖ ❖ ❖ ❖ ❖ ❖

Barbara Shaw spread the Wall Street Journal options page out on the counter and ran her finger down the column to Tuscarora preferred. She jotted down a straddle of reciprocating puts and calls, planning to close out the losing leg next week, before the market learned anything. She got hold of her broker in the Caymans—he was there, it seemed, 24/7—and placed the order, on margin.

Her ex-husband, an options trader in Chicago, taught her all this. After the move to Washington, she bought some books and worked out the strategies first on paper, using the knowledge she gained from the law firm about public companies. She made money, at least on paper.

There were, however, two problems: first, it was illegal, and second, she had no money. For a while, all she did was play at it, eventually getting pretty good. Then, her father's medical problems popped up leaving her to cover his expenses for at least three years. Gideon Aubrey stepped into the picture, got her to transfer to the Justice Department, provided the cash and showed her how to move it to the account in George Town without the IRS picking it up. The last two years, as Gideon's money flowed in, she followed the strategies she had worked out.

One more to go. And now, this Tuscarora scheme, whatever it really was, looked real dirty, not just cash-register-fraud like she thought. She was a potential government witness against Gideon if this ever came out. He had to realize that all along. Now, those clients of his knew who she was. Maybe they always did and just wanted her to see that—Christ, the damn telescope!

She used the remote to turn up the sound on the television and filled the wine glass again.

Tess, she thought. Blonde hair. Gray eyes. She still kept wishing she had asked Harry to see his wallet photos. She turned to her computer screen and pulled up a list of flights to Miami with connecting flights to George Town. She already had one from Baltimore-Washington for tomorrow. She booked another out of Atlantic City.

Gideon had violated their whole arrangement. Now, she would have to come forward first and tell Harry, but she wasn't sure how much. She started to call the number from Harry's Rolodex for the Durham Bryce law firm, and then remembered it would be closed for the holidays. She needed some time to think anyway.

That was it. She went back to the television without seeing or hearing the broadcast. She put the straddle out of her mind, too. All of it was on autopilot.

Bryce parked in the driveway of the white Victorian house in Winchester. The baseball field across the street lay under a thin crust of snow. It was where, every spring, he played Little League, his father coached and his mother sold snack. The porch of the house was draped with evergreens and the windows glowed with candles.

Bryce and his daughter took the gifts, luggage and briefcase out of the car. The front door flung open. His mother drew them both inside, into the warmth of her embrace and the smell of balsam from the living room and turkey from the kitchen.

The blue Taurus stopped by the right field foul line. Bryce's gray Honda was parked in front of the house Kauffman told them to look for. They drove back out of town and checked into a motel on the bank of the Delaware.

CHAPTER FIVE

Larson spotted Bryce on a street corner outside a church with a small group of people, singing a carol. He was holding a little girl. When they finished, people drifted apart. From a block away, Larson followed Bryce and the girl down the street to the next intersection across from a baseball field. Three other adults were with Bryce, two women and an older man, the one he figured was the father. He watched which house they entered and went back to the Dodge, moving it to a spot along the right field foul line.

Harry and Durham watched a college bowl game in the den while the women worked on dinner in the kitchen. Soon, they shooed Tess out into the den. She switched the television to a cartoon and sat on the carpet in front of the couch by her father.

Durham went to the built-in bookcase, opened a small cabinet door and poured himself a Scotch.

"Do you mind?" he asked Harry.

"No, of course not."

"How are things down in Washington?"

"Okay, so far. Not sure how long I want to stay, though."

"You don't like it?"

"Well, what else can I do for the time being? Thanks for the help, by the way."

"Yeah," Durham said. "I didn't like it much, either. Eight years. But, Winston keeps recycling back."

"The Professor? He mentioned he needed to keep his criminal procedure courses updated."

Durham sat down with his eyes on the television screen. "There's more to it than that, Harry. I don't know how much of this I should tell you now. A few years ago Justice asked him to review some cold case files. He contacted me and some others he used to work with. He organized us into a team to go over them."

"You never told me about this."

"I never told anybody." He gestured toward the kitchen. "Winston said to keep it hush-hush. We got together in that Solarium he built in the back of his townhouse in Center City, where he paints those sea battle pictures he hangs all over the place."

"Those sailing frigates and all?"

"Yeah. Somehow they fascinate him. Never asked why."

"And you met in Philadelphia? Not in Washington?"

"It's a quick train ride between New York and Washington. But mainly, Winston said. No Justice Department red tape or surveillance."

"Surveillance? Who? CIA? FBI?"

"And foreign agencies."

Harry got up and went to the bookcase. He looked at the Scotch, but took a bottle of warm soda water. "What kind of cold cases?"

"Fraud, white collar, mostly, but then terrorist stuff."

"Doesn't sound like I should be hearing about this, now, Dad. Was it all legal?"

"He assured us it was, that he had the authority. I dropped out of it over a year ago. Something came up with a petition he got me to file in federal court. Since then I haven't talked to Winston except about your transfer a couple of months ago." Durham picked up his granddaughter and took her back to the recliner.

"Anything else you should tell me about the Professor?"

"How much do you want to know? He's probably still meeting in that Solarium with new people." Durham caressed his granddaughter's hair. "When I contacted him about your situation, he said something about wanting to get together again, go over some new matters. But I didn't pick up on the offer and he let it slide."

Harry took a long swig of the soda. "Well, he hasn't mentioned anything to me about some Solarium."

"Ah, good." Durham returned his daughter to the carpet. "Then it's all in the past for us. Let's keep it that way." He looked at his son again. "So, any further thoughts on my proposal?"

"The Professor just assigned me to a new case and I think I need to work on it for a while, if just to clean up my record. But, yes, I see what you mean about Washington and all. And, I'd be closer to Tess up here."

The TV cartoon broke out into a song. Tess jumped up and sang along, beating out the rhythm with her arms. The men smiled at her, and then at each other.

"Well," Durham said, "it'll take me a year or so to get things wound down to retirement. How long do you think that case will take?"

"About the same, unless there's a trial."

"Can you say anything about it? Within the rules, I mean."

"Oh, it started out as a routine fraud case. Now, I don't know. That's part of the problem."

"Something's happened?"

"I got a call yesterday from a lawyer in Pittsburgh who claims to represent an insider, an informant who wants immunity. I have to fly out there the day after Christmas to take the proffer. I meant to tell you earlier. It's not overnight. I should be back in time for dinner. But can you and Mom watch Tess for me?"

Durham said they would be happy to, went back to the bookcase and topped off his Scotch. He kept his eyes on the spines of obsolete volumes of Pennsylvania statutes. "Can you say who the lawyer was? In Pittsburgh?"

"Harlan Moan. Said he used to work in the Department same time as the Professor and, I guess, you."

"Did he say he knew me?"

"No. Just that he recognized Kauffman's name. Say, do you mind if I run upstairs and make a quick business call?"

"Go right ahead."

Bryce closed the front bedroom door and dialed the number.

"Did you get anything, Pete?" he asked.

"Not much. As you reminded me earlier, Harry, it's the holidays." O'Shea passed on the name of the brokerage firm in George Town. "The other is a direct line to Gideon Aubrey at the Herrick law firm."

"Okay. Can you check out a few other things?" Bryce took the Christmas card list from his pocket and ran his finger down to Barbara Shaw's home number. "This is a private line. Check it against those George Town numbers."

"Private line. You going to get me an official request?"

"Later, if you find anything. Just the last thirty days or so."

"And this is all official business, right? Tuscarora? Not some skin you're chasing?"

"Official. And I hope it all comes up empty. Oh, and check any calls to Area 412, Pittsburgh."

"That it?"

"How about the telescope Barbara Shaw asked me about?"

"Nothing there. But you thought that, didn't you? When do you need this other information?"

"Tomorrow, if possible. I'll call you."

Bryce rang off. He looked out the front window and saw a black Dodge Challenger parked on the street near the right field foul line with the exhaust pipe puffing.

"You did not enter the phone number on that damn computer of yours, did you Peter?" Kauffman asked.

"No, didn't have to. My source used the Postal Service computers. Anyway, it's Barbara Shaw's line. Listed."

"Keep all this on paper. Then shred it."

"Harry's going to call me tomorrow. How much should I tell him?"

"Only what you find. Nothing more. We already have some idea of how she's laundering the money, but don't mention that."

"He's entitled to some kind of warning, don't you think?"

"We can't do anything to compromise Harlan's proffer. You've got him covered out there by Saad and Khahil so the meeting in Pittsburgh should be no problem. Harry needs to be kept clear of everything for now, especially since he's up there with his father."

"And if Harry starts asking me some questions?"

"You know how to answer prosecutors' questions, Peter. Don't let Harry become a problem."

"Yes sir."

O'Shea continued pumping on the Stairmaster. He still had fifteen minutes to go on his routine. He changed the page on his computer screen to and continued scrolling the data on Barbara Shaw.

Harry's mother called them to the dining table. He sat next to his daughter on the side facing his sister and his parents sat on the ends. After a blessing, the meal went according to ritual with some exchange of local gossip, his sister's complaints about graduate school and his mother's reminder to avoid all politics. His father mentioned that Harry might be able to take over the law practice in a year. His mother and sister looked at each other without speaking.

"Don't worry," Durham said to them. "All that stuff with Maureen, the divorce..." Harry's mother moved her head sharply in Tess's direction. Durham coughed and looked down at his plate. Well," he said, "it's gone."

After dessert, they cleared the table and returned to the parlor. The gifts were arranged under the tree, the stockings hung on the stairway railing and a plate of cookies put out for Santa Claus. Then, they all watched "Peter Pan." When the film was over, Harry walked Tess around the house unplugging the window candles. They ended in the front bedroom and he helped her into her pajamas.

"Can you finish the Dracula story, now, Daddy?" she asked.

He sat next to her on the bed. "Where did we leave off?"

"Dracula just invited us into his castle."

"Oh, right. Dracula said they would have to order something out for dinner, and he asked what they wanted."

"And we said pizza. Triple cheese pizza."

"Yes. So, Dracula called out for pizza. It took a while for it to be delivered, but when it came the delivery boy was a werewolf. But they took the pizza anyway and sat in the middle of the great hall and ate it. Dracula, of course, did not have any. 'I vill eat later,' he said.

"After they finished the pizza, they cleaned up the box and the dishes and the dust and toys, like Dracula told them to. Then, he showed them up to their room. It was way, way upstairs. Up three or four flights of stairs. The window to their room looked over the mountain top."

"Just like Uncle Jack's," Tess said.

"Yes, just like that. And Dracula left them alone in the room." Bryce glanced toward the baseball field and stopped.

"And then what happened?" Tess asked.

Bryce got off the bed and placed his face closer to the windowpane. "Tell you what, Honey," he said. "Let's finish this tomorrow. I need to talk to your grandfather."

He tucked her under the covers and took another, longer look out over the porch. The black Dodge was still there, and this time he thought he could make out Virginia license plates. Downstairs, he took his father aside and quietly asked if any neighbors owned a car matching that description. Durham said he didn't think so.

"A car like that seemed to be following me, or my paralegal, yesterday down in Washington," Harry said. "Tinted windows and Virginia plates. Can you get the Borough cops to make a quick check?"

Durham made the call. A few minutes later, a police cruiser pulled up behind the Dodge with flashing lights. An officer got out and approached the driver's side window. The other officer walked around the car's rear. The Dodge left and the officers returned to their cruiser. After a few more minutes, they came to the door and said the driver was from out-of-state, Virginia, and lost. They gave him directions and warned him he would get a ticket for the tinted windows if they saw him in town again. There was no theft report. Durham asked them to check the ownership and let him know what they found. Harry and his father went inside to the den.

"Satisfied?" Durham asked.

"Not really."

"Me neither."

"I guess we wait until we hear back from the police."

"Anything else you want to tell me about that car?"

"I told you all I know."

Durham switched on another college bowl game. Harry's mother and sister stayed in the dining room.

al-Fasi and Aziz watched the police cruiser stop behind the Dodge and the officers speak to Harry and his father. The Dodge was gone, but they waited for two hours until the house lights went out, then went back to the motel and reported to O'Shea over the room phone. He gave them their, and Bryce's, flight information.

The convoy of trucks sat with their headlights on and engines idling behind the barbed-wire-enclosed base as the dawning sun began to shine over them. A hard, cold wind blew down from the Arctic across the Caspian Sea just outside the base. The soldiers standing near the trucks leaned against them and pulled their parkas close. The convoy commander looked up at the brightening sky, down at his watch and back at the headquarters shed.

Inside the shed, the base commander also looked at the sky, the horizon and the wall clock. His orders were to have the convoy moving by now, but the security escort was nowhere to be seen. They weren't supposed to leave without a guard, but he made his decision. He stepped out of the shed and signaled the convoy to start. The troops climbed back into their trucks, the barbed wire gate swung open, and they struggled off.

Twenty miles from the base, the last truck dropped back by degrees and eventually fell out of sight. It left the main road and followed a trail to an abandoned fishing village. The truck stopped and the Hetman stepped out from behind one of the shacks. He wore American military surplus clothes and a white burnoose that flapped in the wind. The driver climbed out, looked around, but saw no one but the man in the burnoose.

"If you have the substitutes and we confirm payment, the cargo is yours," the driver said. The other man nodded.

"And," the driver added, "it is understood that the guidance mechanisms were destroyed back at the base on orders from Moscow. We had no control over that, but the warheads and all are intact."

"That was taken into consideration."

The driver removed a laptop from the truck, set it on the step, opened it and pulled up the antenna. He tapped in the code and the message popped on the screen.

"Confirmed," he said. "You can start loading."

The man waved behind him. Another truck appeared on the dirt street and stopped next to the Russians. A swarm of uniformed men also in burnooses came out from behind the abandoned hovels. The driver and his aide stood aside, lit cigarettes and watched while they moved cargoes between the trucks.

When the transfer was complete, the men climbed aboard their truck, hanging on wherever they could. The truck coughed its way south.

"The funds have been deposited in the account in Israel as you instructed," the driver said, pointing at the laptop screen.

"Very good. Now return to the convoy." The Hetman pointed to another dirt road leading out of the village. The driver folded the laptop and climbed into the truck cabin. He and his aide took the shortcut to the main highway. They caught up with the convoy and fell in last as before. Later, they explained that they had engine trouble and stopped to fix it.

The convoy reached its destination outside Orsk as planned. It would remain undocumented.

The Ossete took his morning exercise by climbing up the parapet and walking around the fortress walls five times. A dry breeze blew off the Indian Ocean. The roosters had crowed and the prayers already cried from three distant minarets. He watched the natives moving on the ground below among their tin and cardboard shacks under clouds of dust and charcoal smoke. He kept the space open for the helipad, even though the helicopter itself was off in Maputo.

His satellite dish sat in the middle of the fortress between two date palms. All the rooms face inward toward the courtyard. There were no outer windows and there was only one outside door, double bolted.

In an hour or so, he would open it for the Cairo University dropout who actually understood all the technology needed to communicate with the world outside his stonewalls. The other staff, the four mercenaries, boarded in second story rooms inside the fortress and were already patrolling the parapet with shouldered Uzis.

He patted one of the iron cannons aimed inland. The forged lettering on the barrel said it was cast in Lisbon, the date long since worn away. He pulled his white cotton robe around himself and looked at his real defenses, the Israeli light machine guns, also pointed inland. The bankers in Tel Aviv had given him good advice.

When he finished his exercise, he walked down to the air-conditioned communications room. A signal bleeped on the screen that the funds from the Caspian had cleared. It remained now for Vrenc and Ingram to complete their part in America.

He walked out to the courtyard. The air was already growing rank. He stopped by the fountain, dipped his hand in the water and patted his brow. The doctors warned him about the extreme heat and fetid air in this part of the world, even in the shade and within the fortress walls. He went inside to his private quarters and dropped on a pile of cushions. Still an hour before the young Egyptian arrived. Time enough for his therapy. He clapped his hands twice.

"Jagodja," he called out.

The girl parted the beaded curtain that separated her chamber from his. Her body was hard and black. Her wide eyes looked at him sideways and her face lacked all expression. The Ossete patted the cushions next to him.

Christmas Day at the Bryces' began early. Tess got up first and made sure all the cookies were gone. Finally, the adults came down and they all opened their gifts. Santa Clause left Tess a sled. There was still a thin layer of snow on the baseball field, so in the afternoon Harry showed her how to make short, safe runs down the slope across from the house. He waved each time the police cruiser drove slowly past.

That night in bed, she asked him to finish her Dracula story.

"Well, let's see if I can remember," Harry said. "Lady Tess and her Daddy were alone in their room in Dracula's castle after dinner. Is that where we ended?"

"Yes. After we ate the pizza delivered by the werewolf."

"Of course. Pizzas are always delivered by werewolves. They were not sleepy yet, so they walked around the room looking for some books to read. But the books were all in Russian or something. They just sat around and told themselves some pirate stories. After a while, they heard some flapping wings against the window. They went to look and saw a big bat. Daddy opened the window to shoo the bat away."

"That wasn't very smart of you," Tess said.

"No, it wasn't. But remember, this was a long, long time ago before they knew anything about Dracula. The bat got into the room and then, wham, it changed into Count Dracula. He closed the window and he smiled. And then, for the first time, they saw his fangs."

"They didn't see them before?"

"Because he didn't smile before. And he said, 'I vant to drink your blood.' 'Why?' they asked. 'Because I am a vampire,' he said.

"Well, Lady Tess and her Daddy knew something about vampires, at least. She screamed. And Daddy ran at Dracula and wrestled him to the floor. Lady Tess looked at the window. She ran over and pulled aside the drapes and opened it to see if there was a way down the castle wall. But there was not. Then, the sun just started coming up over the mountain. Some of the sunlight came into the bedroom. Dracula screamed and Daddy jumped away. And slowly, slowly, Dracula turned into dust."

"Did they have to clean up that dust, too?" Tess asked.

"They just ran out of the room, down the stairs, got on their bikes and rode quickly down to the village. All the people there cheered because they knew if they got out of that castle, Dracula must be dead. The villagers reopened McDonald's and they all had French fries for breakfast. End of story."

"Oh good," Tess said. "That's just how I remember it. So, what was the moral?"

"Well, let's see. Don't tell your Mommy this, but I guess the moral is you don't really have to clean up all the dust. Just leave some of it to take care of itself."

He reminded her about his trip to Pittsburgh the next morning, hugged her and said good night.

Back in the parlor, he sat across from his father. Durham put down his book.

"I just heard from the police," he said. "That car last night is owned by a firm in Virginia called Miltech. Mean anything to you?"

"No. But it sounds like something to do with military contracting, doesn't it? Can the police get any more?"

"Not today, but I'll check with them again tomorrow. I gave my secretary the week off, but I'll be in the office. Did you tell me everything you can about this?"

"Well, something else. The other night, when I saw a Dodge just like that one outside my paralegal's apartment, she said there was a telescope in an apartment across the street she was worried about. I didn't think much of it at first, but with that car, tinted glass and all, it started to seem odd. So, I asked my case agent to look into it, as a courtesy to her, really."

"What did you hear from him?"

"He said he couldn't find anything. That was last night."

"And this case Winston assigned you to—it's military contracting?"

"Yes, fraud."

Durham turned from the window and faced his son. "I tried to reach Winston this afternoon, but I could only leave a message."

What about?"

"What I mentioned last night."

"That Solarium group? You said you broke off contact about that. You want to tell me anymore? Only cold cases now? Not any of mine?"

"No, of course not. I told you, it was a while ago." Durham went back to the chair and picked up his book. "But if Winston brings any of that up with you, talk to me. Maybe then I can tell you more." He put the book down again. "Oh, and this proffer tomorrow. What did you negotiate about immunity?"

"Just Queen-for-a-Day."

"No Department clearance?"

"Just a verbal report."

"To Winston?"

"Yes."

"And the memo of the call? Did you file that?"

"I'm going to write it on the plane."

"Good."

"The Professor said it was best to keep it out of the system until I got the proffer nailed down." Harry started toward the den. "How about we see if there's another game on?"

Durham followed his son. "Well, then I guess I should mention one more thing, Harry. About that memo and all. The last time I met with Winston and this Solarium group, he did say there was a security problem with the Department computer system. Doesn't sound like they fixed it. It was one of many reasons why I dropped out of it. Maybe you should consider dropping this case. Come back here. Take over the practice. I can speed up retirement. I can't be more specific, but I don't like what I'm hearing from you. I've begun to regret getting you involved with Winston."

Harry turned on the television. "I'll take the proffer tomorrow," he said. "We can talk about this some more when I return."

Everything should be all right in your meeting with Harlan Moan," Durham said quietly.

Harry could not hear him over the color commentary from the game on the screen.

A shaft of sunlight leaked through the curtains. Barbara Shaw did not bother to open them. She looked at the time on the clock next to the second empty wine bottle by her nightstand. She missed the flight out of Baltimore-Washington. She made a pot of coffee, showered and dressed. She had time to make the call.

"Hello, Gideon," she said.

"Barbara? Where are you? Miami?"

"No. Still here. Something came up with my father."

"Is he all right?"

"Yes. I'll leave tomorrow."

There was a silence while Aubrey waited. Finally Shaw said, "I am still having problems with that meeting yesterday."

"Do I need to say it again? They wanted to be sure you were committed, Barbara."

"Trapped, you mean." Another brief silence. "I'll ask again, Gideon, why did they want to know about Harry's daughter and father?"

She waited out another, longer silence, until Aubrey said, "I have no actual knowledge of any of that."

He confirmed what she thought last night, drinking her wine. She hung up and called Durham Bryce's law office. It was still closed, but this time she left a message. She waited until ten-thirty and called the Bryce home. Harry's sister told her he had already left for Pittsburgh.

So, one option was canceled. She would drive up there, meet Harry's father face-to-face, maybe make some kind of contact with Harry from there, and take the Atlantic City flight.

She made the other calls. The broker was open. She could access the money. Her Chevy Cavalier was back, parked in the building lot. She picked up the bag she packed the night before, threw on a coat and left. The traffic was lighter than she expected and she got right through Baltimore.

Bryce arrived at the airport two hours before flight time. The terminal was crowded with noisy families returning home. He bought a newspaper and coffee and took a seat in the lounge facing out at the airplane. He focused on the puzzles first and did not see two men standing just outside the special security checkpoint waiting to retrieve their handguns. The speaker announced boarding. He got up to stand in line, and the two men followed.

CHAPTER SIX

Tom Gould stood in the terminal next to the down escalator holding a sign, "Fine Art Carpets." The monitor showed the flight from Newark had arrived. When the passengers finally came down, he saw who he was waiting for—two men in dark coats, with pale, alert eyes. They looked like brothers, but one who was shorter, seemed older and noticed the sign first. They approached Gould, but exchanged no words. He ushered them past the baggage claim and into his BMW.

The men from Newark sat in the back seat. When they reached the highway back to Pittsburgh, Gould said, "We can talk now. The pistols Mr. Vrenc specified are on the floor."

The older man picked up a magnesium camera case and opened it. Inside, in blue foam, were two black Cobrays. The passengers took the guns out and balanced them in their hands.

"They have been modified?"

"Yes. Fully automatic. Mr. Ingram took care of that."

"Ammunition?"

"In the top there. Six clips."

They fitted a clip into each of the pistols and put the others in their coat pockets. Gould had test-fired one of them in Virginia. Thirty-two rounds in a second-and-a-half. He could barely control the aim and hoped he would never see the pistols or the men from Newark again.

"Silencers?"

"In the side pocket."

They screwed the silencers on the gun barrels, balanced them again, and then separated the pistols, silencers and clips and put them back into the case.

"I got shoulder holsters, too, if you need them," Gould said. "They're in the door compartment."

The men took out the holsters but did not put them on.

"I have a question," Gould asked. "Why specify those guns?"

"They use ordinary ammunition," the older man said. "Hard to trace."

"But what about escape? They have no range or accuracy. I know. I tried."

"Escape is for you to arrange. You just get us there."

"Well," Gould said, "you shouldn't need them anyway. You two are just back-up."

They crossed the bridge into Pittsburgh, and Gould drove the BMW to a high-rise building and down the ramp into the garage.

"We meet Mr. Bennett here," he told them.

One man took the camera case. The other put the holsters under his coat. Gould left the car for the attendant. They took the elevator up to his suite. Bennett was waiting for them at the dining table.

"Did you tell them who we think it is, Tom?" he asked.

"No. I thought you should do that."

Gould took a seat by the window above the marble Federal Courthouse. The men from Newark sat on the couch by the interior wall, keeping both of the others in view. The camera case sat between them on the floor. They examined Bennett with penetrating but indifferent eyes.

"It is a woman," Bennett said. "We are certain of that now. Her name is Caldwell. She is, or was, an administrative assistant, and gave notice of resignation effective this morning. No prior notice, retirement plans or anything. She is the only one, besides Tom and me, who would have access to some of the key information, especially some documents, the government is after. Not everything, of course, but enough to cause us major headaches."

"Where is she now?"

"At home, we think." Bennett pointed out the window behind Gould. "Up there, on Mount Washington."

"So, when do we go?"

"Half an hour or so. Wait for the neighborhood to empty of commuters."

"You're sure the woman's there?"

"She has a week off. She's flying to California late this afternoon," Gould said. "I overheard that from the secretaries."

The older man touched the other on the arm. They took off their coats and put on the shoulder holsters, removed the pistols from the camera case and reassembled them. Gould offered coffee, but they asked for tea. He started for the kitchen to boil the water.

"You need to tell them about the documents," he said on the way past Bennett.

"Oh, yes. This woman had access to documents about this transaction. We kept as much as we could off the computers and removed all the incriminating papers we were able find in the files. But she might have copies, and those documents are the only way the government can make a case. That's what our lawyer said."

"Yeah, her lawyer." Gould said. "Tell them about that."

"Yes," Bennett added. "We are pretty sure who he is, but we need to confirm that. He also might have copies."

The kettle whistled and Gould brought out the tea and coffee.

Bryce parked his rental car in an open lot on a side street behind the Federal Office Building. He found the address Moan gave him a few blocks up Grant Street—a restored Gilded Age monument with the original marble on the ground floor. He rode a clanking brass cage elevator to the fourth floor. He walked across the red Persian carpeting on the reception room floor and showed his identification to the secretary behind a high desk. She spoke his name into a telephone, then told Bryce that Mr. Moan would be available in a moment and to please have a seat. He settled in a rigid armchair. Across the room, a woman, her hair tied in a tight bun and dressed in a gray tweed business suit, glanced up at him over an open copy of Forbes. She had one bag of luggage on the floor next to her. Bryce looked at the large painting of Fort Pitt on the wall above her.

The secretary reached under the desk and a security lock buzzed. The door behind her opened and she told Bryce to go in. Inside, a man introduced himself as Harlan Moan. He looked part of the same generation as Bryce's father and the Professor, gray hair combed back and wide suspenders holding up pinstriped pants. But no suit coat.

They went down a corridor flanked by cubicles with young men and women staring at computer screens under fluorescents. Moan

stopped, opened a door and showed Bryce into a conference room—
warmly lighted, unlike the corridor. Bryce chose a seat at the long
mahogany table facing the door with his back to the wall. He set his
brief case on the table but left it closed. Moan sat down on the other
side of the table. A small manila file was already in front of him.

"How long have you been with the Division?" Moan asked after
he settled in.

"Just a few months," Bryce said. "In Washington. Been with the
Department for about six years."

"I think I mentioned I was down there. Long time ago, though.
Been to Pittsburgh before?"

"Couple of depositions. No trials. Never been in the
Courthouse."

"Not in winter, I hope?"

"No, thank God. I've heard about your winters."

"They say there's a big storm on the way from Chicago. Good idea
for you to get out of town before it hits."

"I plan to."

Moan offered coffee and placed the order through the speaker at
the far end of the room. In a few minutes, another secretary came in
with a tray holding a china tea set and a carafe. When she left, Moan
poured. Bryce started to sip it black, but Moan stopped him.

"You'll need cream with that," he said. "It's Cuban. The coffee, I
mean."

Bryce added the cream, took a taste and agreed.

"We have a corresponding firm down in the Caymans," Moan
explained. "One of our clients is a bank with a branch down there.
Heavy Cuban influence, they say. They introduced us to that."

"You mentioned you knew my boss, Winston Kauffman, when
you were in Washington. Did you happen to know my father,
Durham Bryce? He was there about the same time."

Moan looked down at the manila folder and opened it. "Now
that you mention his first name, it does sound familiar. No doubt we
ran into each other. Sounds like you've got a legacy."

He turned over a few pages and looked back up. "Well, let's get
down to business so you can catch your plane before the snow hits.
My client can, I believe, significantly advance your investigation with

information that, again, I believe you do not have. That is from my review of the subpoena and various things my client has told me."

"Information?" Bryce asked.

"And evidence. Also, leads."

"And the evidence? Direct or indirect?"

"Both. Some hearsay, of course. Some admissible, some maybe not. And background, naturally. Plus codes to help you with those disks they submitted."

"Okay," Bryce said. "What's the price?"

"Immunity, like I said."

"And, like I said, I need a proffer. You can make it a hypothetical attorney proffer, if you like." Bryce opened his brief case and removed the yellow pad with his notes from the previous conversation with Moan. He flipped to a blank page and wrote down Moan's name, date, time and place.

"That is acceptable." Moan looked at his file. "Hypothetically, my client is well-placed on the financial side of the subject of your investigation, Tuscarora Industries."

"Well-placed?"

"Let me finish."

"If he's too high up, immunity's a tough sell. You know that. Does he incriminate himself?"

"To a degree, yes. I would not indict, myself, as a matter of discretion. But possible? Yes. Conviction? Unlikely, in my view."

"So, this is out of an abundance of caution."

"That's the way to put it."

"All right. Go ahead, hypothetically."

Moan got out of his chair, hooked his thumbs on his suspenders and moved around the room. "In brief, my client is in a position to provide evidence, corroborated by documents, of meetings, phone calls and other communications in furtherance of a conspiracy to defraud the government, to obstruct audits as well as the grand jury, money laundering and, possibly, illegal export of strategic materials. In other words, national security. Arms smuggling, in effect."

"Who does he implicate?"

"At Tuscarora, George Bennett and Tom Gould."

"I know who Bennett is. I don't recall seeing the name 'Gould'. What's his role?"

"My client can explain that."

"Anybody else?"

"An export broker in Virginia. Firm by the name of Miltech. Possibly controlled by foreign nationals."

On hearing the word 'Miltech,' Bryce laid down his pen.

"That name mean anything?" Moan asked.

"It just came up in another context." Bryce returned his attention to his notes. "You said foreign nationals?"

"My client actually has nothing very specific on that, Harry."

"My notes say you mentioned 'tribal.'"

"Yes. The Caucasus. All those 'stans.'"

"And something about a Trust. And some Washington types. What's that?"

"Lawyers."

"Well, there are a lot of us back there."

"Big firm types."

"Come on, Harlan. This isn't Twenty Questions. Who?"

"The Herrick firm. No individuals. I don't know anybody there myself anymore. And nothing direct."

"Well, we both know they represent Tuscarora. Anybody in Justice? You hinted at that."

"With Herrick, I may have a conflict because we used to represent Tuscarora. But now, we're out of it, and I felt I could represent my client in this limited manner. On Justice, nothing direct, either."

"But, what?"

"Call it triple hearsay. A hint. And intimation that the investigation might be compromised on the inside. But it's best you hear that from my client."

Bryce exhaled. He heard allegations like this before and nothing ever came of them. But this time, his thoughts raced back to Barbara Shaw and Gideon Aubrey in Washington, the black car the police reported was owned by Miltech and his father's comments about Professor Kauffman and that Solarium group. Still, Moan was right. He needed to shut it all out for now and just listen to his client.

"So, tell me about the meetings." he said.

Moan sat down again and flipped through his file. "Pittsburgh, of course. New York. A private hunting lodge Bennett controls in

Bedford, a hundred miles or so east of here. Corinth, Mississippi. Grand Turk, in the Bahamas. And some place on the East African Coast."

Bryce wrote this down and asked, "How does he know this?"

"Duties included signing off on travel vouchers and other expenses. Access to financial records. And daily, direct contact with the principals."

"How current is it?"

"Up to the date of service of your subpoena. Then it all stopped."

"Alright. Now tell me about the alleged murder."

Moan grinned. "Officially, heart attack. You'll hear about that."

Bryce took a two-page typed letter from his briefcase and shoved it across the table. "That's the Queen-for-a-Day. If your client confirms what you've said, in the proffer, we'll take the testimony in court-ordered immunity, if that's necessary."

Moan looked at the letter. "It's been a while since I did criminal work," he said. "Is this the standard form?"

"Right off the computer."

"Just printed? You didn't enter it into the system?"

"No. Not yet."

"Okay," Moan said. "I'll recommend that my client accept it. But I need a few minutes to speak to her." He got up and left.

When the door closed, Bryce made a quick note of Moan's use of the pronoun 'her,' refilled his cup with Cuban coffee and made a call from his cell phone to his father's work number.

"Harry," Durham Bryce answered. "I'm glad you called. You're in Pittsburgh?" Bryce said he was, in Harlan Moan's law offices. "I just checked my messages. There's a long one from a Barbara Shaw. Your paralegal, right? She said there's a problem with that case of yours, maybe up here in Winchester. Something about Tess. She also got your sister at home, and learned you already left town. Shaw said since she can't reach you, she's coming up here."

"What about Tess?"

"That's all she said."

"When is she coming?"

"Today. She's probably on the way."

"Well, I have no idea what that's all about. I called because the name 'Miltech' just came up in the proffer—you know, that car up the street. Ordinarily, of course, I shouldn't tell you any of that. Maybe that's what Barbara wants to talk about. Maybe they're tailing me. But that's a stretch. I'm getting way ahead of the facts. At least, be careful with Tess until we find out what she means. I should be home for dinner. We can sort it out then."

"I'll tell the police a bit of this. Put them on alert. And I'll make sure Ms. Shaw stays until you get back so you two can talk directly."

Bryce looked up at the conference room door. It was still closed, but he spoke quietly. "Be careful about what you tell the local police. You know that. One more thing, Dad. This guy Harlan Moan says he knew the Professor when he was in Washington, and he recognizes your name."

"Yes. It's something else we need to go over," Durham said. "That and part of my case load out of Kauffman's Solarium meetings. But, we can't do it on the phone. Just finish the proffer."

The door opened. Bryce said, "Right. I've got to sign off now."

Moan escorted a woman into the conference room—the one Bryce saw in the reception area. Her face had a wary expression and, if real, she looked like a good witness. She dropped a red rope envelope on the conference table. Moan made the introductions: her name was Allison Caldwell. They shook hands and she sat down next to Moan who handed her the letter and told her where to sign it. She did and gave it to Moan.

"Will I be called to testify?" she asked.

"Before the grand jury, probably. I'll let Mr. Moan know the date. It'll be here in Pittsburgh."

"Is it secret? Harlan told me it is."

"Yes. It's sealed until the indictment is returned." Bryce motioned at the red rope envelope in front of her. "Are those the documents Mr. Moan referred to?"

She pushed it across the table to Bryce "Yes," she said. "Glad to be rid of them."

"I have a subpoena for them." He handed it to Moan and asked to have Caldwell's name typed on it. Moan made a call on the speaker. The secretary came and took the subpoena away.

"So, now you can honestly say you're under compulsion," Moan explained.

"Let's start with your employment history at Tuscarora," Bryce said.

al-Fasi and Aziz waited in the cafeteria on the first floor of the old bank building until 11:00, then took the elevator to the law office and asked the receptionist if Harlan Moan was in. She said he was occupied with another client and asked for their names. They said they would call again and went back down to their table with a clear view of the elevator doors.

Gould drove up the mountain incline and stopped at the top in front of a single wood frame house. A Chevrolet sedan sat in the drive. Gould pressed the doorbell. When he got no response, he waved back to his BMW. The two men came out. One of them jimmied open the lock. Inside, Gould called for Allison.

They moved rapidly through the house looking for the documents, but Gould did not expect to find them in the time they could stay. He went to the telephone on the kitchen wall and found Caldwell's personal directory on the counter. When he picked it up a business card fell out. It was Harlan Moan's. He dialed the number and told the operator he was trying to reach Allison Caldwell.

"It's an important personal matter," he said. "I understand she is a client of Mr. Moan's."

The operator said they were in conference with instructions not to be disturbed, but she could take a message.

Gould hung up. He gathered the other men and drove back down the mountain to the city. On the way, he called Bennett to tell him they were headed downtown.

She joined Tuscarora, Caldwell said, in the 1970's right out of high school as a secretary. She took night courses in accounting and eventually got promoted to administrative assistant.

"Besides the pay raise, that meant doing some personal chores for the firm's founder, Mickey Bennett, and later, for Harlan." She stopped.

Bryce glanced up at both of them from his note pad. Moan nodded at her. "Go on."

She explained that Mickey and Harlan were both from West Virginia. Mickey, she said, was a genius at electrical engineering. He teamed up with Harlan in the 1980's and turned Tuscarora into, mainly, a defense contractor.

Moan interrupted. "I was General Counsel. I should have made that clear earlier. I retired a little over a year ago from there and this firm as well. I moved back to Morgantown, but they let me keep an office here for any old clients that want to see me."

Bryce looked at him for a moment after he finished, then returned to the informant. "Continue, Ms. Caldwell," he said.

"Well, when I first met Mickey he was in his forties. He was always optimistic, brilliant, wonderful to work for." She smiled down at the tabletop. "But, he smoked, oh, three packs a day, and I think he put away at least a fifth of Jack Daniels, too. I'd be in the office with him on a conference call or something, and in half an hour he'd fill the ashtray with butts. I had to keep cleaning it out."

"Is he still there?" Bryce asked.

"No. About eighteen months ago, he had a heart attack and lung surgery. He's been in a nursing home ever since. His mind's clear as ever, though."

"What happened next?"

"His son, George, took over and started making changes in the business."

"What kind of changes?"

"More business outside the government. Brokers, exporters. Mickey didn't like it, but he couldn't do anything. Harlan had some problems with George, too."

Moan stopped her and said they needed to consult. They left the conference room and came back after a few minutes. Moan spoke first. "Let me clarify what Allison just said. I thought George was pushing some things too close to the line between legal and clearly illegal transactions over goods produced, at least originally, under

Defense contracts. I had no actual knowledge while I was still connected to the firm that George stepped over the line. But I retired a few months after Mickey went into the home."

"All right," Bryce said. "We might get to that later. Mr. Moan mentioned some obstruction. What can you tell me about that?"

"That was after the subpoena arrived."

"Which was a year after I severed my relations with the company," Moan added.

"And George and Tom—" Caldwell started again.

"Excuse me. Who is Tom?"

"I'm sorry. I've known these people for so long. Tom Gould. He's the chief financial officer. George brought him in when his father got ill. His title is Treasurer of a subsidiary they set up, Blue Mountain. George made me its Assistant Treasurer, but basically I do the same things I always did. Tom plugged George into some investment bankers, a whole new source of money."

"Okay. And the obstruction?"

"Well, George and Tom took control of the whole thing, the document search, over a weekend when nobody else was in the office. I volunteered to help because I knew where all the records were. See, I handled all the bills, travel receipts—all that stuff. On Monday, when I came in, I found the paper shredder burned out. Then, later that morning, I got a call from Mickey asking me to see him in the nursing home."

She stopped, and Moan said, "Go on, Allison."

"Okay. Mickey knew about the subpoena. In the home, he showed me a clipping he had saved. It was several months old, but it reported that a Mississippi subcontractor George and Tom used had a fatal heart attack at an old hunting lodge Mickey still owns near Bedford, Pennsylvania. I told him about the paper shredder. Mickey said he was afraid George had gotten too deep into something and he told me to go see Harlan. To protect myself, he said."

"Protect yourself? Why?"

"Mickey thought there was something suspicious about the contractor's death even though the newspaper didn't say anything like that."

Moan interrupted again. "Dennis Fancher was a partner in a

subcontractor, Pickwick Industries, they were using in Corinth, Mississippi. You'll see the name on a bill of lading when we go through the documents. I checked out the story and couldn't find anything in the official reports not already in the paper. There didn't seem to be a thorough autopsy. But, with that and the document search and the other background noise in the company, I advised Allison to get out and cover herself if she could."

Bryce made a mental note to check the anonymous note from Memphis again. He touched the red rope envelope. "Okay, so where did you get those documents if George and Tom shredded everything?"

"I found them in my own personal files after speaking to Harlan. I took them home. It's all from Blue Mountain, which wasn't mentioned in the subpoena. I finally showed them to Harlan last week."

"Down at my place in Morgantown," Moan said. "Not here."

Bryce turned his note pad over to a fresh page. "We'll get to Blue Mountain in a few minutes. What can you tell me about George?"

Caldwell seemed relieved to change the subject. She began with how George was the only child of Mickey's first marriage. "He used to say George came out of college talking about nothing but Shakespeare and Plato. George worked for some other company for a while, but eventually ended up with us."

She stopped and leaned over toward Moan who told her she could not hold anything back, now. She asked for some water. Moan filled a glass from a pitcher in the middle of the table. She took a long drink.

"You see, Mickey was a big, well, the term used is womanizer. They argued about it all the time, even though Mickey and George's mother were long divorced."

"Did he marry again?"

"Yes. Four times."

"Does George have any siblings?"

"One. A half-sister. She lives in California. No connection to the business."

There was another long pause that Bryce let linger. Finally, Moan said, "Go ahead, Allison. It's okay to tell him. He'll find out sooner or later anyway."

She looked up at the ceiling, inhaled and exhaled slowly. "Mickey always had somebody. He kept an apartment downtown just for that purpose. His first wife found out about it, and that led to the first divorce."

Bryce waited. He did not want to ask the question.

"I was one of them," she whispered.

"And George's half-sister?"

"My daughter." She finished her water and Moan refilled the glass. "Mickey offered to marry me when I got pregnant. I thought about it, but I knew him too well. I said no. We broke up. He kept on with his apartment—womanizing, I mean. I've always been sure I made the right decision. And Mickey did help me out raising our daughter, financially, at least."

"Was your affair a factor in the first divorce?"

"One of many."

"Does George know about all this?"

"Oh, yes." She paused, then added, "We never discussed it. I always assumed I'd be out when Mickey dies, because of all that past ugliness."

Bryce flipped to another fresh page on the note pad. "So," he said, "tell me about Blue Mountain."

Gould parked in the alley behind the old bank building. He stationed the two men outside the street exits and said he would give them a signal when Caldwell appeared. He went back to his car and made another call to Bennett.

"So, it was Harlan," Bennett said. "And I thought he was off in West Virginia all this time. He'll have those documents all figured out for the prosecutor. Do whatever you have to, but keep them from getting that stuff to the Courthouse."

CHAPTER SEVEN

Bryce pushed the red rope envelope back at Caldwell. She undid the knot, without removing any of the documents.

"Blue Mountain is a corporation," she said. "George formed it about a year ago, with Tom's help, after his father's first heart attack. He owns all the stock. There is no relationship, legally, between it and Tuscarora. It won't show up in any of the D&B's."

Moan interrupted in a low voice. "This was just before I retired. I was not advised of any of this."

Bryce looked at him, then back at Caldwell. "What does it do?"

"Exports."

"What kind?"

"On paper, rejects. Stuff rejected by DOD inspectors."

"Who are the buyers?"

"Third World countries. Some governments. Some private firms. George uses that broker in Virginia—Miltech. The proceeds go to Blue Mountain."

Bryce circled the word "Miltech" again on his pad. "Tuscarora doesn't get paid? Not even on the account books?"

"No," Caldwell said. She took a ledger book out of the envelope. "Tuscarora's books are on computer. The government requires that for auditing." She opened the ledger and ran a finger down a page. "But these are Blue Mountain's books. All manual. It stays away from any government business." She flipped the page and ran a finger down again. "Purchase orders. Accounts payable. None of it appears in Tuscarora's computer—or any computer, for that matter."

"Who makes those entries?"

"Mostly me."

Bryce glanced up and asked, "So, Ms. Caldwell, what is the point of all this paper shuffling?"

She sighed. "Look, the purchase orders and the bills of lading are just there to pick up the shipment from Pickwick Industries, that subcontractor in Mississippi. Down there, all they want is the paperwork before they hand over the goods. There are no transaction documents between Blue Mountain and Tuscarora. The only record is here." She tapped the ledger. "And down there in Mississippi, if they keep them."

"Okay," Bryce said. "The goods are picked up. Then what?"

"They're picked up by a Miltech truck. No common carrier. The bill of lading disappears. They're delivered to a warehouse, inspected, then shipped out by air, I think."

"What airport. Do you know?"

"I know the warehouse is near Baltimore."

"But why go through all this? You said they're rejects."

Caldwell pursed her lips. "Mr. Bryce, it's the type of contracts Tuscarora has, classified strategic electronics. Used in things like those drones and missiles. They cannot be exported without a special license and DOD clearance, which they never requested or received."

She plucked a wrinkled piece of blue and white carbon paper out of the envelope and handed it across to Bryce. "Purchase order. See, it's called microwave oven components."

Bryce scanned the document. It was a form with the names "Miltech," "Pickwick Industries" and "Blue Mountain," handwritten across the top.

"Where's it going?"

"Best as I can make out, somewhere in Africa. Normally, what I am given is just a check from Miltech. That's the only purchase order with Miltech on it I've ever seen. George and Tom seemed to be especially concerned about that one and they wanted the documentation preserved. That's what Tom said, anyway."

She opened the ledger book to a different section and spun it around to face Bryce. She indicated a set of handwritten columns.

"George takes only a nominal salary of $50,000 a year from Blue Mountain. Tom told me to create this account, a loan account, and list it as an asset. George draws $50,000 a month from this account. And, of course, he never makes payments."

"Or reports it as income, I presume," Moan added.

"Where does the money go? Do you know?"

"The checks come back endorsed by a bank in Grand Turk."

"It never runs through a U.S. Bank," Moan said. "No Suspicious Activity Reports."

Bryce looked down the ledger page. "I see entries here for you and Tom Gould, as well."

"I get $5,000 a month."

"And you don't repay it either?"

"No."

"What do you do with the checks?"

"I endorse them and send them to my daughter in California. She takes care of it."

"Is this why they trusted you with these records?" Caldwell nodded without reply. Bryce said, "You'll have to answer the question in the grand jury, Ms. Caldwell."

"I've explained that to her," Moan said. "She understands."

"How long before they realize these records are missing?"

"Five days. Definitely by year's end. Tom hinted they might need them at that point."

"What can you tell me about this firm on the purchase order?"

"Pickwick. George had it incorporated two years ago and made the plant managers nominal owners. He transferred a plant in Corinth to them and took back a mortgage. So, he still controls it."

"What was the point of that?"

"George said small business set-aside."

"And you believed him?"

"I didn't question it."

"What about now?"

"I think it's another decoy in the paper trail."

Bryce leaned back and spoke to both of them. "They had to have some fairly sophisticated legal advice to structure something this complex."

"They did not consult me," Moan said. "I got wind of this only through Allison."

"When?"

"When she asked me about the obstruction issue and described her meeting with Mickey."

"Who did they use?"

"Herrick," Moan said.

"Who at the firm? Do you know?"

"I heard the name Gideon Aubrey," Caldwell said. "Never saw him. George always met with him in Washington, never in Pittsburgh."

Bryce circled another name on his pad, trying to show no reaction. "Why is George going through all this, Ms. Caldwell? Wouldn't he inherit the business soon?"

"No, he won't," Moan interrupted.

"Go ahead."

"I redrafted Mickey's will two years ago. We reorganized the company. Tuscarora now has only one share of voting common and Mickey holds that. He's willed it to the University of West Virginia. The rest is non-voting preferred, mostly held by George and some by Allison's daughter, and some traded publicly."

"I see."

"Control passes out of George's hands when Mickey dies. Doctors say maybe a year."

"University of West Virginia?" Bryce asked.

"We're both alumni. I serve on the Board of Trustees."

Bryce stood up and rubbed the back of his neck. He was running out of time for the flight back to Philadelphia, and this could take several interviews before Caldwell would be ready for the grand jury. He'd come back in January. However, she already supplied important details to take up with Barbara Shaw tonight.

"One more thing for now," he said and sat back down. "Mr. Moan said something about travel abroad."

Caldwell pulled papers from the envelope and spread them out. "This is a travel voucher George and Tom submitted about eight months ago. They went to some place in East Africa. Look at the names."

Bryce picked up the first voucher. It showed a flight to Maputo, Mozambique, and listed as clients "Milos Vrenc" and "Vana Djugashvili."

"Do you know who these people are or why they had the meeting there?"

"No, George and Tom did not say." She pointed to two more vouchers. "Then there are these. Tom Gould's trips to Mississippi and Virginia."

"Pickwick and Miltech?"

"Yes. And this is the newspaper clipping Mickey gave me. Dennis Fancher— one of the plant managers down in Corinth. He had that heart attack during a supposed business meeting with Tom at the hunting lodge in Bedford. The next day, Tom left for Mississippi."

"What was their business?"

Caldwell pulled up straight against the back of her chair. "Pickwick has a subcontract right now, making guidance systems for one of our prime contracts using Tuscarora's licensed technology. Production started last summer. It should be coming off the line, ready for shipment. These are all firsts and should go directly to the Air Force, not Tuscarora or Blue Mountain."

"What are they for?"

"Smart bombs. Drones. Missile guidance. Look at that again." The purchase order from Blue Mountain and Miltech to Pickwick was dated two days after Fancher's death. It listed twenty crates of microwave oven components, but with no dollar amount entered as cost.

"Mickey told me he knew Dennis Fancher," Caldwell said. "He said Fancher wouldn't go along with any of this."

Bryce opened his casebook to the anonymous letter.

"I shouldn't show you this, Harlan, but I need your input right now. Come around and take a look."

Moan inspected the document. "Whoever sent you this note did not know about Blue Mountain, either. That's why it wasn't in your subpoena. This will require a whole different paper trail to follow, won't it?"

"And there's no delivery date. Is there a bill of lading in there?"

"No," Caldwell said. "No more paperwork came past me."

Bryce looked up at the wall clock and told them he needed to catch a plane, which meant they would have to meet again after he went over the documents. Caldwell said she had a flight, too, so Bryce offered her a ride to the airport. She accepted, with Moan's consent, and then excused herself.

When she was gone, Moan said, "The immunity will have to cover the IRS, too. I forgot about that loan account."

"I'll make the change and get it to you."

"How'd she come across?"

"Looks like a good witness."

Bryce stuffed everything into the envelope and retied the knot. "You have copies?" he asked.

"No. I thought it best not to."

"Does she?"

"I told her not to make any."

Bryce put his notes and the casebook in his briefcase. Then he thought about his odd contacts with Barbara Shaw the last few days. "Anything you want to add about the alleged source in Justice, Mr. Moan?"

"Nothing from me. Ask her." Moan said he had to make a call, and left.

When he was alone, Bryce tried to reach O'Shea, but could only leave a message. Bryce asked him to check on Pickwick Industries and any sales of electronic parts to Blue Mountain or Miltech, to find out what facilities Miltech had near Baltimore, and to reexamine the reports on Fancher's death in Bedford. Moan returned and they made tentative plans to meet again in January.

Caldwell was waiting for them in the reception area. There was something she forgot to pack for her trip and asked if Bryce minded driving her home first. He agreed, and Moan let them leave together.

Alone in the elevator, Bryce asked her, "Do you remember who signed those checks you mentioned from Miltech?"

"Yes," she said, "they were stamped Robert Ingram, president."

"And another thing. Mr. Moan mentioned you thought somebody in Justice might be involved in this. What was that?"

"Oh, yes. Tom said when the subpoena arrived he was sure their lawyers in Washington could get it all buried."

"You mean Mr. Aubrey?"

"Yes. And Tom mentioned that Aubrey knew somebody in Justice."

"Did he say who?"

"No. Why didn't you bring that up in the conference room?"

Before Bryce could answer, the elevator door opened.

al-Fasi and Aziz watched Bryce and an older woman step out of the elevator, and then followed them outside and down the back street toward the parking lot. Caldwell pulled her luggage bag behind her and Bryce held a briefcase in one hand and a red rope envelope in the other.

From the street corner, Gould saw Caldwell, too, with a man he did not recognize but assumed was the DOJ lawyer. There were more people in the lot, getting in and getting out of cars, than Gould thought there'd be. He waved the two gunmen back to his BMW, and waited as the lawyer's rental car headed out across the bridge toward Mount Washington. Gould tailed them from a safe distance.

Caldwell directed Bryce to her house. He turned into the driveway behind a late model sedan, locked the car and decided to leave the case files in the rear seat with her luggage since they'd only be in the house a few minutes. Gould drove past the house and stopped a block away. He told the gun men from New York to recover or destroy whatever documents Caldwell had in the car and the house. They turned quickly down the block and at a signal from the older man split up—he went to the back door and his partner took the rental car, hefting his Cobray by the barrel to smash the window.

When al-Fasi and Aziz arrived they saw the two gunmen approaching from the BMW they'd made downtown. Aziz jumped out and moved toward the one next to the car, calling out "FBI" as he removed his service pistol. The gunman spun around and fired the Cobray. In less than a second, the gun emptied all twenty rounds, spitting bullets across the agent's chest and face. Aziz catapulted backward and dropped on the grass next to the drive with his unfired weapon still in his hand. al-Fasi came around from the driver's side of his car with his pistol already out. He stopped, steadied and fired. The shooter was trying to reload his Cobray, and al-Fasi's first shot caught him in his left eye. He dropped down on the other side of Bryce's car. al-Fasi rushed to Aziz' side, praying that his Kevlar vest had absorbed the shots and saved his life. Although it protected his torso, the vest offered no shield from the spray of bullets that hit his face. al-Fasi made sure the shooter was dead, too, then ran into the house. He yelled for Bryce and Caldwell to hit the floor, and moved past them to the kitchen.

From behind the house the older gunman heard the shout "FBI" and the gunshots. He backed away and sprinted toward Gould's car.

al-Fasi broke through the back door, looked toward the street at the running gunman and got off another shot. It hit him in the arm, but did not stop him from jumping into the BMW. He fired another round at the car racing quickly out of sight. He returned to the house.

Bryce and Caldwell were standing, not lying on the floor, staring back at him. He held up his left hand with his badge.

"Get out of here," he shouted.

"But..." Bryce started.

"Get out, both of you," al-Fasi repeated. "Take that rental car. I'll clean this up with the locals. You weren't here, understand?"

Bryce grabbed Caldwell by the arm. Outside, she stopped, paralyzed for a moment by the sight of the two shooters with face wounds, but he managed to get her into the front seat. He backed out between the two bodies, shifted into drive and shot down the local street. "First," he said to her, "show me how to get out of Pennsylvania."

She said nothing. This time he shouted. "Out of Pennsylvania. Tell me how."

"Okay, okay." She directed him through a few turns. "Now what?"

"Western Maryland. I have a friend in Savage River. Local cop. Nobody can find us there."

"Who were all those guys back there?"

"I have no idea." Caldwell's knuckles were white from squeezing her hands together. "You heard what I did. A guy yelled 'FBI.' Then the gunshots. The bodies. Oh, my God, the bodies." Her throat tightened. "The one in my house looked like he had a badge. Did you know they were following us?"

"No."

"Did you recognize the badge?"

"Yes. And after what you said in the elevator, about something going on in Justice, we should stay clear of all of them. I was supposed to meet one of my staff tonight. Now, shit. I don't have a clue."

"I was going to see my daughter. And there's Tom Gould. I thought I saw his car, a BMW, in back of the law office building downtown. Okay, damn it. I can get you out of Pittsburgh. Then you navigate to that cop friend of yours in Maryland."

al-Fasi made sure they'd left, then placed a call from Caldwell's kitchen phone. The secretary put Harlan Moan on the line.

"Saad, is that you?" he said.

"Yes. There's been a shooting at your client's house."

"My God. Is she all right?"

"Yes. She and Harry Bryce are on their way out of town. You need to go, too, before I report in. I'll contact you again, later."

"Yes," Moan said. "You're right of course. I'm headed for Morgantown. Reach me there." They rang off, and al-Fasi waited a few more minutes before calling the police on his FBI cell.

Gould recrossed the Allegheny and moved quickly past the downtown area, deeper into the old steel workers' neighborhood full of boarded up corner stores and signs in various languages. The gunman next to him pressed his arm where the bullet hit him. The bleeding stopped and he felt no bone injury. Gould asked him what happened.

"I heard someone shout 'FBI,' then gunshots. I took off."

They said nothing more, but finally Gould announced, "Here we are."

He aimed the BMW at the closed steel garage door, got out and pressed a bell on the disintegrating brick wall. The steel door whined up. Gould drove the BMW in. A large black man in overalls pressed a button on the inside and the door scrolled back down. Gould got out and left his passenger in the car.

The air in the shop reeked of motor oil and ozone. Acetylene torches hissed blue flames in the rear as they cut through metal auto bodies. Another black man greeted him with laughing eyes and bright white teeth. He extended his hand after wiping it with an oil rag in his hip pocket.

"What can we do for you?" he asked in a singing accent.

"Make that car go away," Gould said.

"Expensive car." The Nigerian bent toward the passenger window, looked at Gould's passenger and noticed traces of blood around his coat sleeve. He smiled back at Gould. "Okay," he said.

"How soon?" Gould asked.

"How much you want to pay?"

"I'll pay your premium, whatever it is."

"Then right now." The Nigerian snapped his fingers. Two more black men came out from the rear of the shop. The gunman stepped out of the car still holding his left arm and retreated toward the garage door. One of the black men drove the BMW further inside over a hydraulic lift.

"The police..." Gould began.

"No contact. Until they do, we just go about business."

Gould gestured toward the gunman. "He'll need to stay here a while. Maybe overnight."

"How much?" the Nigerian asked.

"Two thousand?"

"Three."

"Done. "

The Nigerian shifted his eyes to the gunman. "He speak English?"

The gunman heard the question, nodded yes. He took Gould aside and said he had to make a report.

"Tell them delivery is still on schedule," Gould said. The gunman walked away to a stool in a corner of the shop, still holding his left arm.

Gould turned to the Nigerian who kept his smile. "I need a loaner," he said.

"Of course." The Nigerian snapped his fingers. A freshly painted Ford sedan rolled forward. Gould got in. The garage door clattered up and he drove it out. Back in his apartment building, he buried the Ford in the basement garage without waiting for the attendant. At the front desk, he found two messages. Upstairs, he poured a triple Scotch, neat. When he finished, he called Bennett with the news. He refilled the Scotch tumbler and ransacked his desk for his passport.

Ingram put down his phone and looked at Aubrey sitting in the steel and plastic chair in front of him. "They made contact with the informant, out in Pittsburgh. But they could not get the documents or prevent the meeting. Bennett says the FBI intervened. One of the FBI and one of the men Vrenc sent are gone. The other escaped and is in hiding."

"Where are Bryce and the informant, now?" Aubrey asked.

"Don't know."

"In custody?"

"Don't know."

"How did they identify it was FBI?"

"George said they just heard a shout, then gunfire."

"Christ," Aubrey said. "We can't be sure, then. Well, Harry's got to be heading east as fast as possible right now. Who was the informant, did he say?"

"George says the informant is Allison Caldwell. Acts as their bookkeeper. He thinks she produced a ledger and other documents about this transaction. Maybe even Bedford. She may have heard something in the office about you, too. She must know you're their lawyer. How long before Bryce reports in?"

"About the proffer? Twenty-four hours."

"And if he does, how long for Justice to respond?"

"With the red tape, a week or more, normally. But this isn't normal." Aubrey got up. "We can't assume it was FBI. And if not who? Or even if it was, what were they doing there?"

Ingram remained seated, steepling two fingers on his lips. "It's all about timing, Gideon. Milos will be here tomorrow with the transfer papers. The goods are being picked up in Mississippi now, I hope. They should be here tomorrow, too. Then, it's just house cleaning." He waved around at the stacks of taped cardboard boxes on the floor.

"Nothing I know about Harry gives me any clue how he'll react to this," Aubrey said. "I mean he gets assigned to a routine white collar fraud case and ends up getting shot at in Pittsburgh, with one of the shooters shouting 'FBI.' He's got a drinking problem. I've known that since law school. So he might just disappear in a bottle of vodka for a few days. On the other hand, he may try to contact somebody, but I bet he's not sure whom to trust. And if he does come back East, he'll drive, not fly."

"Yeah," Ingram said. "Airports are traps."

"And he may have heard there's only a few days to stop the delivery. If he decides to do that he'll need help from somewhere. I've got an idea where he'll look. I'll see what I can dig up."

"What about Harlan Moan?"

"I'll get you that, too."

They settled onto Interstate 68 East, and once out of Pennsylvania, Bryce picked up his cell phone and hit his father's office number. A message came on and he switched to the home line. His sister, Kathy, answered and told him Durham was out. Bryce asked if she heard any word from Barbara Shaw, but Kathy didn't know anything about Shaw. Bryce said he would be delayed and not to hold up dinner.

"What was that about?" Allison asked.

"Trying to reach my father. That's all."

"I mean that woman you mentioned."

"She's my paralegal. I told you I was supposed to meet with her tonight. Until now, I suspected she was the insider you talked about."

"And now?"

"Maybe she got religion."

"Maybe." She waited while a few more miles of highway slipped past, and asked, "Why did you bring up the insider in the elevator, away from Harlan?"

"He said to ask you. Plus," Bryce added, "Harlan and my boss, Winston Kauffman, both know more about this case than they've told either of us. And that damn near got us both killed back there."

O'Shea scrolled the computer screen over the real estate records in Corinth, Mississippi. He found a deed transfer to Pickwick Industries for "one dollar in hand paid," and a mortgage held by Allegheny Factor for land and buildings. A Dun and Bradstreet report on

Pickwick led to an executory subcontract with Tuscarora. He made a note to check his contacts at the Defense Criminal Investigative Service for details of the prime contract.

Next he entered "Ossette" and of the many entries there he found an old Financial Times of London piece on one Vana Djugashvili, said to control an investment bank in Karachi, Pakistan, with branches in the Cayman Islands, Grand Turk and Nauru. The article linked him to a trading entity called the "Trust" started by a Scottish Jacobite, John Allen, in St. Petersburg, Russia, in the Eighteenth Century. Allen, it said, had also commanded a Russian frigate in the Black Sea before leaving Russia for Rhode Island during the American Revolution to become a privateer. O'Shea printed out the entry.

He knew it was a security risk, but he entered "Djugashvili" and another location came up: Bur Mtavo, Mozambique.

The unmarked panel truck stopped in front of the real estate office on the Corinth town square across from some Civil War cannons. Two men went inside and asked for the manager. Charles Farley came out of an inner office. The men showed him the bill of lading and asked for the warehouse keys. When they left, Farley entered their visit in his daybook.

The drive to the warehouse took ten minutes. They backed the truck up to the loading dock of a prefabricated steel building. They tried the key, but found the roll-down door unlocked. It spun up with a clatter. The gray late afternoon sunlight poured into the bay. The sound of shuffling bodies on concrete was clearly audible as they walked in. The smell of urine hit them.

The cartons they came for were stacked on pallets in one corner with a pair of ragged men crouched behind them.

"Get the fuck out of here," one of the truckers said.

The men moved slowly around the pallets pulling two black plastic trash bags. They continued down the loading dock and onto the service road. The truckers watched until they were gone, then went to work. They spray-painted over the labels on the cartons, and used stencils to spray on new ones identifying the contents as microwave oven components.

They loaded the truck and tried, without success, to lock the warehouse door.

Nearby in the industrial park one of the vagrants punched a code on his cell phone, confirming delivery.

CHAPTER EIGHT

Shaw pulled up in front of the converted bank building on the main street. As she walked toward the brass double doors, an older man came out.

"The office is closed," he said. "Are you looking for someone?"

"I came to see Durham Bryce. I called and left a message."

"That's me. Are you Ms. Shaw?"

"Yes. It's very important I talk to you."

"So I gathered. This is about that case Harry's working on, isn't it?" he said.

"Yes. Something happened yesterday. I had a meeting. There's more going on than Harry knows and I decided he needs to be told about it. Maybe some real danger."

"A meeting? Who with?"

"With a potential subject of Harry's investigation and his lawyer."

"And you're Harry's paralegal, right? Sounds like we do have a lot to talk about. I'm on my way home, why don't you follow me?"

Shaw parked her Cavalier beside a baseball field backstop opposite a white Victorian frame house where Durham Bryce left his car in the driveway. As they walked up to the porch, Durham asked, "What was this meeting about, Ms. Shaw?"

"I'm on the take, Mr. Bryce. I decided after the meeting I had to tell Harry."

"But the meeting itself. What was it about?"

"Your name came up, Mr. Bryce."

He reached for the door knob, but as he did Tess stepped out in a snow suit and reminded her grandfather he promised to take her sledding.

"Is this Harry's daughter?" Shaw asked.

"Yes. Tess, this is Barbara Shaw. She works with your father."

Shaw stooped down and extended her hand to the girl. "I'm so glad to see you," she said. "Your father told me all about you."

"We should talk about this over there," Durham said, pointing back at the field. "Tess, get your sled."

The girl took her sled off the porch and they crossed the street. "I don't want my wife and daughter to hear any of this," Durham told Shaw. "What kind of danger are you talking about?"

They circled the visiting team dugout and walked toward third base and the small slope by left field. "They mentioned you and Tess. Nothing specific that I heard."

"But why would we be part of the conversation?"

"They seemed to know something about you. I didn't hear what." Shaw looked out and saw a man in a black leather jacket walking toward them over right field. "Oh, my God. That's him."

"Who?"

"The guy who was following Harry the other day."

"Driving a black Dodge with tinted windows?"

"Yes. You heard about him?"

"I don't know who he is, but I know what he is, Ms. Shaw. Take my granddaughter and get out of here."

"Where? To your house?"

"No. Too late for that now. Not safe. Put her in your car and find Harry. I'll do what I can here. Tess," he called out. "Go with Ms. Shaw. She's going to take you to your father."

She lifted the girl up and ran with her back to the Cavalier. Shaw held Tess on her lap in the driver's seat, started the car, made a U-turn and drove up and over a rise in the street. She came to an intersection with a numbered state highway, turned right and took it north.

Durham waited and watched them go, then started out across the diamond. He saw the man reach behind his back and withdraw a pistol as he neared second base. Durham had to hold the guy's attention, even for a little bit, away from his granddaughter and away from his family. He kept walking toward the man, keeping himself between the gunman, the house and Shaw's car.

Shaw kept just under the speed limit with one eye on the rear view mirror. She saw no sign of the black Dodge. When the State highway leveled off, she wrestled Tess off her lap and into the passenger seat and flipped on the child door locks.

"Who are you? I want my Daddy," Tess screamed over and over.

Between the child's cries, Shaw said, "I work with your father. We're going to see him." She touched the girl on the knee and she recoiled. Shaw told her to fasten her seat belt.

"Where's Grampa?" Tess demanded.

Shaw kept her attention straight ahead as the two-lane road curved around some hills lined with bare, black tree branches still holding some of the light morning snow.

"I don't know, Tess. I'm sorry. You heard him, he told us to find your father."

She hoped to just drop this all in Harry's lap, head for the Caymans, wait it out, pay whatever fines she had to, and get another job somewhere. But with this, back there on the ball field, she saw that Aubrey's clients would be soon coming after her, too. For now, she could only concentrate on this little girl.

"Is my Grampa all right?" the girl asked.

"I hope so, Honey."

"Where are we going?"

The road leveled out and they came to a lighted intersection. There was still no sign of the Dodge. When the light changed, she continued north, and took a two-lane bridge into New Jersey. Shaw reached into the glove compartment for an old New Jersey map. She yanked it out and it fell apart at the folds. At a convenience store out of sight of the approach road, she pulled over and spread out the pieces on the steering wheel. There was enough left of the map to figure out where they were. Turnpike straight ahead a few more miles. After that, she knew how to get to Newark. And from there, she—or they, she reminded herself—could get to Pittsburgh, or Philadelphia. Whatever Harry said.

She let the map fragments drop on the floor under her feet and headed for the turnpike.

Finally, she answered the question Tess had asked. "We're going to the airport, Honey."

Larson fired off one shot when they got close enough and ran back to the Challenger. He raced over the hill, the way Shaw had gone, but her car was nowhere to be seen on the other side. He reached the state highway, knew it led to New Jersey, but after the shooting he needed a quicker way out of Pennsylvania. He took I-95 across the Delaware and exited on US 1 North. Fifteen minutes later, he came to a shopping center and parked in the employees' lot in the back. He removed the Virginia license plates and wiped the steering wheel, door handle and dash. He picked out a green Plymouth Volare station wagon, jumped started it, and drove north another thirty miles. He pulled into a non-chain motel with a neon sign, 'Shangri-La', paid cash and checked in.

He called Ingram from the room.

"Aubrey's whore was there," he told him. "Did you know about that?"

"No. Another fucking problem."

"I hit the old man you told me about, but the bitch got away with the girl." Larson told Ingram he scrapped the Dodge.

"I'll report it stolen," Ingram said. "Now we've got to speed things up."

Larson told him where he was, in a fleabag motel somewhere in New Jersey with a fleabag Volare, and that he had to get further away. Out of the country for a while, maybe. Larson told him to stay there overnight, give him time to check on a few things, including Aubrey.

"His whore's not going back to D.C. any time soon. You figured that much, didn't you?"

"She could be headed anywhere. No way to tell. Aubrey said she had plans for the Caymans, but she can't fly anywhere with the girl. No ID. I'll get back to you. Sit tight for now."

Larson tossed his cell phone across the stained bed covers. It did not bounce. He walked out to the diner on Route One and ordered a cheeseburger platter and a beer from the waitress with big, floppy tits. Even a fucking fleabag diner couldn't fuck that up, he thought. But he was wrong again. He left a twenty on the table and went back to his room.

Aubrey said to meet him in a small Chinese restaurant. They took a back booth. Ingram poured the tea while Aubrey removed a sheet of notepaper from his jacket and slipped it across the table.

"That's the information you requested."

Ingram looked at it quickly and folded it into his pants pocket. "I saw the credit card and cell phone numbers. Barbara Shaw, right?"

"Yes."

"I'll get that to those geeks in Africa. What's the rest?"

"Harlan Moan in Pittsburgh and Morgantown. And a contact Bryce might make in western Maryland. Local assistant police chief. Harry and I knew him in law school."

"Where'd you get that?"

"Don't ask. Tell me what happened," Aubrey said.

"You know I sent Larson tailing Bryce up to Philly?"

"So? Now what?"

The waiter came over. They ordered egg rolls and won ton soup to get rid of him.

"Your source, Barbara Shaw, was there," Ingram said.

Aubrey stared up at the ceiling. She was there to turn, he knew.

The waiter returned with soup and water, then left.

"Larson said she took off with Bryce's daughter. He thinks she's in New Jersey. That's where he is now."

Aubrey stirred his soup and tried a sip, but it was too hot. He put down the spoon.

Ingram leaned across the table and whispered, "Larson said he offed Bryce's father."

"Oh, Jesus fucking Christ. Is he nuts? Now it's felony murder."

Ingram shrugged. "Keep it down. Yes. He'll need to be cleaned out when this is over."

Aubrey took a long drink of water. The waiter returned with the egg rolls and refilled Aubrey's glass. Ingram spread mustard on one egg roll and took a large bite.

"I thought your call was something more about Pittsburgh," Aubrey said. "The obstruction."

"I told you they didn't get the documents, didn't I?"

"Yes. But that's not my problem. All they'll show about me is that I'm counsel of record."

"That woman, Caldwell, might have overheard something. George and Tom talking."

"Just hearsay. I could have dealt with that. Not this." Aubrey pushed his plate aside. He could not think about eating.

"That's not what I wanted to see you about. Our people wanted me to ask you about those FBI agents. What does your source at Justice say?"

Aubrey gulped down the rest of his water. "I don't know. The subject never came up. It would be crazy to even think about that. FBI?" Aubrey's attention had been focused on his office, where mentally he was already cleaning out the files. Now, a murder prosecution. If Justice got Shaw's testimony, he was finished. She was the only witness who could connect him to all of this. That and the notepaper in his own handwriting he just handed to Ingram tying him to Harry's friend, the police chief. No chance of getting it back now.

"Another thing," Ingram said. "We need to find out if Bryce has reported in."

The waiter dropped the tab on the table and Aubrey picked it up. "Anything else?"

"We have to move up our deadline. I'll need the corporate documents in twenty-four hours. Bring them to the hangar. You'll get your money then."

"To my personal account. Direct, right?"

"Of course. Meanwhile, keep tabs on Bryce, if you still can."

"And you'll clean the rest up? Barbara Shaw? If you don't, I'm toast."

"I know," Ingram said, "We will."

Aubrey dropped cash on the table and left Ingram with the egg rolls.

When Shaw reached the turnpike, she stayed in the local northbound lanes. The sky grew grayer over the brown salt marsh invisible beneath the refinery towers. A passenger train screamed past on one side of the highway and jet aircraft roared crossing over the other side. She exited at the airport service road and followed signs to a chain motel just outside the airport complex. She parked and registered with her personal VISA card. The desk clerk told her where to put the car. Once settled in their room, she ordered two dishes of chocolate ice cream from room service. She opened the drapes over the balcony window facing out across the access road to the air terminal to let in what sunlight remained of the day.

Tess found the television remote and sat with it in the middle of one of the double bed. She managed to get the set on, but the screen displayed a menu instead of program channels. Shaw punched up a cartoon.

"When will I see my Daddy?"

"Maybe tonight, Dear."

Room service arrived. Shaw signed the receipt and gave Tess her dish. She left hers on the tray and went over to the balcony again, looking out at the jets taking off and landing. Get her back to Harry she thought, in Pittsburgh, if they can make contact. Then to the Caymans. She did not think she could take Tess back to Winchester. Durham Bryce said not to, and she feared returning to Washington, too. For now, at least.

"Can we talk to my Grampa, now" Tess asked.

"I'll try, Hon." Shaw called the Bryce home number she saved on her cell.

Bryce's sister answered it. Barbara told her who she was and that she had Tess.

"Who are you?" Kathy screamed. "Did you kill my father?"

"What?"

"I said, did you kill my father?"

"I didn't know anything about that. We saw a man out on the baseball field and your father asked me to take Tess. That's why she's with me."

"Where are you?"

Shaw waited and finally said, "I can't say. Does Harry know about this?"

"No. You bring her back, right now."

"I can't do that either. Tell Harry to contact me on my cell phone."

"Please, bring her back."

"I told you, I can't." She hated to cause them even more pain. Her first duty was to protect Tess best as she could but she faced her own risks, too. "Tell Harry to call me."

"Wait," Kathy said, and Shaw thought she heard another person on the line.

A man's voice asked, "What did he look like, the guy on the baseball field?"

It had to be the police, so she folded up the cell phone and walked back inside. She told Tess she left a message and her father would call soon. She sat down and dipped into her ice cream. Durham Bryce knew a lot more about this case than he had time to tell her. Maybe about her, too. He took the hit to save his granddaughter. And now, Aubrey's clients will figure out she turned. Harry was her only protection, but only as long as she had Tess.

Kauffman sat alone in the study. The rented townhouse came furnished, and the Queen Anne reproductions the owner provided were nice enough. So was the townhouse itself, and so was Georgetown, but he and his wife were ready to get back to their own place on Spruce Street in Philadelphia. This would be his last tour in Washington and they both hoped it would not last much longer. They left almost everything back there, but he did bring along a few things to hang on the walls—mostly his amateur paintings of Eighteenth Century naval battles.

He sipped his brandy while the Second Brandenburg Concerto played on the local PBS radio station, and fingered the piece of paper sitting under the brass lamp on the desk that his secretary had brought over from Main Justice. It was a hand-written fax. The telephone rang and he picked it up.

"You get it?" al-Fasi asked.

"Yes. Any word on Harry Bryce out there?"

"No. And you?"

"Nothing."

"Well, there is something here," al-Fasi said. "I'm in the FBI Field Office. A State Police report just came in on the wire. Durham Bryce was murdered outside Philadelphia. It says the suspects and his granddaughter are missing."

"Oh, God. When?"

"Just says today."

"I got a message from Durham, but didn't get back to him. Is it in the news yet?"

"Not out here. Police are looking for Harry and the informant. And the car I told them was at the scene. They're crawling all over the law office and suspicious as hell of me."

"What about Harlan?"

"Gone home. Morgantown. I got word to him before calling in the locals."

"What about the informant?"

"Allison Caldwell. She owns the house and the car parked there, so the police have picked that up."

"Okay, Saad. As soon as you can break loose from all that, run down to Morgantown and contact Harlan again. Find out what you can about the proffer, especially what documents he produced. Maybe he has copies. Where did you send this fax from?"

"Store front notary down the street."

"Good. And Bryce?"

"Locals are checking the usual things. Airport, turnpike. I've heard nothing."

"He's heading East, I'm sure. And when he finds out about his father and daughter, if he hasn't already, he might call in here, but I don't know. After you see Harlan in Morgantown, get him back here—Georgetown, not Main Justice. We have to keep all this out of there for now."

"Right," al-Fasi said. "But I might be delayed. That storm out of Chicago is just hitting here,"

"Do your best."

They ended the conversation just as the radio interrupted the music with a weather report. The storm would reach the East Coast in a few hours, but they predicted the heaviest snow would fall north of Baltimore. Major roads in western Pennsylvania were closed. Kauffman looked out across the backyard brick patio. Brown leaves scattered across green moss on the bricks and the branches of a single dogwood tree stood silhouetted in the porch light. He wondered when the highways would open again.

The Ossete pinged the numbers from Ingram into the computer in his old Portuguese fort. The information he was looking for popped up; he emailed it to Manhattan. When the Cairo University dropout got him the new algorithms, he would send them to Manhattan as well, and Vrenc could deal with the new security problem coming out of Maryland.

The shadows lengthened as they drove along the bank of Savage River. The snow began to fall heavily, but the road was still open. Bryce turned right onto an unpaved path leading into the woods, marked only by the mail box with the name Whitten. The cabin loomed in the headlights through the snow, with a white Jeep Cherokee and a blue pick-up truck in a clearing by the door. Two dogs barked from a pen on the side of the house. Bryce parked beside the Cherokee. He went with Caldwell to the door and knocked. A man taller and heavier than Bryce in a red woolen hunting shirt opened it with a wide smile.

"Harry. How the hell are you? You said you were coming after Christmas, but I didn't hear from you." He drew them both inside.

"Whitten. Jack," he said to Caldwell with an extended hand.

She took it and said, "Caldwell. Allison."

Whitten led them past the gun rack on the foyer wall and into the living room. Bryce and Caldwell both sat on a sofa beside a blazing fireplace. Whitten sat in a swivel chair and twisted it around to face them.

"You both look worn out. Take a few minutes to relax. Where's Tess, Harry?"

"Back in Philadelphia. I'll get to that. Let me tell you what I think happened today in Pittsburgh, because I—we—may need help from you. And not Federal."

Bryce told Whitten as much as he thought he could about a federal grand jury investigation, why he was in Pittsburgh and who Caldwell was. "Then, after we finished the proffer, I offered to take her to the airport with me, but we stopped at her house first. We were inside, so we didn't see what happened. We heard someone shout 'FBI.' Then some shots. A man ran in the house, out the back, more shots, came back, held up a badge, said he was FBI and told us to get out of town. It seemed like a good idea. On the way out, we saw two bodies down by her drive. We managed to find our way here. I need to borrow one of your trucks if I'm going to get back East."

"Yeah. Whoever they were, they'll trace the rental," Whitten said. "How about her? Is she going with you?"

"I hadn't even thought about it. Ms. Caldwell?"

They both looked at her. "I'm still in a state of shock. I've tried not to think about anything, except how to fly to California."

"Well, stay here for now," Whitten said. "Take some time. Get your heads straight. No problem, Harry, with you taking one of the trucks, but this storm is looking like you'll have to wait a bit." He offered them drinks and went out to the kitchen.

Whitten returned with an unopened Coke bottle and a fifth of Jack Daniels. He filled two glasses with ice and whiskey. He gave one to Caldwell. He handed Bryce the Coke. "Sorry, Allison, I should have asked what you like." She said Jack Daniels was fine with her. Whitten sipped his drink. "Was that guy who chased you out of town really FBI?"

"He held up a badge and he had a service weapon. I didn't inspect them."

"You didn't know the FBI was tailing you?"

"No. And I'm not absolutely sure it really was FBI."

"Sit tight," Whitten said. "I'll try to make some contacts in Allegheny County. Off record." He went to the kitchen again and picked up the wall phone. Bryce tried to hear what he said into the receiver, but Whitten moved around the wall and spoke too low. He came back and said, "They'll get back."

Bryce asked if he could use that phone to call home. Whitten motioned and Bryce retraced his friend's steps back to the kitchen. Caldwell and Whitten sat in silence in the living room, listening to the fire. They heard Bryce shout, "Oh my God, Kathy. What about Tess?"

Whitten leaped up and ran into the kitchen next to Bryce.

"And you and Mom?" Whitten listened through another pause until Bryce said, "I'll be there as soon as possible. I'm still in the mountains. No, don't call Maureen yet. Wait for me."

"What is it?" Whitten asked him.

Bryce turned around, his face was sheet white. "My father's been killed. Shot. My paralegal ran off with Tess. My God, what the hell's happening?"

"Who was it? Do they know yet?"

"No, they don't. They made it sound like Dad recognized the shooter."

"What about Tess?"

"With my paralegal, Barbara Shaw. Kathy says Shaw wouldn't tell them where she and Tess are. Christ All Mighty, Jack."

Whitten grabbed him by the shoulders. He looked back over the kitchen counter at Caldwell on the sofa, who stared at them both, stunned.

"Come with me," he said. "Into the bedroom. So we can talk." When he closed the bedroom door, he asked, "Can you reach your paralegal?"

"Yeah, yeah, I think." Bryce fumbled in his pocket and got out his cell phone.

Whitten put a hand on his arm. " Don't use that. Use the land line there." He pointed to the phone on the nightstand. "Calm down, first, Harry. Take a few breaths. Think about what you're going to say. Play along with her."

Bryce found the number on his cell, and dialed it on the land line.

"Barbara?" he asked. "What happened?" After hearing her out, he asked to speak to his daughter. His tone shifted even lower. "I love you, Honey. I love you. I'll be with you in a few hours. Trust me."

"Tell her you're here with me," Whitten said. Bryce did. "Now ask to speak to your paralegal again. We need to straighten out some priorities. Find out where they are."

Bryce asked and added, "Why don't you bring Tess back home?" He listened and only said, "Okay," then turned to Whitten. "They're in a motel at the Newark Airport. She says my father told her not to take Tess back, but to get her to me. She thought of flying to Pittsburgh. She doesn't want to say too much with Tess in the room."

"Ask how she paid for the room."

Bryce did and held the phone against his chest. "VISA, personal." he said.

"Christ, Harry. Tell her to get the hell out of there."

"Where should I tell her to go? She can't make it here in the storm."

Whitten walked around the unmade bed with a hand on his brow. "New Jersey? You still have that family place at the shore?" Bryce nodded. "Tell her to go there. You'll meet them there. And for God's sake tell her she has to turn off her cell phone when you're done talking."

"Okay Barbara," Bryce said. "You have to leave right away. Take the Parkway, south. Go all the way to the end." He gave the directions to the house. "The keys are under the doormat. Tess will feel safe there. She's been there a lot, every summer. It's my parent's place. But look, get moving before this storm hits the coast. And Barbara, one more thing—"

He pulled the phone away from his ear and replaced it. "Lost the signal," he said. He wiped his eyes with his sleeve.

Whitten placed an arm over his shoulder. "Turn off your cell phone, too," he said. "Cut the power. You know anything about her car? Make, model? Anything I can pass on?"

"Nothing. Last time I saw her she said it was in the shop and asked for a ride."

From the bedroom, Whitten saw Caldwell by the fireplace holding a cell phone in her hand. "What the fuck do you think you're doing?" he shouted.

"Tried to call my daughter. And now, I should talk to my lawyer."

"Turn it off. You're a fucking government witness. Don't call anybody right now. And not from here, for God's sake."

She put the phone away. "Well, it doesn't matter. No signal anyway."

"Local towers are probably down in the storm." Whitten returned to the swivel chair. "Sorry for the language, Allison. It's just what I use with the kind of people I usually have to deal with."

"I think I heard it once or twice in a ladies room back in Pittsburgh," she said.

Bryce walked over to the window facing the down slope of the mountain behind the cabin. The snow started blowing straight across, nearly horizontal, and nothing else could be seen past the flakes. "My father and I talked about this case last night, Jack. He used to work with my boss, Winston Kauffman, in his days in Washington. Later, Durham joined a group of consultants on cold cases until about a year ago. He said he would tell me more about it when I got back. Then, in Pittsburgh, I got a message from him that Barbara Shaw was on her way to see me. Something about this case. Now, she thinks the guy who killed my father was the same who tailed me back in Washington a few days ago, and that my father seemed to know who he was. But she didn't want to say much. She hasn't told Tess about her grandfather."

He swung around and looked at Whitten. "Jack, I've got to go. Let me have the Cherokee."

Whitten took up the television remote and clicked on the weather channel. Behind an image of snow blasting across the Pennsylvania turnpike, a female voice told everybody to stay inside and off the roads."

"You're not going anywhere right now, Harry. You'll just get blown off that mountain. Good thing, too, because I'm not letting you go anyway. Come on over here. Sit down. Go over this fucking case, with me. Every freaking detail. Before you even think of heading back east. So I know what to tell my contacts and more important, what not to tell them."

Bryce moved away from the window and sat at the dining table angled toward the fireplace. They listened to the snow hitting the cabin walls. Bryce moved his hand toward the bottle of Jack Daniels Whitten left on the table.

"You touch that, I'll break your arm," Whitten said.

"That'll still leave me another one."

"Then I'll break that, too."

Bryce withdrew his hand and smiled. "Thanks, Jack. Sometimes, I need a kick in the head from you."

Tom Gould slouched on the stool in his kitchenette. The window drapes were pulled shut and the only light came from the florescent lamp over the counter and the muted television screen across the floor. An open bottle of Ballentine's sat on the counter with a half empty glass and a passport. After one more sip, he took the message out of his pocket. Call the FBI Field Office.

He opened the passport. Due to expire in two weeks. He would have to renew it. To expedite it, he would have to go to the federal building where the FBI had its offices as well.

Reports of the storm out of Chicago flickered across the television screen. The scroll said it had just reached the East Coast and that the airports and Interstates were closed, but the center had shifted north of Baltimore.

Bennett called and told him to get the gunman out of town. Gould tried the number at the chop shop. He let the phone ring ten times before hanging up. He went back to the bedroom, took the lock box out of the closet and set it on his bed.

Larson wrote down the information Ingram passed on from Manhattan. Shaw was less than an hour away, weather permitting. He watched the first snowflakes drop past the parking lot lights from his room at the Shangri-La. He went out to the Plymouth and started up US 1 North. The flakes drifted across his headlights from left to right in the wind.

CHAPTER NINE

Karev sat on the stool in the body shop watching as the crew cut up the BMW, leaving only the frame on the lift. The radio behind them, blaring heavy metal rock, broke in with a news report about a shooting on Mount Washington. A reporter quoted a neighbor who claimed to see a BMW on the scene. The workers kept their attention on the torches. The announcer moved on to the snowstorm, then back to music.

Karev went over to the desk and picked up the telephone. The Nigerian started to object, but Karev stared back, patting his shoulder holster. The Nigerian backed away. After dialing the number, he waited until a machine answered the call, and then carefully replaced the receiver on the cradle. Karev walked to the door and looked out on the street. The slanting snow was accumulating and he saw no tire tracks or moving vehicles. After a few minutes, however, a rusty Peugeot rounded the corner and slid to a stop in front of the garage. He pressed the button and the garage door scrolled up. Behind him, the telephone rang. Karev looked back and signaled the Nigerian not to answer it. When the ringing stopped, he climbed into the Peugeot, which reversed out of the drive and moved slowly away.

"It is on the news," the driver said.

"I heard it."

"They said one of the dead was a federal agent. Did you know about that?"

"No. We were not warned."

"The news reports said little, but there have been police inquiries in the community. So they must have something."

"Did you report this to Vrenc?"

"Yes."

They drove on through the littered streets, past abandoned houses, all of it purified under the fresh snow. Karev said, "The American left me alone back there with those Africans. He was not aware we have other resources."

"Forget about him," the driver said. "You've got to get out of here. The shipment was loaded in Mississippi and is due in Baltimore tomorrow—weather permitting."

The Peugeot turned down an alley and parked in the rear of a three-story brick building on the corner. It once was a row house, but now it sat next to a vacant lot, with the side wall stuccoed over. They entered through the back door of what Karev realized at once was closed grocery store with iron gates outside across the windows. The room smelled of chlorine.

Karev removed his shoulder holster and gave it to the driver. "Dispose of that," he said. The driver tucked it under the cash register counter.

"I told Vrenc you do not have the documents. He gave me some new orders to pass on." The driver handed over a slip of paper.

"You can confirm we didn't get any documents." Karev looked at the paper. "Morgantown? Then Baltimore? I'll need cash and a clean gun."

"How much?"

"A couple of thousand, to be sure."

In a dark corner by the back wall, the driver kicked aside a cardboard carton of toilet paper and reached into the shelf behind. He pulled out a strong box, set it on the counter and unlocked it. First, he removed a plastic-wrapped automatic, then a small fold of uncirculated hundred dollar bills. He closed the box and replaced it.

"That should be ten thousand, but I haven't counted it." He pointed at the location where the box was hidden. "Security. The neighborhood knows to stay away, and we have to clear out after this anyway."

"I need a different coat," Karev said.

The driver opened a closet and pulled out a red ski jacket. "Use this, you'll look like a local. He folded Karev's black overcoat around the leather holster. "I'll dispose of these," he said. "And, I've got a VISA you can use."

He rang open the cash register and found the card. Karev examined it and a slip of paper taped to the other side. "That's the PIN," the driver said. "The card's aged three years."

"Car?" Karev said.

"Take the Peugeot." He dropped the keys on the counter. "It has road maps, but no GPS. Head south out of State."

"And the weather?"

The driver shrugged and led Karev back to the car. He gave directions through the local streets to the bridge out of town. He stood in the doorway until the Peugeot disappeared down the alley, then called the Nigerian and told him to close up and send his men home for a few days.

The steel gray Mercedes with diplomatic license plates reading "Republic of Serbia" turned into the space for visitors in front of a one-story building marked Miltech. A new sign advertising AVAILABLE hung on the wall. A heavy man in a tweed wool overcoat got out of the car and pressed the door button. He heard a muffled ring inside and saw the red light come on by the doorjamb. He let himself in.

The only light in the room shone over the desk. Ingram stood up behind it and motioned toward a steel and plastic chair. The man from the Mercedes sat down. Apart from the metal desk, the only unpacked items in the room were a telephone, fax machine, Rolodex and a note pad. Everything else was in the thirteen cardboard boxes around the floor.

"You are ready, then?" Milos Vrenc asked.

"It all goes into storage tomorrow."

"Under a new corporate name? Not linked at all to the past?"

"Of course. That lawyer arranged the paperwork. He is delivering it tomorrow as well."

Vrenc wondered how many other details the lawyer knew. Ingram might be losing control, he thought, but he was forced to stay with him. He unbuttoned his overcoat and removed a sealed envelope. There was a small penknife attached to the watch chain from his vest. He used the blade to cut the diplomatic seals.

"It arrived from JFK yesterday," he said.

Ingram took the envelope and leafed quickly through the contents. "Good, this confirms the money transfer."

"Take that with you. Show it to your lawyer and whomever else you need to prove that the funds have arrived in Grand Turk."

"The lawyer has not heard of any contact by the prosecutor, Harry Bryce, with Washington since the meeting in Pittsburgh. Nothing routine. No documents. Nothing. He did give me information about a place Bryce might have gone to, and I sent Colovic down there from Bedford. I asked Bennett to get Karev back to New York, but that may be complicated by the weather."

"I send him orders to go to Morgantown first. Try to get the documents," Vrenc said. He did not add that he also had him go to Baltimore, not New York. "So, as far as we can tell, the prosecutor has made no contact with the Justice Department since Pittsburgh? Is that right?"

"All I know is what the lawyer told me. The prosecutor may have sources he can't track. We weren't informed about the agents following him in Pittsburgh."

"Maybe outside Justice. Yes."

The fax machine buzzed and a message crawled out. Ingram picked it out of the tray.

"The shipment at Corinth is loaded and on its way. I'll notify the aircraft to prepare for take-off." Ingram pushed the fax paper across the desk. "There is one more thing. The prosecutor will probably give priority to reconnecting with his daughter, in New Jersey. Anything you can trace on her?"

"Is that phone secure?" Vrenc asked.

Ingram shook his head and took a cell phone from under the desk. Vrenc placed the international call, pulled the pad over and jotted down the notes. He showed them to Ingram.

"I'll get some coverage down there, too," Ingram said. He looked at the time and date on his wristwatch. "In twenty-four hours, we should rendezvous at the warehouse in Maryland. Then we shift everything to Cold Spring. In forty-eight hours the deal should be closed."

The carpet merchant from Manhattan put his palm on the diplomatic envelope.

"After you get the papers from the lawyer and confirm the delivery, break off contact. Clean things up, and get that back to me," he said.

Whitten brought the dogs in from the storm. They shook off the snow, sniffed at Bryce and Caldwell, and curled up next to the fireplace. Whitten added a few more logs then put a pizza into the microwave.

"Okay, Harry," he said. "Are you ready for some thinking? Out loud?"

"The only thinking I'm doing right now is about Tess and how to get to her."

"You know what I mean. This case of yours."

"Fuck the case."

The microwave buzzed. Whitten brought out the pizza. The three of them sat at the table.

"Smart guy like you, Harry," Whitten said, "knows that fucking case of yours caused all this, so tell me about it."

"I probably told you more than I'm allowed."

"Yeah, well, all those rules just went out in a shit bucket. I can't make any calls for backup. Not yet, anyway. And if I do, I have to disclose you're here. Both of you. And why. So, I need to know all that you know at least."

Bryce chewed on a slice. "You're probably right," he said.

He started with background Whitten already knew: the transfer to Washington, the assignment to the Tuscarora investigation, the call from Harlan Moan, how he reported the call verbally to his boss, Professor Kauffman, who then informed the Deputy Assistant Attorney General. He continued with a description of the party at Gideon Aubrey's house with Barbara Shaw.

"Gideon?" Whitten interrupted. "The tax guy back in law school?"

"That's the guy. I had a minor matter with him a few years ago. And, it turns out, according to Allison, he's counsel of record for one of Tuscarora's subsidiaries."

"Christ." Whitten said. "Okay, go on."

Bryce continued to the last conversation with his father.

Caldwell decided to explore the cabin while Bryce talked. She started in the foyer, examining the gun rack, and moved to a work room with a small table with a vise for tying flies for trout. She examined the book rack, the DVD's and novels—all westerns and mysteries. She overheard Bryce end with the shooting in Pittsburgh and the phone calls with Barbara Shaw and his sister. She decided it was okay to return to the dining table.

"It appears," Whitten said, "that the shooters in Pittsburgh didn't know the FBI was tailing you."

"I guess not."

"Doesn't sound like the guy who said he was FBI was on official duty. Or he wouldn't have said to get out of town."

"No."

"If they were FBI, or Feds of some kind at least, who do you think sent them?"

"It would have to be Kauffman. He's the only one who knew I was taking her proffer today in Pittsburgh."

"Nobody else? Where and when, I mean?"

"Christ, I forgot that I mentioned it to the paralegal. Just the call from Moan, I think."

"Date, time and place?"

"I'm not sure—might have."

"And the killer who showed up at your parents'. He was after you, I guess. Didn't expect to run into your paralegal. Or did he?"

"I assume not."

"Why do you think he went there?"

"To make contact with me, I assume. He wouldn't have known I was already on my way to Pittsburgh. But before you ask why again, I'll tell you—I haven't a clue."

"Who sent him? Any ideas?"

"The only people who knew anything about the proffer, in Justice anyway, were Kauffman, Barbara and the DAAG."

Whitten pushed aside his plate and wiped his mouth with a paper napkin. He pointed to Caldwell. "She gave you documents in the proffer? I mean, your kind of cases, you get piles of that shit."

"Right."

"Were the shooters in Pittsburgh after them?"

"Well, one of the bodies was right next to the car where I left them."

"And you have them here?"

"Sure. Still in the car."

"Give me the keys." Bryce laid them on the table. When Whitten left, Caldwell came over to Bryce and took both his hands in hers.

"You're keeping those documents, aren't you?" she said. You're not giving them to those creeps in Washington you just told your friend about."

Bryce tried to draw back, but she held tight.

"Harry," she said, "let the Feds handle this. That's what Harlan told me."

"Trust Harlan Moan?" Bryce said. "He sent you to me. I'm a Fed, or so I thought until a few hours ago. Now, who knows? Look at what it got us. Me. You. My father. My daughter." He stared back angrily at her. "We can't trust any of them, Allison. Or, to put it better, we don't know who we can trust."

"You're going to use those documents to protect your daughter, aren't you?"

"If that's what it takes."

"And what about me?"

He looked at her but said nothing.

"Am I in the bargain, too?"

"You're headed for California."

She pulled her hands away. "That's no answer, Harry. I'm going to Morgantown to see Harlan. I have to make changes in my plans. Maybe I should say they've been made for me. Just like for you. I know what it's like to have a daughter. We both face the same tough choices."

Bryce got up and crossed to the fireplace. "Nobody knows what his real price is until something like this comes along, Allison. Now, I know. I'll sell out the whole United States of America if that's what it takes to make my daughter safe and to get the bastards responsible for my father's death. And whoever else is involved in this mess." He turned to look at her. "But not you," he said. "You're not to blame. Wish I could put it better than that. Maybe later. I hope that's good enough for now."

She let a moment go by, then asked, "What about the girl's mother?"

"I'm hoping to get Tess back safe before she finds out about this."

"You're not going to call her?"

"No."

A glimmer of anger flashed across her face. "For God's sake, she deserves to know."

"If I tell her anything too soon, she might put herself in danger, too."

Caldwell went to the patio door to look out at the snow. The thought hit her for the first time—her own daughter might be in danger.

"I'll call Maureen as soon as I have Tess back with me," Bryce promised.

Another reason, Caldwell thought, to somehow reach Harlan as soon as possible. Instead of talking about her fears, she said, "I like the mountains better in the summer, with all the leaves on the trees."

"Yeah, they hide a lot, don't they, the leaves" Bryce said.

"But the winter snow helps," she said. "Covers some of that, I mean, for a while."

Gould counted the cash first. He had just $25,000 on hand. He took out the old bearer bond from Vrenc. He never could read it—it was in Cyrillic script. The vellum was old and heavy. Vrenc assured him it was worth $100,000, but the only place he knew to redeem it was in Philadelphia, a small shop on Jewelers' Row. He scanned through a couple of other documents. Worthless to him now, he decided. The rest of it, certificates of deposit, shares of stock and Treasury notes, would be lost, but he was due a large cash payout in Baltimore. And after that, he would not return to Pittsburgh, anyway.

He pocketed the cash, carefully rolled the bearer bond into his jacket and left everything else in the safe deposit box on the bed. He packed a travel bag, and took it with him out to the kitchenette for another drink. He couldn't stand putting it off any longer. He forgot about the drink and went down to the garage to the Ford loaner.

The snow was still building up, but city trash trucks with plows were quartering the city streets under yellow flashers, scattering salt and cinders behind them. He followed one slowly out of the business district until he could cross the Allegheny and get to Bennett's place.

"Where's that guy from New York?" Bennett asked when Gould arrived.

"I thought we should pick him up on the way the airport," Gould told him. "We don't want to spend any more time with him than we have to, and you wouldn't want him here. We might be stuck with the storm for a while."

Bennett explained the arrangements he made for a private flight. "It can take off as soon as the snow stops. No tickets. No security to go through. We have to be in Baltimore when the goods arrive or we might miss the contact. Let's have a drink while we wait."

They sat in Bennett's entertainment room and nursed their drinks, but after a few minutes of mutual silence, they both decided that they could delay no longer. Gould drove them back to Pittsburgh, into the neighborhood with the body shop.

The shop was dark like everything else on the block except the streetlights. Gould got out of the Ford and pushed the doorbell. The street itself was silent and unplowed. No sound came from within the building. He knocked on the metal doorframe, and the door swung open on its own. He reached for a light switch, walked in and found the shop empty except for the car frames on the hydraulic lifts. Outside, he noticed for the first time a set of tire treads leading up to the garage door.

Gould got back in the Ford. Bennett asked, "Was he there?"

"Nobody is."

"What do you think?"

"Maybe they closed up early because of the storm."

"But where's that New Yorker? Maybe they heard the news report about the shootings. Stashed him somewhere. You notice anybody following us?"

They looked back and saw nothing moving, not even trash trucks plowing snow.

"We can't waste time looking," Gould said.

They headed back out of the city toward the airport. The snow began easing up. Get across the bridge again, Gould thought to himself, and then it's all in George's hands. "What's next?" Gould asked.

"At BWI we rent a car and go to Ingram's hangar. That's where they told me the truck's coming."

"BWI might be closed in the storm."

"We don't have to be there until tomorrow morning."

"What about our money?"

"Ingram said he's got the confirmation. They need to inspect the stuff first."

"And then we're out of it? No more dealing with Ingram and the others?"

Bennett did not reply. The drive was slow, but they were able to keep moving. After a while, Bennett said, "I hope Vrenc arranged to get that guy to New York, or whatever."

"At least out of Pittsburgh."

Whitten set the brief case and the red rope envelope on the dining table. He opened the envelope and spread out Caldwell's documents. He picked up the purchase order first.

"What's Blue Mountain?" he asked.

"Something they set up to handle exports," Bryce said. "That's the subsidiary I mentioned. Gideon Aubrey, counsel of record."

"And Miltech and Pickwick?"

"Miltech's the export broker. Pickwick is a subcontractor."

"Were they in the subpoena?"

"No. I never heard of them until Allison told me about it this morning."

"So, you probably don't have obstruction."

"Agreed."

"There's no date on the purchase order. How about a bill of lading?"

"Nope."

"Okay. Can I see your notes?" Whitten asked.

Bryce shrugged. "Might as well. We've already violated all the grand jury regs." He spun the brief case locks until they clicked. Allison went to the fireplace and sat by the dogs.

Whitten scanned Bryce's notes. "So, this guy Bennett set the whole thing up to screw his father."

"That's right," Allison said. "With Tom Gould's help."

Whitten flipped open Bryce's case binder and read the anonymous letter from Memphis. He returned to the purchase order, the newspaper clipping and then looked at the travel records. "Well," he said, "even if you can prove this guy Fancher's death wasn't natural, what you have so far won't make a case even against Gould, let alone Bennett."

"Or anybody else further up the chain, if any," Bryce added.

Allison turned back at them. "What do you mean? Why do you think they were all over my place? You said they were after those documents."

"It's all circumstantial," Whitten told her. "Business meetings, Contracts. Microwave oven parts. At most, tax evasion, from what I can see."

"But, it's obvious," she said.

"Sure to you. And to Harry and me. But not to a judge and jury. Reasonable doubt. You heard of that?"

"What about my testimony?"

"You haven't testified yet. And when you do, you're impeachable."

"What's that mean?"

"It means," Bryce broke in, "Mickey Bennett. Your affair. Your daughter by him. The money they gave you that you sent to her. Conflict with George over the divorce from his mother. You're implicated. Maybe your daughter is, too."

"Oh, Christ," she said. "Harlan knew that all along, didn't he?"

"Of course."

Whitten broke in. "Harry needs more direct evidence than you can provide. But there is this." He dropped a finger on the travel voucher to Mozambique. Allison got up and came over to look.

"Hear about that worm in the Justice Department computers they've been trying to break for about a year now, Harry?"

"I've been out of the loop, remember? Just got back full time about four months ago."

"Computer worm," Whitten said. "Infected hundreds of U.S.

Government programs. They keep coming up with security fixes, but the worm mutates and breaches them. They think it originated somewhere in the Caucasus because of their network addresses. And they think lately it's moved to somewhere in East Africa."

"How do you have access to all that secret stuff?" Allison asked.

"You'd be surprised what we figure out on our own here in Savage River."

"So, that's why the Professor never turns on his computer," Bryce said. "And that's why he set up Pete O'Shea in the suburbs."

"And why they insisted I keep all those records only on paper," Allison said. She went back to rub the dog's necks.

"Harry," Whitten said, "it's my guess these people you mentioned don't care about the Fancher case now. They care about East Africa."

"But I could have used the Fancher allegations to turn somebody else," Bryce said.

Allison lifted her hands off the dogs and looked at the two men. "You might try Tom Gould."

Whitten refilled his glass of Jack Daniels. He offered Allison one and she accepted. He gave her a fresh glass and got Harry another bottle of Coke. Then he said, "What if those parts really are missile guidance systems?"

Barbara Shaw moved around the room, turning off the lights, but she left the television on. She told Tess to get ready to leave but did not explain why. Tess protested she had to finish watching the show. Shaw wanted to keep the girl calm, so she waited and struggled to calm herself and collect her own thoughts. Thirty minutes after she ended the call with Harry, she pulled aside the drapes and looked out the porch window again, keeping herself in the shadows. The snow outside was falling harder, but wasn't accumulating. Planes were still taking off and landing at the airport across the six-lane highway from the motel. She noticed a green Plymouth station wagon draw up to the lobby entrance and recognized the man getting out: blond crew cut, black leather jacket.

"Tess," she said. "Get your coat on. We have to go now."

"But where?"

"To meet your Daddy. Let's go."

She bundled Tess up in her coat and carried the girl out into the hall. As she pulled the door behind her to fully engage the lock, she heard the telephone ring inside. Ignoring it, she went down the hall to the fire exit, taking each step as carefully and quietly as she could until they reached the bottom. She touched the metal door. The security bolt was cold. She took a deep breath, recited a quick prayer, and pushed it open. The rush of the on-coming storm and roar of jet aircraft hit them. She ran with Tess to the car.

Larson used his universal card to open the door, sneering all the time at the stupid desk clerk and the stupid door lock and then congratulating himself on his luck that the deadbolt wasn't thrown.

He stepped inside. He did not need to hit the light switch. The airport and parking lot lights shone through the parted drapes at the porch window. Empty. He could see from the rumpled bed and dirty dishes that they had been there. He slid open the porch window and leaned out. She was down there in plain sight, carrying the girl, getting into her car, pulling away. Fuck. He should have thought to yank off the distributor cap.

He ran down the back stairs two at a time and made for the Plymouth. The wagon bounced over the exit speed bumps and he heard the bargain shock absorbers give way, cracking the muffler underneath. He could see that she was out on the service road, receding rapidly from view in the heavier snow. When he got to where he'd last seen her, he faced a maze of exits, ramps and ambiguous signs. East, west, north, south. He could only guess which one she took. He continued east bound on the airport access road, but he knew he'd lost her.

Screwed. And for the second time. Won't be a third, he swore. He made his way back to his motel on Route 1 to report to Ingram. Get some new directions, some idea where she was going, maybe. That'd take time. For now, he'd wait and see if the diner waitress was off duty yet.

CHAPTER TEN

al-Fasi knocked on the door. There was no response. He knocked a second time, and again nothing. He moved aside the doorjamb and took out his service pistol.

"Federal Agents, Mr. Gould. We have a warrant. Open up."

Still, no answer. The other agent signaled to the assistant building manager waiting down the end of the corridor. He came up with the key, turned the lock, and hurried back. al-Fasi tapped the door open with his toe. It hit the interior wall and swung halfway back. No sound of movement inside. The agents nodded to each other. al-Fasi entered first in a crouch, waving the pistol barrel ahead of him. The local agent followed. They had the floor plan from the assistant manager, and al-Fasi headed straight for the bedroom. The local agent covered him from just inside the door, sweeping his pistol across the kitchenette and living room.

al-Fasi carried out the open lock box and dropped it on the kitchen counter. He leafed through the papers quickly. Most of it was routine bank stuff.

"Take that back with you," he said. "Have it inventoried. I'll look at it more closely later."

While the other agent turned away to report in, al-Fasi removed two of the papers. Whatever else was there, he knew Gould would not be coming back for it. The locals had insisted he get a search warrant, and they were lucky to get the magistrate to sign off. It all took time. A check with the parking garage camera downstairs showed they were several hours late.

The pick-up truck moved quietly down the private drive toward the cabin. Deep snow covered the stone paving and Colovic used only the parking lights. The wind tore through the tops of the trees. He was sure they could not hear him approach from inside the cabin. He slowed when the odometer rolled off two-tenths of a mile, out of sight of the cabin itself, and steered the truck into the woods. He shut off the lights, but left the engine running.

It took him half the night to get through the mountains from Bedford in the storm. He could not stop on the way, and when he finally reached Savage River, he went past the drive twice before seeing the mailbox.

He took the Remington deer rifle from the Bedford hunting lodge, made sure it was loaded with hollow points and mounted the sight. He pocketed a spare box of solid shot cartridges even though he was confident the five rounds already loaded would be enough. He wished they'd had some explosives at the lodge.

He walked another fifty yards down the drive, staying to the edge of the tree line, stepping over branches blown down by the wind. When the cabin lights came into view, he moved further into the woods. He saw three vehicles parked in front—a Jeep, a pick-up and a sedan—all under a floodlight.

He spotted the telephone line dangling down from a pole, moved to where he could reach it and cut it with a serrated combat knife. Then he retreated back into the trees.

He knew he could not break in with just a deer rifle. Even the knife would not be fast enough for three of them. He raised the sight to his eye and scanned the windows, but could spot only one person, a female, alone at the fireplace. He swung the sight across the cabin front and noticed, for the first time, the dog pen. No animals. No barking. He checked his watch, deciding to wait. If they went to bed, maybe he could them get them inside.

"Jesus Christ," Harry said. "A worm. A fucking computer worm. I've read about those things but nobody in the Department ever said anything to me about that. There were clues I might have picked up, maybe, like the Professor telling me keep the proffer off record for a while. But the case itself? You're suggesting the hardware in the contracts is involved, too? Professor Kauffman led me to believe this was just a fraud case, just about money. My father hinted there was more. He was going to talk about it when I got back. Maybe that's why he got killed. And my daughter Tess? Barbara Shaw? What the hell else didn't they tell me, Jack?"

"More important," said Whitten, "why?"

Caldwell broke in. "Wait a minute. How about what Harlan knows that he didn't tell me. What about my daughter?"

Bryce looked at her. "You implicated her with those checks. If Jack's right, the documents you gave me are key to something else. Like you just said, Gould is the guy. He's the one, you said, in contact with the money, the angels."

"You have a case agent on this you can trust to a contact?" Whitten asked.

"I don't know who to trust. But we have to take a chance now and trust somebody. Plus, I should officially log in. Can I use your land line again?"

Whitten waved him toward the kitchen. "Try the phone again. See if it's back on. When you're done, I'll try some of my own contacts. Definitely not federals."

Bryce picked the receiver off the wall and returned it. "Line's still dead."

"Let me try mine," Caldwell said. She took out her cell before Whitten could stop her, but she put it away. "Dead, too."

They all looked at the muted television screen. It still carried scrolls and images of the storm. The dogs stirred in front of the fireplace. Then they leaped up, barked and darted to the door, clawing and sniffing at it.

"Hit the floor," Whitten yelled. "Get away from the windows." He flipped off the lights in the kitchen and dining room before dropping to his belly. Bryce was on the floor by the table. Caldwell fell next to the fireplace and crawled over to the others.

Whitten kept his attention on his dogs. "Who would know you're here, Harry?" he whispered

"You're not a complete secret, Jack. Gideon may know we're still friends. And I listed you in my security clearance file, remember?"

"Yeah. They called me about Maureen's divorce charges."

"You think somebody's out there?" Caldwell said, trying to keep a low voice like the others.

Both men ignored her. Whitten said to Bryce, "Somebody leaked my address from that file. Your boss? Your case agent?"

"Don't know. It doesn't much matter right now, does it?"

"Yeah. Whatever's out there..."

"Who?" Caldwell broke in again. "Oh God. Tell me what we got into."

Whitten held a finger to his lips. "Friends of your friends in Pittsburgh is my guess."

"Your police radio, Jack?" Bryce asked.

"Out in the truck." Whitten crept up to the front window. Taking an angle without the fireplace or the television behind him, he raised his head above the sill half expecting a rifle shot. The outside floodlight threw a circle out over the doorway and drive. Nothing moved inside the circle except the last of the storm's snowflakes. He slid over the floor to the foyer gun rack, pulled down a pump action shot gun and laid on his back, feeding in the shells.

"What the hell are you doing, Jack?" Bryce asked. "You can't go out there. We don't know how many there are."

"That's what they want—for us to just sit tight. They might have explosives. Burn us out, maybe. We have to do what they don't expect." When he finished loading the pump action, he reached up for the double-barreled shotgun and the bolt-action deer rifle. He handed them to Bryce.

"Slug shell in the shotgun," he said. "You used that rifle the last time we went out."

Bryce loaded them both. He kept the rifle with the box of bullets and handed the shotgun and a few extra shells to Caldwell.

"You know how to use that?" Whitten asked. She nodded yes, she did.

"Good. It's short range. At least it's something for you to think about. Now, calm down."

She took the shotgun and cradled it on the floor. "I've started to," she said.

Whitten rubbed his dogs by their necks as they kept pawing and sniffing. "Okay," he said. "Here's the plan. Give me two minutes after I get out the back door. I'll slip around to the front. Then, you let the dogs out. They'll go straight for the intruders, wherever they are. Look for the muzzle flashes from their guns, Harry. Aim at that. Shoot and keep their attention. You," he pointed at Caldwell, "back up Harry. I'll work my way around behind them while you're shooting."

Bryce put his hand on the pump action shotgun in Whitten's hands. "I got you into this. You do the cover."

"We don't have time for that macho shit, Harry. I know the ground, they don't. I've killed people. I don't like it, but I have. You haven't. Last time we went hunting, I don't remember if you even got off a shot."

"A couple, I think."

"Well, you didn't hit anything. And besides," Whitten added, "I'm not a Daddy; you are. Whatever happens, get out of here and get to Tess."

Whitten crawled to the kitchen and the back door. Before he opened it, Bryce said, "They might have both doors covered."

"It's a forty-five degree uphill shot from back here."

He slipped out. Bryce and Caldwell listened. There was no gunfire. The second hand on Bryce's watch read two minutes since Jack left. He switched off the outside floodlight, reached up for the door latch and pushed it open. The dogs bounded out in full cry. Bryce lay down in the darkened doorway, braced and shouldered the deer rifle.

Colovic heard the dogs. He knew he was blown when the interior lights went off but forgot about the dogs. The wind eased up as they ran out. He hadn't planned on using hollow point rounds on dogs; now he didn't have a choice. He squeezed off two of them. The lead dog fell dead in the middle of the clearing in front of the cabin. The second fell wounded, a few yards from him. He left the dog where it was and concentrated on the cabin door. No one came out, but a few rounds of rifle fire ripped through the branches overhead and he saw the muzzle flashes. He expected an attack from his flank and tried to see through the trees on both sides. He needed night goggles, explosives, and an automatic instead of a light deer rifle with 30.06 ammo. Three rounds of hollow point left. With the shots from the front door, he thought he only had one flank to worry about. He moved further back in the woods, keeping the drive on his left.

Whitten saw the muzzle flashes from just one gun—probably a deer rifle, he thought—coming from where he expected. It looked like only one shooter, so far. He worked his way from behind the dog shed and up the drive through the trees, keeping wide of Bryce's line of fire. The wind stopped for a moment. He tried not to make any sound. The sudden calm air gave him a small margin of visibility. He still believed scatter shot was his best bet, but he needed to get closer, and he needed Bryce to keep holding the shooter's attention.

He found the pick-up truck off the drive, engine running, headlights off. He passed behind it, stopped, crouched down, and raced across the drive to the next tree line.

A sudden gust of wind hit him in the face from the left. He used his hand as a shield and kept moving. A dead branch cracked under his boot. He froze and listened. The wind picked up again, cracking the branches overhead. Whitten thought he saw a man close to the ground, about ten yards left of Bryce's line of fire. He stayed crouched and moved nearer.

Colovic made out the shape of a man some twenty yards behind him. He looked back at the cabin to be sure no one else was coming out. Then he shifted position again to increase the angle of fire between himself, the cabin, and the figure in the woods.

Whitten saw the movement. Bryce's shots were still hitting the branches above. He brought the shotgun to his hip and fired. The shot went wide. He pumped and fired again.

Colovic spun on the first report. The buckshot whistled through the brush next to him. He dropped to one knee, and the second blast cut through the air above. He let off two quick rounds.

The first shot hit Whitten square in the chest and hurled him back. His trigger finger discharged the shotgun one last time, up in the branches. The second bullet caught him in the chest, too, and he dropped down on the forest floor. The night, the wind and the accumulated snow swallowed him up.

After a few minutes with no sound or movement, Colovic crept over to the body and stood up. He could save his last chambered hollow point. He returned to face the cabin and fired at the door, then reloaded with solid shot.

Bryce and Caldwell waited. They counted five rifle reports and three shotgun blasts since the dogs ran out and they heard moaning from one dog.

A rifle shot hit the wall behind the open door. Bryce caught the door with his foot and pulled it shut. He started to bolt it, but two more rounds slammed in. The door swung open on its hinges. Another shot pierced the front window.

Bryce pointed Caldwell back toward the kitchen. They crawled along the floor with their guns. Another fusillade of rifle fire smashed the front door hinges and it sagged against the jamb. Bryce lay on the floor with his back against the refrigerator door and his rifle pointed to the open door. Whitten hadn't turned off the florescent light over the kitchen sink. They couldn't risk reaching up for the switch.

"He'll come after us," Bryce said. "He can't wait us out. Doesn't have time. Needs the storm for cover. He knows we're armed. Like Jack said, he might have grenades or something." He pushed himself part way up against the refrigerator. "We have to go outside. It's our best bet. I remember the layout. Back of the cabin, the ground drops down to the river. There's an abandoned railroad track along the riverbank. Only the locals know about it. We get there, go about a quarter mile or so along the tracks. One of Jack's neighbors has a boat landing and nearby is his place. If we can reach it, we might get some help. Hold on to your gun."

Caldwell followed Bryce out the door onto the deck. The wind and snow had stopped. They crawled down the steps to the ground. It was steep and cold, but they moved lower from tree to tree while Bryce kept turning back to look up at the cabin. Halfway to the river, the kitchen light flicked off.

Colovic thought the shots at the door and window would draw their attention for a while. He moved toward the cabin, found the power line and cut it. That should distract them a little longer. He went around the house to the rear and found the deck out over the mountain slope. He looked at the steep grade. If anybody was down there, they were hidden in the trees. He started slowly up the deck steps and then saw the door was open. He spun around and stared back down the valley. He had to move.

Bryce made out the shape moving along the side of the cabin, saw him hesitate halfway up the stairs and turn in their direction. Bryce took cover behind a tree. Caldwell was below Bryce on the slope and could not see the cabin, but stopped when he did.

The wind died down again. Yelps of the wounded dog and the sound of their shoes on the dead leaves just under the snow cut through the stillness. Bryce checked to make sure the safety on the deer rifle was off and started back for a better line of shot.

"Where are you going?" Caldwell whispered.

Bryce waved at her. "Keep going. That way." But she stayed where she was as Bryce moved up the slope.

Colovic took his hand off the rail and cradled his gunstock. Bryce picked a spot, knelt, and brought Whitten's rifle to his shoulder. Caldwell tried to make out what he was aiming at—then she saw the sniper silhouetted on the deck. Another blast of wind raced through the trees as she heard Bryce's rifle go off. The bullet struck the foundation and sprayed pieces of concrete into the air. She had to help Bryce. She had to be sure they got the sniper.

Colovic leaped down and tried to regain his balance on the ground. Bryce loaded and fired again. The bullet grazed Colovic above the ankle and smashed into the bottom step. He yanked his leg, tripped, and rolled a few feet down the mountain until he hit a tree trunk. He lost his grip on his rifle and it slid down past him.

Bryce tried to reload, but in the cold his hands dropped the fresh rounds one after another into the snow. Now, only a few yards separated him from the sniper. Bryce closed on him, swinging the rifle butt at his head.

Colovic stood up, stumbled and kicked his 30.06 further away. He ducked inside the arc of Bryce's gun and tackled him just below the rib cage, knocking Bryce's rifle out of his hands. Bryce grasped the sniper by the neck and shoulders. They rolled down the mountain until they crashed against a moss-covered boulder.

Bryce tried to get to his feet, but the other man was quicker. One karate kick, delivered by steel-tipped boots, struck Bryce in the chest. He fell back against the boulder and tried to raise himself. Another kick hit him in the thigh and he dropped to one knee.

One of Colovic's hands gripped Bryce by the belt. The other held him by the neck and lifted Bryce up to his feet. Some guttural words spat into his face. The sniper released his grip on Bryce's throat and squeezed that hand into a fist, drawing his arm back. Bryce jerked his head aside and took a glancing blow on the temple. A red haze melted down in front of his eyes. He locked one leg behind the sniper's knee, jammed an elbow into the sniper's groin and pushed forward.

Bryce twisted free, crouched and groped along the ground for a branch or stone. Colovic hauled him up from behind and shoved his face hard against the rock. Colovic felt in back for his knife, but couldn't reach it. He closed both hands around Bryce's throat; his fingers probed in to crush the windpipe.

Bryce heard the muffled blast and lost consciousness just after his face hit the snow.

After watching Bryce fire twice and miss the gunman each time, Caldwell climbed more quickly up through the trees, only to have Bryce and the sniper roll past her on the snow. The storm clouds finally broke. Now able to see the sniper strangling Bryce clearly in the moonlight, Caldwell stood up.

She raised the shotgun and struggled to balance the butt against her shoulder with her feet on the sloping ground. She aimed at the sniper's back and fired. The recoil pushed her away several steps. She saw a puff of red mist explode over the top of the sniper's left shoulder. He threw Bryce down and turned to look at her. He started toward Caldwell, straight over branches and half-buried tree trunks. His left arm hung limp by his side, but the right one reached across his waist and drew out a serrated combat knife.

She stared at his face as he came, the snarl and the blood making a frightening mask. The cries of the wounded dog faded in the distance. Without knowing why, she felt calm. She remembered old family stories of frontierswomen defending themselves and their families against French and Indian terrorists. She took a breath and brought the shotgun back up. She aimed at the center of the sniper's chest and pulled the trigger.

She heard nothing but the shot. The sniper jerked back toward the boulder. He seemed startled. He dropped to one knee and tried to keep looking at her while the hand still holding the knife reached for the wound in his abdomen. Caldwell cracked open the shotgun, dropped out the spent shells and loaded two more. The snarl had left the sniper's face; all that remained was hatred as he attempted to stand. She remained calm and fired again. The sniper's head jerked back and his body slumped against the boulder. The knife fell on the snow next to Bryce.

Bryce's line of vision ran even with the surface of the chessboard. The chessmen loomed in enormous life-size scale in front of him. The king looked like his father, one of the rooks like Professor Kauffman. He saw his daughter's face on a pawn. He struggled to stay level with the board and make out whom the others represented, but he began to float above them all. He tried to look back down at the chessmen and recognize them, but he kept moving upwards. The chessmen looked small now, and the individual faces were gone. He reached out for the pawn.

"Oh, thank God," Caldwell said.

Bryce opened his eyes. "Allison?" He barely croaked the word out. His throat was sore and strained, but he felt the cold air again and heard the rustling forest. He tried looking past her, but her face was too close to his. He made an attempt to sit up, but she pushed him back down.

"Don't move," she said. "Let me check you over." She ran her hands over his arms and legs and flexed his neck.

"What happened?" Bryce finally managed to ask.

"The guy's dead, Harry. I thought you were, too, until just now." She pressed a wool scarf against his temple. He reached up to touch it. It was wet. Blood, he knew.

"I used those slugs, like Jack said. It took three of them. Guess I'm not a very good shot. You've got a gash on your head—have to watch the bleeding. You feel in one piece otherwise?"

"How long was I out?" He started to recall the fight, the grunts, the crushing fingers. "Just a few minutes. You scared the hell out of me, Harry."

He tried getting to his feet. Caldwell stopped him again.

"Wait," she said. "What about your ribs? Any sharp pain?"

"No. Seems good enough for now. It'll be plenty sore tomorrow, I guess."

"Nothing feels broken?"

"No."

"All right. Try to stand." She helped him up and let him lean his left arm over her shoulder while he got his legs under him and gained some balance.

A wave of dizziness swept over him. She gripped his waist tighter as he reeled unsteadily uphill.

"You sure you're okay?"

"Yeah." He licked his lips. They were dry.

"Can you make it to the cabin?"

"Have to try, don't I?"

Together, they staggered up the porch steps to the deck and made it inside. She led him to the sofa, let him drop and started to re-stoke the fire. She came back to look at his head wound as best she could in the dim light from the fire. There was no new seepage, so she went into the kitchen. Over running water, she called out, "How do your ribs feel now?"

"About the same."

She returned with a damp towel. She removed the wool scarf. They both saw it was blood-soaked. She looked closer at the wound. "Bleeding seems to have stopped," she said.

Bryce rested his neck against the sofa cushion, staring up at the cedar ceiling and blinking his eyes while Caldwell wrapped the towel around his head. "I thought I died," he said. "I mean, I thought I was dying. And then I thought I did."

She finished with the towel and drew away.

"I was playing chess," he said.

"Chess?"

"Then you brought me to. Didn't see who I was playing against before I woke up. But I saw some faces on my pieces. My father, my boss, my case agent, my daughter." He sat up straight. "We need to check on Jack."

"I'll go. You should rest a bit. Make sure your head's clear." She went out the front door.

Caldwell moved slowly over the clearing in the dark. The first dog was dead. She found the second one just inside the trees and it was finally silent and lifeless as well. It took more time to locate Whitten's body. The sight hit her with a wave of nausea but she suppressed it. She did not want to look anymore, but knew she would have to. She hurried back to the cabin and lifted Bryce up from the sofa.

"He's dead, Harry," she cried. "Your friend is dead. We have to bring his body inside. We can't leave him out in the snow like that."

Bryce steadied himself by the mantel, then followed her into the woods. They tried to move Whitten's body, but it was too much with Bryce's injuries. He looked back at the cabin, almost fifty yards away. "We can't do it," he said. "Too heavy. Too far. Not enough time."

Caldwell was still holding Whitten's ankles. "Yes, we can," she cried. "We've got to bring him back to his house."

Bryce saw her tears and put a hand on her shoulder. "The door's gone, shot off, remember? Won't do any good. We'll have to leave him, Allison. Too many people we're dealing with know about this place. We have to get out of here. Jack would understand." He stepped away from the body and lowered the tone of his voice. "We'll take Jack's trucks. You drive the pick-up over to Morgantown, see Harlan, and get in touch with your daughter. Decide what to do next after talking to them. I'll take the Cherokee."

She let Whitten's legs drop to the snow. Harry was right. She had to see Harlan. She had to reach her daughter. And they both had to get out of Savage River. The calm she felt earlier returned. Bryce led her from the woods into the clearing.

"I'll find Jack's keys," he said. "Get those guns. Just the ones we used. Leave the others."

Caldwell walked around the cabin and back down the mountain. Bryce found Whitten's keys under the truck floor mats and then went inside the cabin. He pocketed a few handfuls of rifle bullets and slug shells and retrieved his briefcase with Caldwell's documents and his notes from the dining table. When Caldwell returned she handed him the guns. He gave her the keys to the pick-up, put an arm around her and held her for a moment.

"Can you drive, now?" he asked. She said she could.

Bryce dropped the guns in the back seat of the Cherokee and the briefcase on the passenger side. On the way out they came to the sniper's pick-up, still idling. Bryce got into it, engaged the gears and drove it deeper into the trees. He left the keys in the ignition. As he climbed out, a cell phone rang in the glove compartment. He opened the phone, made a note of the number and took it with all the documents in the compartment.

The main highway was drivable, at least in Jack's 4-wheelers. Bryce turned left, heading east. Behind him, Caldwell went right, heading west. She stopped in the town and placed a call.

Ingram hung up. "Something must have happened to Colovic. His orders were to call us an hour ago. That means someone probably has his phone."

Vrenc's earlier thoughts on Ingram grew firmer. "So, we assume the prosecutor still has the documents," he said.

"And headed for Washington. If he reaches the wrong people, he shuts us down."

"But, maybe he's not going to Washington. Maybe your back-up plan will work. You must be ready for the worst."

"Yes. And hope Colovic is dead. Or at least not in custody somewhere. We are changing our base anyway after the truck arrives and we confirm delivery. If the FBI does come here, or to Baltimore, they will find nothing. We'll have the new corporate papers. I've told the plane to fly closer to the coast."

"Where to?"

"Cold Spring. Over in New Jersey."

"Ah," Vrenc said. "You've covered all the contingencies, Robert. Of course, after this, we have to start again. New suppliers and all."

"There's still a few left," Ingram said. "Contingencies."

They both looked at their watches. The truck was due in a few hours.

CHAPTER ELEVEN

Shaw drove south on the Garden State Parkway in the storm, listening to the weather reports. She moved Tess into the back seat, hoping she would sleep. Plow trucks worked their way along and kept one lane open. Staying several car lengths behind another sedan, she managed to move at a slow but steady pace.

The fuel gauge was just about half-full when she left the airport, and it had dropped below a quarter. She approached an exit with a Shell gas sign, turned off, passed through the EZ pass tollgate and found the station was open. She paid in cash and returned to the Parkway. Tess woke up and asked where they were. Shaw told her the last highway sign said Asbury Park. Now, there were no plow trucks in sight and she let the cars in front of her determine the safest route. Further south, the snow melted on the windshield and began changing to slush on the road. The lane markers became visible. She picked up speed. By the time she reached the end of the Parkway the snow stopped, the sky started to clear and a beam of moonlight danced over the inlet. The dashboard clock showed 5:00 A.M. The drive had taken six hours.

She stopped on the shoulder, picked up her road map fragments and the notes from her conversation with Harry. She continued through the city of Cape May, its Victorian homes festooned with holiday decorations, on to Cape May Point and turned down Yale Avenue. She located the house by number, pulled into the drive, found the keys under the door mat like Harry told her, tucked Tess into the thick down-filled covers of the bed she was familiar with, turned up the heat and sat on the sofa waiting for the warmth to put her to sleep.

The call came while Kauffman was in bed. He slipped on a robe and took it downstairs in the study.

"What is it, Harlan?"

"I hope this is secure, calling you at home, Winston."

"I've been assured it is. Go ahead."

"Your agent, al-Fassi, reached me at my law office after the attack in Pittsburgh. I told him I'd leave right away for Morgantown. I just got a message from my client. She and Bryce were attacked again in Savage River, Maryland. They were in a place owned by a friend of Bryce's."

"Are they all right?"

"Yes, from what I could make out, but his friend was killed and so was the assailant. Ms. Caldwell said she's on her way here."

"How about Bryce?"

"He's headed east, to meet up with his daughter at a family place in Cape May Point. His paralegal is with her. Did you know about that?"

"Some of it. Does Bryce have the documents you gave him?"

"The message didn't say anything about them."

"I have not heard from Bryce. How did your client reach you in Morgantown?"

"I presume by cell phone."

"God, Harlan, then they can track her. That goddamned worm. Anything else?"

"She's worried about her own daughter, out in California. Wants her protected."

Kauffman took a moment to gather his thoughts. "Listen, Harlan, you're probably not safe in Morgantown now, but you should have some time. I've told Saad al-Fasi to get down there to give you some security, but he may still be tied up in Pittsburgh. He should contact you. Wait for Ms. Caldwell, then bring her back here. And I mean here to my home, not Main Justice. Get what information you can about her daughter, and I'll see what I can do about that."

The call ended, and the front door rang. Leah Kauffman led Special Agent O'Shea into the study. He handed over a stack of letter-sized papers and Kauffman leafed through them.

"This is from the Internet?"

"Yes. Some public. Some not."

"And you used that equipment in your home, right?"

"Yes. Neither the Bureau nor the worm can trace it, so far at least."

"Okay. Explain what you've got here."

"Miltech is controlled by a man named Robert Ingram."

"I see that."

"There is a suggestion he may have origins in the Caucasus. My contacts at Immigration hinted he may be illegal, but impossible to trace right now."

"Why Caucasus?"

"He uses a foreign language page on the Internet, in Ossetian."

"The worm and the Trust. Is the page public?"

"Yes, but of course it's probably coded anyway. What he does there looks innocent enough."

"Okay. What else?"

"There appear to be no fixed assets in Miltech."

"Ah, just like the Trust. Nothing to be confiscated."

"Yes," O'Shea said. "However, it is affiliated with several other concerns, two of them particularly interesting, if you've done drug cases."

"That is why I had you transferred to my Section, Peter." Kauffman reached for his humidor and tilted it toward O'Shea who took out a cigar. Kauffman did, too. They both snipped the ends and lit them, exhaling plumes of blue smoke over the desk.

"One's a plane hangar at Baltimore-Washington International called Technical Transfer," O'Shea said. "The other is a hangar, too, called Techair Maintenance, located in Cold Spring, New Jersey."

"Where's that?"

"South Jersey. Down near the end, about a hundred air miles from Baltimore. I know the place, as a matter of fact. Fly there on weekends sometimes to keep my air miles up and practice my instrument checks. I've seen this hangar, too. Real isolated. Never saw anybody there. And nobody is at the airport at night. Runway lights and beacons all on automatic."

"So, if you're smuggling something in..."

"Or out.."

"As the case may be. What's the connection between them?"

"Ingram is listed as the incorporator in each case."

"Which States?"

"Each one different. Virginia, Maryland, New Jersey. And,"

O'Shea puffed cigar smoke and grinned, "counsel of record in each case is Gideon Aubrey."

"The Herrick firm."

Kauffman laid his unfinished cigar down in the ashtray. "Does Savage River, Maryland, mean anything to you, Peter, in connection with Harry Bryce?"

"Yeah. Bryce's security clearance last summer listed a guy out there, assistant police chief, as a reference. Agents interviewed him. I saw the memos in the file. Why?"

"I just heard from Harlan Moan. Bryce and the informant were attacked in Savage River last night. Bryce's friend was killed, but both of them got out safely. Another question. Cape May Point. What do you know about that?"

"Couple of miles from Cold Spring. A lot of birdwatchers."

"Harlan said that's where Bryce is headed." He opened the top drawer of the desk and handed O'Shea a one-page document with FBI letterhead. "I just got this 302 last night."

O'Shea scanned the report. "Goddamn. Barbara Shaw. Durham Bryce. And Harry's daughter."

"She's with Shaw. And Harlan thought they're trying to meet at Cape May Point."

"Jesus Christ, Professor. Do you think Ingram could pick that up?"

Kauffman raised his cigar and puffed the coal back to life. "We have to assume that, don't we? The Savage River incident shows somebody got access to Bryce's security file."

"You think it was Shaw?"

"No. She was up in Philly then. Somebody higher."

"Does Harry have the documents Harlan gave him?"

"Harlan doesn't know. I hope he does."

"If he has them, it could lead to another source. Turn him, maybe we break up the whole conspiracy. Maybe even get all the way to the worm. But what Ingram needs, right now, is time to complete this transaction. That's his main job. Bryce is his most immediate threat, at least from his point of view, not the FBI or Main Justice. And then, to cover the Trust, he has a lot to clean up after that. So, he must have the documents."

"Here's a hypothesis, Peter," Kauffman said. "Bryce believes that his daughter is with Barbara Shaw. He can't really trust her, but he has to set up a meeting and he picks someplace he considers safe, Durham Bryce's cottage in Cape May Point. And that's near where Ingram is going to try to consummate the shipment."

"Maybe."

"We have to assume the worst about Bryce, like he does about Shaw."

O'Shea looked at Kauffman who stared back without reaction. "So, I have to get down there. Secure the documents. And with the timing, I'll have to fly, which means I can check out the hangar at BWI first."

Kauffman had managed to keep his cigar alive. "Good. And, Peter, you will enter none of this on that computer of yours. Nothing traceable."

"Just what I printed out for you."

"Good. Ingram, you know, has a sophisticated operation, or he thinks he does. He has access to some sources we cannot track yet, at least not securely, but with all his blundering we have picked up a lot. That was just stupid, not to say tragic, to go after Durham Bryce. And his granddaughter, for God's sake. Then those bungled attacks in Pittsburgh. He has a lot of house cleaning on his agenda, I imagine."

"Maybe," O'Shea said.

"Maybe what?"

"Maybe blundered."

"Yes. If he delivers, the Trust won't care. At least in the short term."

"And long term?"

"I've told you that I believe they have sources inside Justice. Not just that computer worm. Now, they must suspect something rogue, unofficial, after Pittsburgh and Savage River. They're trying to divert attention away from Bryce, Durham and Barbara Shaw."

"Down there I won't have much to work with except surprise."

"I'll send al-Fasi as soon as he reestablishes contact. It's time to reactivate your surveillance tapes."

"Now that we have their attention, it'll be detected."

"A risk we have to take."

"And Bryce?"

"What about him?"

"He could be some help, too."

"We're not sure what side he's on now."

"Until his daughter's safe, he's in business for himself."

"Exactly."

"But when she is, he might be willing to pitch in."

The Professor stood up to show O'Shea out. "I should have told him more about this case, Peter. It's all been quite shadowy—the worm, the Trust, the moles in Justice, the consultation with his father and Harlan a couple of years ago in my Solarium. Initially I thought it best to defer to Durham, keep it off-record that way. Maybe if I had taken the lead, Durham would be alive."

"Add that to the rest of the maybes," O'Shea said, and left.

Larson reported to Ingram that he missed Barbara Shaw again, this time at Newark. Ingram would have to deal with Larson later. For now he just gave new orders.

"Cape May Point?" Larson said.

"We picked her up going through an exit north of Atlantic City. The rest is coincidence. There was a call between her and Bryce. And his family has a place down there."

"So, that's how she got out ahead of me. Bryce made any other contacts? Official?"

"Nothing we picked up. Go down there, get the documents and clean everything up. Bring the documents to the airport. You know where it is."

"Yeah. When?"

"Evening. After dark. That's the best I have right now."

Larson snapped shut the cell phone and laid it on the night table. He would throw it out on the way down and buy a new one. He checked the digital clock next to the phone. Plenty of time. He lay back down and rolled over, looking at the woman on the bed. He took her by the throat and caressed her neck. She looked back, reached between his legs and tried to make her face look hungry.

Larson pivoted over and mounted her. She made a nice pretense of having an orgasm. Larson liked that. Lots of experience, this one. Worth the time and money.

When finished, he got up, and so did she. She approached him standing and rubbing her really huge nipples against his chest. She purred. Pretending to want to do it again. Very expert. Very entertaining.

He rechecked the clock and then looked out the window. The snow had eased off, drifting now against the neon signs outside. Plenty of time to get there with the weather clearing. Driving would be better in a couple of hours. Some daylight, anyway. He could drive faster to make up for it.

The waitress suggested another position, and he decided to stay a bit longer.

When Kauffman arrived at Main Justice the next morning, he was almost alone on the third floor. He switched on the lights to his own office and then, without going in, went down the hall, past the reception alcove and into Pickering Thayer's private office. He assumed the AAG's secretary was late or, like his own, on holiday leave. He noticed the personnel file tabbed 'Bryce' on the desk.

"Looks like we both got in early today."

Kauffman tried to look casual when he turned. Thayer stood in the doorway. His eyes shot over to the desk. Kauffman took his eyeglasses off his nose and wiped them with a handkerchief from his breast pocket.

"Makes the drive easier, doesn't it," the Professor said. He moved over near a coat rack, refitted the glasses and refolded the handkerchief so the points showed again on his suit jacket. "I came by to report the latest on the Tuscarora matter."

Thayer dropped his overcoat on a chair. "Yes?" he said.

"Something serious."

"You could have emailed it."

"My secretary's off. I never learned how to type."

"What is it, then?"

"Bryce took the proffer in Pittsburgh and afterwards he and the informant were attacked."

Thayer stood up. "What the hell? Who? What happened?"

"No details yet. You should get a copy of the 302 soon. But no arrests. Two bodies."

"Bryce? Is he all right?"

"I've been told both he and the informant survived, but I've had no contact with them."

"Leads? Suspects?"

"Nothing yet."

Thayer walked around behind his desk and sat down, keeping his eyes on Kauffman. "Who's on the case?"

"Local police and Resident Bureau Office."

Kauffman was not telling him everything, Thayer realized, but he knew not to attempt a cross-examination. "Well, Winston," he said, "I appreciate you getting this to me right away. If they need any extra resources out there just ask. Let me know as soon as you hear anything more on Bryce."

Thayer looked down at his desk, signaling dismissal, but Kauffman said, "One more thing, Pick, since you asked about Harry Bryce. He was spending the holidays with his parents and daughter near Philadelphia. Harry's father was killed while Harry was in Pittsburgh. I got a 302 on that as well. It says Harry's daughter was taken by his paralegal, Barbara Shaw. The family says Shaw tried to reach Bryce. No arrests on this, either."

"Christ, the paralegal? Any contact with her? Did she...?"

"No. The report says the shooter was a white male."

"What the hell is the connection here, Win? Is there any?"

"Don't know. The Philadelphia office is working on it separately for now. But I wanted to add, since it might pop up in the press, that Harry's father and I worked together here in Washington years ago. He had a small private practice outside Philadelphia. The informant's counsel, a man named Harlan Moan, also worked here back then. He's listed as retired from a firm in Pittsburgh now. I didn't want you to be taken by surprise by any of this."

"Well, thank you for that. Oh, did the firm in Pittsburgh have anything to do with the informant?"

"The report says no. They just let Harlan use office space when he's in town. They claimed he left right after the proffer meeting and didn't leave any records behind."

"All right. Keep me up to date." Thayer turned on his desktop computer and as the hard drive wound up, Kauffman decided he had done as much as he could on this front and without another word returned to his office. Thayer listened to his steps down the corridor until they faded out, then exited the building down the corner stairs.

Out on the Mall, he typed "Kauffman, Moan, Bryce" on his cell phone and asked for a link. Instead a text message came back from Virginia. "Checking. Delivery this PM. BWI. Inventory."

Thayer crushed the phone under his foot, threw it in a waste bin, and walked back to Main Justice where he spent the rest of the day.

Vrenc's cell phone vibrated in his pocket. He checked the screen: "Virginia tracked."

He typed back, "Government?"

It answered, "Private. Maryland."

"Location?" he asked.

The address appeared. Vrenc showed it to Ingram, who marked it down and said he would take care of it. Vrenc decided he had to risk using his voice line. It was evening on the Indian Ocean when the call came from North America.

"Did you get the message?" the Ossete asked.

"Yes. We will follow up on it. The shipment is due to arrive at 3 P.M. local time."

"Everything is arranged?"

"They are using a different airfield. Better security, they say."

"They have made several changes recently."

"Yes, they have. It is that investigation."

"Will this one cause any more delays?"

"Allow for twelve hours. They have some other details to clear up."

"Ah," the Ossete said. "But you have received the funds?"

"Yes. And everything will be purged after confirmation."

"That is in your hands," the Ossete said. "When you confirm the delivery, I will transmit the data and purge everything here."

"There is a new matter. I have been asked if the names Kauffman, Moan and Bryce are linked in any way?" Vrenc waited a few moments for the Ossete's answer.

"All three were involved two years ago in the situation that cost us a great deal of money. They have surfaced again?"

"Yes. I knew about Bryce and Moan. Just out of Philadelphia and Pittsburgh, I thought. Not Washington. I will pass on your information."

"Go with God," the Ossete said. He then transmitted a directive to Mombassa for the helicopter to be ready on twenty-four hour notice.

A signal came on Ingram's line. "The truck is on the Beltway," he told Vrenc.

They rose to leave. Ingram turned off the one light over the desk and picked up his flash drive. Vrenc handed an envelope to Ingram.

"Your new identity papers," he said. "Your name is Richard Issler. Your driver's license in Florida."

"I'm due to get the other paperwork from Aubrey at the warehouse. Mr. Issler will need a new lawyer, of course, but that can wait."

Outside, they got into their separate cars.

"Leave me a message in Manhattan," Vrenc said before they left. "Use the land line."

"I've been pinged," O'Shea reported. "Somebody traced back that Miltech search."

"Back to where?" Kauffman asked.

"Here. My house."

"And from where?"

"Africa."

Kauffman sighed. "All right, Peter. Get out of there. Erase everything first. Everything, you hear? Take as much hardware as you can. Smash what you can't take. Better yet, burn it. Melt it. Then take a look at that BWI hangar, before flying down to Cold Spring.

No more insecure contact. Especially not here in Main Justice. I'm going back to Georgetown. You can reach me there."

"Okay, but I sure as hell hope they haven't tapped your office, because if they have we're screwed," O'Shea said.

Kauffman spun his chair around and looked past the wrought iron bars and through the glass. Morning was now a fact. No rose tint reflected off the building windows across Pennsylvania Avenue or off the rapidly melting snow on the sidewalks. He turned back and placed a call from Main Justice to Morgantown, but there was no answer.

Police cars closed off the residential block. Allison kept moving until she found a spot to park, and walked back. Halfway down the street, she saw a group of neighbors staring across at a dozen police officers milling about in front of Harlan Moan's house. It was wrapped in evidence tape, and an ambulance waited with its back doors open. She asked the young man beside her what had happened.

"I don't know for sure, lady, but they say someone got shot in the house."

Harlan Moan lived alone, she knew, which meant that... "Oh Christ, it can't be, please don't let it be," she prayed, knowing that Harlan Moan was dead. "Now what am I supposed to do?" She turned away and almost made it back to Jack's pick-up.

"Ms. Caldwell?"

She looked at the man standing under a street lamp.

"You remember me?" She shook her head no, but she did.

He held up a badge in his left hand. "Pittsburgh? FBI?"

"I don't know what you're talking about." She took out the ignition keys and moved to the truck.

"Stop. I'm taking you into custody."

"What for? I have nothing to do with anything here."

"It's for your own safety."

"Safety? Why the hell should I trust you? Who are you?"

"My name is Saad al-Fasi. I'm a federal agent. I don't expect you to trust me, and I don't care if you do. But I did save your life back in Pittsburgh and now you're coming with me." He took her by the arm and led her away down the street. "Be quiet. Don't make me use the cuffs."

"Why? Why shouldn't I just scream like hell? You have a gun?"

"Of course. And Mr. Moan's killer might still be around somewhere, waiting for you."

"For God's sake, then at least tell me what happened back there."

"In the car." al-Fasi pushed her into a dark sedan, got in himself and started the ignition. "I arrived too late," he said. "Tied up in Pittsburgh. I found his body in the kitchen and the house looked like it was searched. Called 911 and left, hoping to spot the killer somewhere outside. But I didn't and then I saw you."

He steered the car out of town toward Interstate 79.

"Where are we going?" Allison asked.

"Washington. To the only safe place I can think of right now."

She groped in her pocket for her cell phone and took it out.

"Put that away," al-Fasi commanded.

"I need to reach my daughter."

"Did you use your phone on your way here? Call her? Or Mr. Moan?"

"Yes. Or I tried. Didn't get through, but left Harlan a message."

"Well, turn it off. It's traceable."

She put her phone back. "My daughter has to be told about all this. She needs protection."

"We'll deal with that in Washington." al-Fasi let the conversation drop until he reached the on-ramp and they were out of Morgantown. "Any idea what the killer might have been looking for?"

The change of subject caused her to think for a moment. "Copies of the documents I gave Mr. Bryce? Harlan said he did not want to keep copies, but nobody knew that."

"So, Mr. Bryce has the originals and that's it?"

"Yes."

"Do you know where he is now?"

"On his way to meet his daughter."

"I can understand why."

Caldwell sensed that the agent was sincere and softened toward him enough to ask, "I don't think I should be telling you this, but do you know about Savage River?"

al-Fasi admitted he did not.

She related all that had happened.

al-Fasi was silent for a few minutes before he said, "We'll have to stop there on the way."

CHAPTER TWELVE

Karev left the Peugeot in the general aviation lot and walked around the terminal. One of the mechanics servicing a small plane pointed him to the hangar several hundred yards away. The walk over the tarmac seemed long, but it was clear of snow. He was relieved to be out in the cold air after the long drive from Morgantown. There were no trucks or planes nearby and when he got there he tested all the hangar doors and found them locked. He decided to bring the Peugeot close enough to watch for the arrival of any trucks or cars. He had to keep his distance, just make his report. The pistol he got in Pittsburgh was somewhere down a West Virginia mountainside.

Saad al-Fasi followed Caldwell's directions off the Interstate. They went past Whitten's mailbox once, but saw no sign of police, so they turned back and entered the private drive. al-Fasi noted the pick-up truck in the woods and Bryce's rental car at the cabin. He pulled up next to it.

"What evidence did you leave?" he asked her.

"Fingerprints, I guess. Harry took the guns and all the documents I gave him."

"Can't do anything about the prints."

"There was one other thing. A phone rang in that truck back there as we left."

"I'll check that on the way out."

"How about Harry's friend? Can we move the body? I mean, out of respect?"

"Probably not, the locals will want to check it out first, but I'll think about it. See if that car's unlocked while I go around the back."

al-Fasi went through the cabin, scanning around quickly, then out the deck and down the mountain. He found the sniper where Caldwell said he would be. He patted the pockets for any identifying information, and, as he expected, found nothing. When he returned Caldwell was standing by the rental car with the passenger door open.

"This place is so messed up from all of us walking around, I guess it wouldn't matter if we housed the body in the car," al-Fasi said. He followed her out in the woods to Whitten's body, moved him into the car and closed the door. Caldwell seemed more cooperative as they got into his sedan.

On the way out, he stopped at the truck and searched it. Again, he found no identifying papers and also no cell phone. He told Caldwell about it as they headed back to the Interstate.

"Harry must have taken it," she said.

al-Fasi said. "So, now he's got almost everything to make his case. All he needs is a witness."

Ingram found the house at the end of the cul-de-sac. The blue siding was dented and white paint chipped off the garage door. High grass poked through the remaining snow, and no lights shone through any of the windows.

He went to the door and no one answered the bell. He moved around, checking the windows for signs of a security system. The computer station sat in plain sight in the dining room, but in the back yard, he saw the processor melted in a heap of plastic next to a can of charcoal lighter fluid and the satellite dish smashed. So, Vrenc was right, he thought. No teenage hacker. He jimmied open the back door and waited for the sound or light of an alarm. Nothing happened.

All that was left at the station was the dead monitor screen. No evidence of who the hacker was or whom he worked for. The house must have security, but he could not pick it up. Very professional. Ingram had to go. Someone detected the ping from East Africa. Everything needed to move faster now. Outside, the cul-de-sac still appeared deserted. He headed straight for the hangar.

Larson lay on his side and propped up his head watching while the waitress dressed at the other end of his motel room for her shift. She took the cash on the nightstand and put it in her apron pocket.

"Stop and see me the next time you're in town," she said.

He waved as she went out the door. After a few minutes, he got dressed and left. Outside, he looked up at the angle of the sun. He should get there close to sunset. Enough time to find the place, take care of Ingram's business and get out to the airport. The old Plymouth Volare rocked as he climbed in. The engine complained but started, and the station wagon wobbled out onto Route 1.

O'Shea skirted the BWI service road at the northern end of the approach runway, and spotted the hangar with the sign "Technical Transfer." There were no vehicles or aircraft nearby, so he drove back to the general aviation terminal.

He showed his badge at the counter, and learned no flights were listed to arrive at the Technical Transfer hangar. That confirmed what he picked up from hacking Ingram's company, that the flight was destined for Cold Spring. He called the Professor for clearance, then asked to have the Cessna 10 made flight-ready. He sat down with a Washington sectional chart to plot out his flight path. When he finished, he poured a cup of coffee and watched as the crew brought out his plane. They would take a while, so he picked a copy of Time off the rack and sat on a bench with a view through the picture window of the hangar a few hundred yards off.

A Buick with Maryland tags drove past the terminal. O'Shea knew the license plate numbers were serialized to Hertz. He stepped out to watch it go toward the hangar. The driver and passenger stayed inside after the Buick stopped beside the building. O'Shea went around to check the fuel level and tank caps on the Cessna then returned to the terminal.

Next to come was a black Cadillac with Virginia plates and a solo driver who pulled up next to the Buick. O'Shea watched the three men go into the hangar. Then a white panel truck with Mississippi plates moved slowly up the service road. When it neared the hangar the bay door rolled up and the truck entered the building. O'Shea knew he needed support and made another call.

"Stay in the terminal," the Professor said. "Don't go out there. We can't spook them into changing plans."

"How about using just airport security?" O'Shea asked.

"Only if something really blows up. And not something you cause."

O'Shea saw another car arrive, this time an Audi with D.C. plates. He put the phone in his pocket and went back into the terminal.

The two drivers climbed out of the panel truck. Ingram led them into a bare office and introduced Bennett and Gould, explaining that they owned the factory down in Corinth. Then he filled two Styrofoam cups with vodka and handed them over. The deliverymen threw the vodka down the back of their throats and held out the cups for more. Ingram refilled them.

"What is next for us?" one of the deliverymen asked in accented English.

Ingram pointed at the other two men. "They confirm the shipment. If everything is okay, we confirm the payment when the lawyer gets here. At that point, we have to move the shipment to another location."

"Where?" the deliveryman asked.

"New Jersey."

"How much further?"

"About a hundred twenty-five miles. You'll follow me down there."

Tom Gould broke in. "Do you want us to do the inventory now? As long as we have to wait for your lawyer. Maybe save us some time."

"Good idea. Open up the truck." Ingram handed Gould a clipboard with a sheet of paper containing a long printed list of serial numbers. He and Bennett left the office with the deliverymen. Still in the office, Ingram opened a metal cabinet to make sure the pistols were loaded.

Gould followed the two men into the back of the truck. They opened each of the microwave oven cartons, and Gould sifted through each one, checking off the serial numbers. He announced everything was correct. The truck was secured once more and everyone returned to the office. Behind them, footsteps rang through the empty hangar, and a voice called out for Ingram.

"That's Aubrey, the lawyer," Ingram said. "Now we can confirm payment. Take a look at these first." He handed Bennett the cardboard envelope with the broken diplomatic seals. Bennett handed it to Gould who scanned the paperwork inside.

"You're right. Needs a lawyer."

The afternoon sun reflected off the salt marsh and Christmas lights started to shine on the houses along the road. Most of the snow had steamed away. Bryce passed a private harbor with the boats all out of the water up on wooden frames, a reminder of his long aborted plans to get one himself.

It took another hour to reach the turn, then the circle and then the cottage. Its lights were on and a Cavalier with D.C. plates sat in the drive. He drove around the block. The other cottages were dark and he saw no other cars.

He parked the Cherokee at the end of the street, took Whitten's deer rifle from the back seat and got out. He could detect no sound or movement as he came up to the cottage. He held the deer rifle to his hip and kicked the door open.

Barbara Shaw leaped off the couch.

"Don't move," he told her.

She started toward him anyway. "Harry. Thank God."

"I said don't move. Where's Tess?"

"In the bedroom. There." She pointed at one of the interior doors. "Asleep, I hope."

"Anyone else here?"

"No, Harry. What are you thinking?"

"She okay?"

"She's fine. She just wants to be with you. You don't need that." She pointed at the rifle.

Bryce kept his eyes on her and told her to sit down. "I've been shot at twice in the last twenty-four hours. And my father..."

"I told you what happened."

"Without any corroboration."

"Your father told me to get Tess out of there. We didn't see anything. I don't even have a gun."

He kept the rifle on her while listening for any sounds inside or outside the cottage.

"Harry," Shaw said from the couch, "I had no idea Gideon was into anything like this."

"Gideon. His name keeps coming up. So what you told me the other day was a lie."

"Yes. I lied. But I decided I had to come and tell you the truth. What I know of it, at least."

"Later. Right now, I need to see Tess." He lowered the rifle barrel, flipped the safety switch with his thumb and went into the bedroom. He put the rifle against a chair, sat on the bed and lifted his daughter into his arms.

"Oh, Daddy," she cried.

"Baby, Baby. You okay?"

"I'm scared, Daddy."

"So am I, Baby. So am I. But I'm here to take care of you. You're safe now."

He carried her out into the living room, holding her in one arm and the rifle in the other. He took a chair with her in his lap.

"Anybody follow you?" he asked Shaw.

"Not that I saw. But the guy in that black Dodge, the one you noticed in Washington the other night—" she stopped and looked over at Tess, "followed us. He wasn't in the Dodge. He was in a green Plymouth, but I lost him in Newark."

"You're sure?"

"Of course not. I'm not sure of anything anymore."

"Yeah." Bryce could not say much with his daughter in his arms. So, he asked, "Well, I'm hungry. How about you, Honey?"

Tess nodded.

"There's a diner up the road," he said to Shaw. "You drive."

Bryce turned off all the lights on the way out. He laid the deer rifle in the Cavalier's back seat and took the passenger seat with his daughter. Shaw followed his directions to the diner. He told her to park in the rear, where the car would not be seen from the street.

Aubrey walked through the hangar, past the panel truck and into the office.

"George, Tom," Aubrey greeted his clients. He dropped his briefcase but kept his laptop strapped on his shoulder and offered them handshakes. "What are you doing here?"

"We were asked to come," Bennett said. "Tom just confirmed the code numbers on the shipment."

"Everything all right?"

"Seems to be."

"We also need to confirm payment."

"Well, I thought you left that to me. Why do that here?"

Gould handed Aubrey the diplomatic envelope. "Bob just showed us these. Can you check them over?"

Aubrey took the envelope, moved between the deliverymen to the desk, and laid down the laptop. He paged through the documents. "Looks good," he said, and handed them back to Gould.

"Can you confirm that on your computer?" Gould asked.

Aubrey reached out to Gould for the envelope again. He typed in the information, and spun the screen around for Bennett and Gould to see. "There's your account, George."

He hit the tab button. "And there's yours, Tom. Look okay to you?" They nodded that it did, and he said, "I'll fax it to you in Pittsburgh." Ingram started to stop him, but before he spoke, Aubrey tapped another button. "Done," he said, with a smile.

Ingram moved between them. "I have some private business with Gideon. Do you two mind stepping outside for a minute?"

"We'll head to the terminal and check in for our flight," Bennett said.

"No. Please wait a few more minutes. I have a couple of things to go over with you after I finish with Gideon."

Bennett and Gould walked out into the hangar and looked at their watches. Gould asked if they could leave now, change flights, maybe not use BWI, but Bennett shrugged him off.

In the office, Aubrey handed Ingram a flat brown envelope from his briefcase. Ingram opened it and looked through the papers. "Florida this time, I see. These are the originals?"

"Yes."

"You have copies?"

"Of course."

Ingram slid the papers back into the envelope. "Okay, Gideon. I have to end our relationship now that this is done. Remove whatever records you have in your office. Erase everything on your firm's computer base. Understood?"

"I was expecting that," Aubrey said. "What about them?" he tilted his head toward the hangar. "Blue Mountain. I represent them, too, you know, but I've kept it pretty clean."

"Do what you have to."

"And the files?"

"Talk to Thayer about that. You should not have sent that fax, Gideon."

Aubrey gathered up his briefcase and laptop preparing to leave. "Why not? That's what they wanted, and they're my clients, too. Anyway, the government already has access to all the records out there. You still worried about Bryce?"

"Of course.

"And that shipment?"

"Another change of plans, Gideon."

"You're right," Aubrey said. "I'm out of it now. Don't tell me any more." He walked out through the hangar, waving goodbye to Bennett and Gould, got in his car and left.

Ingram gestured at the deliverymen, reopened the metal closet, and handed over the two pistols. They fingered them briefly and held them behind their backs.

"You know what's next. Follow me."

The two men stood beside the panel truck facing Bennett and Gould with the light from the hangar door behind them.

"You done with the lawyer?" Bennett asked. "What more do you need to go over with us? We have a flight to catch." They both started back to the office, but Ingram held up a hand to stop. The deliverymen brought the pistols around.

"What is this?" Bennett demanded. "I thought the deal was closed."

"It is."

"So, if that's all then, we're leaving." They started toward their car, but Ingram held up his hand again.

"We have another change. Sorry, but it's beyond my control."

Gould threw the diplomatic envelope back at Ingram who ducked as it went past. "Then, take the money back," he said. "Give us the keys and we'll take the truck." He turned around and looked at the empty space over the tarmac out the hangar door.

"This is not about that," Ingram said. "It's about house cleaning. Orders."

Gould started running toward the open space outside, but Bennett remained frozen. Ingram signaled the drivers. The shots threw Bennett back and he landed on the concrete floor in a heap. Gould tried to make a turn as he neared the hangar wall. He felt two sharp tugs on his temple and fell unconscious on the concrete with a dark pool of his own blood spreading beneath his face.

"Leave them there," Ingram said. "Nobody will come out here. We're running out of time and have to go now."

He picked up the diplomatic envelope and went to his Cadillac. The drivers followed in the panel truck and pulled down the hangar door behind them. Ingram led them to the service road.

O'Shea saw the Audi leave first. He waited inside a bit longer until he saw the Cadillac pull away followed by the panel truck. The Buick with the rental plates was still there. He walked out to the hangar, tested the door and got it to open. There was enough light coming through the bay door to illuminate the service entryway.

He called out, "Anybody here?" His voice echoed against the steel walls. He scanned the interior and saw the two bodies right away. He pressed a finger on the neck of one, then went to the other. He felt a pulse.

O'Shea put away his weapon, scanned the interior and saw the office. Inside he found a washroom with paper towels and cups. He filled a cup with water, came back and threw it in the face of the second body while pressing the towels against the man's forehead and temple.

Gould's eyes flickered open. He felt the searing pain on his temple and the warm damp blood around his face and neck. O'Shea's face came into focus.

"Keep pressure on that," he heard O'Shea tell him. He held one hand against the towels. With the other, he groped for O'Shea who pulled him up to a sitting position.

"You're one lucky sonofabitch," O'Shea said. "Head wounds always look like hell. Bleed like a pig. They must have thought you were a goner. Lucky for you I got here, or you would have been."

Gould struggled to his feet, holding on to O'Shea's shoulder.

"Pain?" O'Shea asked.

"What do you think? Sure."

"Sometimes head injuries don't hurt. Good that this one does. Didn't see any aspirin back there, though."

"How about whiskey?"

"Just vodka. Not very medicinal. Get steady. See if you can manage on your own."

"O'Shea took his hands away, and Gould slowly recovered his balance. " I think I'm okay now," he said. "Thanks. Who are you, anyway?"

"FBI."

"Oh, fuck. Just what I need now."

"Yeah, fuck you, too. Which one are you? Bennett or Gould?"

"Gould. Tom Gould. How did you know that?"

"You'd be surprised. Can you walk? We have to move."

Gould tried taking a step and said he thought he could. O'Shea left him to return to the washroom. He found a first aid kit and more towels. He pulled the bloody wad off Gould's head and applied the fresh ones. He secured them with a strip of gauze wrapped around his head and tied under his chin.

"All right," O'Shea said. "Bleeding's slowed enough."

"Now, hands behind your back."

"What?"

"Behind your back. Your head's secured. Both hands are free. I'll show you some ID." O'Shea took his handcuffs off his belt and waved them in front of Gould's face.

Gould obeyed. O'Shea shackled him and shoved him by his shoulders out onto the tarmac toward the terminal. Once outside, he used one of the disposable cell phones to call the Professor again.

"Two of them," he said. "Bennett's dead. The rest have left with the truck. I'm taking Gould with me. You surprised?"

"In a way, yes," Kauffman said. "They didn't see you?"

"No."

"Good. They'll stay with their plans. And now you've got the witness. Take care of him."

When they reached the Cessna, O'Shea used the phone one more time again, to call airport security.

"You called me in to the FBI?" Gould asked.

"Can't yet. If I do that, I lose custody, and you need to stay with me for a while."

Karev remained in the Peugeot. He watched the Audi leave, thought he heard shots, and then saw the Cadillac and the panel truck drive off. He reached for the door handle, but stopped when he saw someone walk across the tarmac and enter the hangar. Karev waited until the guy came out with another man in handcuffs. They walked back toward a two-engine Cessna. When the terminal blocked their view of the hangar, Karev went over, noted the one body, and knew he had little time. He found a telephone in the hangar office and placed the call to Manhattan.

"The shipment has arrived and they left," he said.

"Where are you now?" Vrenc asked.

"BWI airport. The hangar."

"That line is not secure."

"No. Someone came in after they left, and took another man out in handcuffs. A second one is dead."

"They were both supposed to be eliminated. So, they were under surveillance?"

"Seems like it."

"How about the lawyer?"

"He left before the shooting."

"Okay. Get out of there right away. Someone is in our computers. We don't know who it is, yet, but the delivery has been changed to another airfield, a place called Cold Spring, New Jersey. Can you get there?"

"Yes, but I need another weapon," Karev said.

"There is a source on the way." Vrenc gave him directions. "He is one of us. You can trust him. When you get there, make sure of the delivery."

Karev walked out and looked across at the terminal. He caught sight of the guy he now assumed was a federal agent pushing the man in handcuffs up into the Cessna. Further off by the International terminal, he heard the sirens and saw the lights of the approaching security vehicles. He ran to the Peugeot and sped away.

Larson found the place on Yale Avenue. The lights were out inside, but the street lights let him see an unmade bed. There was no car parked anywhere nearby, but a thin patch of remaining snow on the drive showed recent tire treads. He hoped to Christ they were coming back. That was his only chance. He drove a block away, turned a corner and parked near a sand dune, hearing the surf on the other side. He had time, he thought, so he walked up the dune and looked out over the bay and ocean. He lit a cigarette with his Zippo, and, in the full moon, watched the waves lapping against the jetty rocks. He pitched the unfinished butt out toward it and started down to the beach. Then, he thought better of it and went back to the green Plymouth to wait. He was sure they would be back soon and he would finally finish all this up.

CHAPTER THIRTEEN

Main Justice was all but deserted. Kauffman decided to take any more calls from O'Shea at home. He closed up his office and drove his black Interceptor out onto Pennsylvania Avenue. Traffic was light and he soon reached the townhouse. His wife met him at the door and directed him right to his study. His guests stood up when he entered.

al-Fasi introduced Allison Caldwell.

"The informant?" Kauffman said. She said she was. "Are you all right?"

"No, of course not. I'm still alive is all. Do you know what happened?"

"Just some of it. Not the details. I'm very sorry for this, Ms. Caldwell."

"What about my daughter? I have not been able to reach her. I have to know if she's safe."

Kauffman motioned them back into their chairs and moved behind his desk. "Harlan told me about her. I'll check San Francisco again."

He lifted up his receiver. "Confirmed," he said into it. "Protective custody for just a few more days. No details. We don't want her implicated in any way."

"What's that mean?" Caldwell asked after he hung up. "Custody? She didn't do anything."

"She is in a motel, Ms. Caldwell, with agents watching her. In another day or two, you will be out there with her and this will all be over, I hope. It's the best I could do for now." She started to say something else, but he held up a hand and turned to al-Fasi who pointed at the documents.

"There on your desk," al-Fasi said. "The top two are from Mr. Gould's apartment in Pittsburgh. On the way here, I found the other five at Miltech."

Kauffman paged through them. "Crumbs left behind in the trail.

They need to be connected. But, we cannot discuss them now. Ms. Caldwell might still be a substantive witness." He held up one of the documents. "You did not show her this?"

"No. And she says Bryce has her documents with him. She also said Bryce has the hit man's cell phone. No identification left at the site."

Kauffman's phone rang. He picked it up and listened. Finally, he said, "I'll send Saad down there, then." When he finished, he said to al-Fasi, "Peter has got Mr. Gould."

Caldwell started in her chair. Both men looked at her for a response, but she said nothing.

"Where are they?" al-Fasi asked.

"On the way to their new departure point in New Jersey. O'Shea's flying there. I guess I can say this without compromising Ms. Caldwell. Peter found him in the hangar at Baltimore-Washington, wounded. The other one, Mr. Bennett, he found dead. Gould confirmed where the shipment is headed, as he suspected."

"George is dead?" Caldwell interrupted. "My God, Mickey Bennett won't survive this news. George? And our old friend, Harlan Moan. How many more are in danger? Couldn't you have warned any of us? How can I be sure about my own daughter? Why didn't you inform Bryce or Harlan about this?"

Kauffman avoided the eyes of both Caldwell and al-Fasi. Instead, he looked down at the documents. "I did not know the full extent of the situation, Ms. Caldwell, but you are right. I did not disclose to Bryce everything I knew. I agree, some of this might have been avoided if I had told Bryce more. At the time, I thought I could not, and I can only ask you to accept my judgment, at the time, that it was safest for everybody to keep it confidential. There has been a problem in the Department, but these documents may help clear that up."

He waited, then faced Caldwell across the room. "As for Harlan, he and I were friends, too. And Harlan knew as much as I did. So did Harry's father. About the risks I mean, as I understood them."

"Harlan? He knew?"

"Yes."

"The two of you spoke about my daughter, and he didn't tell me?"

"I gather he did not."

"Oh my God. And Bryce?" she asked. " He's going for his own daughter. He's got a lot more documents—my documents. He said they're his bargaining chips."

"I assumed that," Kauffman said.

"He doesn't trust you or anybody else in the Justice Department. Now I see why."

"I assumed that, too." The anger and confusion showed plainly on her face but she stayed in her chair. "Mr. Bennett and Mr. Gould were probably removed, after Harry got your proffer, because of their contacts with the higher ups in the conspiracy."

al-Fasi broke in. "This Ingram guy seems to be out of control."

"Him and others in this arrangement of theirs," Kauffman answered. "They panicked when they heard about an informant coming forward. We did not figure that. So, will you confirm Mr. Bryce's destination, Ms. Caldwell?"

She spun away in her seat, looked at the paintings on the walls without seeing them and said nothing. Kauffman turned to al-Fasi.

"She told me Cape May Point."

"I was afraid of that. The airport—the new departure point Ingram is headed for—is not far from there. That's where Peter's flying. He'll arrive ahead of them, but he'll need support, Saad."

"Especially since he's babysitting that key witness, Gould."

"Key witness," Caldwell whispered at the wall. "Harry said that, too."

Kauffman glanced toward her, then scribbled on a note pad, tore off the sheet and handed it to al-Fasi with a set of ignition keys. "That's the Bryce address in Cape May Point, and the airport is at Cold Spring. The car is parked out front. It has the interceptor package, Corvette engine and all the rest. It can give you 120 miles per hour, if you need it. Contact Bryce first, then link up with O'Shea at that airport. You will have to ad lib it from there. Just stop the shipment."

al-Fasi took the paper and the keys. "Just one more thing," he said. "Bryce doesn't know who I am. He just saw me for a few seconds in Pittsburgh."

Caldwell got up as al-Fasi did. "I'll go with him. Harry knows me."

"Oh, no, Ms. Caldwell," Kauffman said. "There's likely to be some shooting. You don't need to be around any more of this."

"I've done some of that shooting myself, if your agent hasn't told you."

"Bryce has the documents, Ms. Caldwell, but they mean nothing without your testimony. I can't put you at risk again. You gave no sworn testimony or affidavit, did you?"

"No. There was just Harlan and me."

"You and Harlan and Bryce. As it was supposed to be."

"And Harlan's gone, so I have to stand in for him. At least for now, we're on the same side. Like you said, you have nothing without me and the documents I gave Harry. For my daughter's sake, Mr. Kauffman, I want to see all this stopped."

The Professor nodded and turned to al-Fasi. "What are you carrying?" he asked.

"Service pistol. But she told me Harry's got two of the guns from Savage River, a deer rifle and a shot gun."

"How about Kevlar?"

"I'm wearing one."

"There's another one in the trunk of my car. One more thing," the Professor said. "If you have to communicate by air, use the radio in the Interceptor. It's the most secure thing we have, but not certain. O'Shea's home computer has been penetrated. We don't know how much they extracted. He's got a couple of throwaway cell phones, and I gave you the number at Harry's cottage. But do as much as you can face-to-face."

Kauffman watched as al-Fasi pulled the pocket doors shut, then dialed the number to the Bryce house in Cape May Point. It did not ring, but a recorded voice came on to say service was discontinued for the winter. He mumbled a curse to himself and went to the bookcase by the wall. He poured himself a small glass of brandy, sipped, and studied his crude copy the exploding battleship 'L'Orient' in Aboukir Bay.

"The boy stood on the burning deck..." he started quoting to himself.

He picked up one of the documents he received from al-Fasi, and sat down with it on the sofa.

"The Trust," he mumbled. "Almost there." The telephone rang again on his desk.

O'Shea wrestled Gould into the plane and secured him. He moved around for a last pre-flight check, then climbed into the pilot's seat. He tuned in ATIS for weather, wind speed and direction aloft, then set the radio back to ground control.

"This is Queen 6560 requesting departure on Runway 27," he called out.

"Queen 6560 hold your position. Squawk 1200 on your transponder and ident."

He leaned out the window, yelled "clear prop" onto the deserted tarmac and started the engines. He let them idle while he checked the gauges. When the oil registered green, he turned on the navigation lights and the rotating beacon. Ground control came back with permission to taxi out to Runway 27. He taxied to the run-up and held. Ground control confirmed wind speed and cleared them for take-off with northern departure.

The Cessna accelerated down the runway, lifted into the air and turned north. O'Shea called Departure Control and told them he was headed east for Atlantic City at 125 miles per hour.

"Roger Queen 6560. Frequency change approved. You'll leave our air space. Pick up Dover Air Force Base at 123.7. Good night."

"Queen 6560. Good night."

He set the Cessna on an eastern bearing when they reached cruising altitude. Then, he pulled out one of the throwaway cell phones and punched in the Professor's number with his right thumb.

"You're still on that line from earlier?" Kauffman asked.

"Yes. A few calls left on it. I've got another as back-up. I'm in the air now, the Bureau's Cessna. Security's a little better up here. Gould is with me. He looks all right. Bleeding's stopped. I told Ground Control we're headed for Atlantic City instead of Cold Spring. Gould heard enough from Ingram to confirm the destination."

"No more details over this line, Peter."

"Right. But when I get there, I'll need help to make contact with Harry."

"Saad is on his way in the Interceptor, with the radio, which I hope is still secure. I gave him the address. He has the informant with him—a woman. She will help Saad make the contact."

"With Harry?"

"Of course. That's the only reason I agreed to let her go."

"Okay. Harry won't trust me, so maybe she'll be useful and not just more overhead getting in the way." O'Shea made a slight adjustment for a gusting tail wind. "Where can I reach you over the next few hours? Here?"

"Yes. Right here."

"Okay. Signing off. Ten-four, Professor." O'Shea returned the cell phone to his pocket.

The cockpit began to darken and the drone of the engines settled in. Gould finally said, "You're not FBI, are you?"

"That's the least of your problems, pal."

"You're chasing something on your own. Freelance, aren't you?"

O'Shea took a minute to answer. "Look, pal. Let me pass on something they teach us down at Quantico. Don't ask leading questions."

Gould took a minute himself. "So, what if I pull a Houdini? Slip out of these cuffs?"

"Then what? Jump?"

"No. Take over the controls."

"You know how to fly?"

"I've seen it in the movies. Emergency landing. Brain surgeon did it once."

"You've got more important things to worry about, pal. You're in the safest spot in the world for you right where you are, next to me in this plane."

"There's something else. It's in my coat pocket. You'll find it anyway."

"Give it to me after we land."

They maintained altitude and heading. O'Shea tuned in the Dover Tower, identifying himself as Queen 6560 at 2500 feet for Atlantic City. They told him to squawk 5194 and gave him barometric reset if necessary.

Gould shut up, twisted in his seat and tried to adjust his hands.

They took a bench in the back of the diner. Bryce sat with his back to the wall and held his daughter in his lap. When the menus and the water came, he slipped her into the seat next to him. She held his arm and said she wanted a hot dog and French fries. Bryce and Shaw ordered cheeseburgers, and they all settled on Cokes.

Shaw watched Bryce. Close to his daughter, they were like she had imagined, but in their physical presence a real pain tore through her chest.

"I'm sorry, Harry," she said at last.

"For what? I'm just so grateful you got Tess back to me. It's been a real mess."

"Careful way to put it—'mess.' It's not over, is it?"

"No. But I hope we're out of it soon, when I turn it all back to the Professor." Bryce looked at her. He waited before saying more, parsing the words in his mind. Finally, he said, "What were you doing in Winchester? My father said you left a message you wanted to talk about the case. Why do it there?"

Shaw pushed aside her plate, took a minute, and then leaned across the table. "I've been taking money on the side from Gideon Aubrey for about two years now. I pass on information about the investigations. I've used the money to help pay my father's medical bills. I can't get into all that right now. Maybe later. But, Gideon asked me for information about the Tuscarora case."

Bryce was surprised by the details of what he began to suspect back in Pittsburgh. With his daughter next to him, it was not a subject he wanted to open now. He had to keep Barbara Shaw cooperative, treat her for now as a victim, like himself and his daughter. She could nail Gideon, if she stayed in this mood, and Gideon, if turned, could give him the whole conspiracy.

"He's not the attorney of record for them. I thought he just does civil work."

"He represents a subsidiary or affiliate."

Bryce hesitated. He should not disclose any of the proffer. He had to assume she was a witness. Finally, he asked, "You mean Blue Mountain?"

"That's it. And Gideon has another client that's involved in this. Bob Ingram."

"Was he at the party?"

"Yes. He's a customer of Blue Mountain."

"Is his firm Miltech? In Virginia?"

"Yes. You're starting to put this together, aren't you? He had that guy following us in Washington, the car with the tinted windshields—the one who showed up in Winchester." Shaw glanced over at Tess and stopped. She leaned back against the booth and sipped her Coke.

"What did Gideon want from you about Tuscarora?"

"The informant. The proffer."

"How did he find out about that? I never filed any memo."

"I don't know. Gideon had a meeting with Ingram on Christmas morning. He made me go with him. He said he needed me for credibility with his client. I didn't want that kind of exposure, but I went. They made a call to some banker in New York."

So, he thought, there is a link she doesn't have, but Gideon does. "While you were there? Is that why you're telling me this?"

"Yes. I suspected that this was something much bigger than I had bought into. I got a real sense of danger at that meeting for the first time, in actually seeing Ingram. I think Gideon was scared, too. There was talk about Pittsburgh, but there was also talk between Ingram and the banker about your father and your daughter. I confronted Gideon about it afterward and he said we'd both be out of it in a few days. I thought about it long and hard, Harry, after that meeting and my talk with Gideon. I had a feeling they were sending that tail after you in Philly. I decided I had to tell you in person, and not in Washington. That was the message I left your father."

"The tail. The one in D.C.?"

"Yes."

"Sent by Ingram?"

"Yes."

Bryce hesitated again, then asked in a low voice, hoping his daughter would not hear, "In this meeting, Barbara, or any other time, did the name Jack Whitten come up?"

The tears were starting to well in her eyes, "No," she coughed.

Bryce believed her and touched her arm. He said, "You know, Barbara, I probably have to report some of this."

The tears broke out, and she took her napkin to wipe them dry, but her eyes remained red as she spoke. "I'm so sorry, Harry. I don't expect you to believe me, but it was all about my father. I needed the money for him."

"And Gideon knew about that?"

"Yes." The word came out with a cough.

"Did he show you how to launder the money, too?"

"Yes. Through the Caymans. I was planning to go down there after seeing you. I booked a flight out of Atlantic City."

"When?"

"Tonight."

"How long do you plan to stay there?"

"I don't know. Use up my accumulated leave time, at least."

"They've really got you hanging out there, Barbara. But you know that. You believe you would be safe down there, now, after all this?"

"I haven't had time to think it through, Harry. I just want to get away."

Bryce said, "Yeah," and waited. Then he asked, "Did my father say anything to you about this case, or about the Professor?"

"We never got a chance to talk."

"He said he was going to tell me something. He said he would wait until I got back from Pittsburgh."

They let everything drop in silence and watched Tess finish her French fries and drain her Coke glass. When she was done, Bryce said, "We can't stay here much longer. Let's go back to the cottage and see if we can figure out what to do next."

Shaw slid out of the booth and stood at the end. "Any ideas now?"

Bryce held his daughter and slid out himself. "Nope," he said. "Not for us."

The restaurant overlooked the mouth of the Severn River as it emptied into the Chesapeake Bay. Sailboats crammed against the docks and it was noisy with tourists. Aubrey was waiting when Thayer arrived, nursing a tall glass with a long straw. Thayer took a seat and ordered a draft beer. Aubrey asked for a refill.

"The documents are out in my car. Three boxes," Aubrey said.

"And the computer?"

"I erased what I could."

"And the hard drive?"

"Well, they'd have to subpoena the processor itself, but I kept as much as possible out of it. Just official stuff. I don't think they'd find much."

"Plus a court fight to get it." Thayer picked up the menu. "What do you recommend?"

"Clam chowder. My funds have been deposited, so I'm out of this, right? Ingram said he's firing me. Moving to another firm. He didn't say which one."

"He's leaving Virginia. So, unless Bryce got something on you in Pittsburgh, you're done—after I get your records. You staying with Herrick?"

"I don't know," Aubrey lied. He had already submitted his resignation.

Thayer signaled the waiter again and ordered another round for both of them.

"We never talked about this," Thayer said. "What can you tell me about Bryce?"

Aubrey looked out over the docks. "Harry? We were drinking buddies in law school. After graduation, we went our own ways—he into Justice and I into private practice. We butted heads on a case in Philadelphia a few years ago."

"Did you ever meet his father?"

"I don't think so."

"He worked with Harry's boss, Winston Kauffman, back in the Eighties."

"Is that how Harry got the transfer? I heard a bit about the divorce."

"Nothing else?"

"No. He handled that old case professionally. That's it." Aubrey brought his eyes back to Thayer. "Did you pass on that information about Jack Whitten, our law school classmate out in western Maryland?"

"Yes."

"Any luck? Did they get the documents?"

"Evidently not."

"So, Harry must still have them. Has he reported in?"

"Nothing I've heard."

Aubrey took another sip. He did not want to continue the meeting, but something compelled him on. "One more thing. Now that I'm out of it, what was this all about, really? Don't tell me anything I shouldn't know. All I did was process the paperwork and collect my fees."

"Right. Red tape."

"I might have guessed more if I gave it any thought."

"But you did not, did you? You have no actual knowledge, other than what Ingram might have said, right?"

"Yeah." Aubrey took the last sip from his drink. "I've probably had too much of this. There is another issue. Ingram mentioned something called the Trust. Oh, forget I asked. I shouldn't have mentioned it. Not my concern."

Thayer pushed aside his beer, laid a couple of twenties on the table and got up. "You're right, Gideon. You've had too much and it's time to go. Get me your documents."

Thayer moved his car next to the Audi and they took the boxes out of the trunk. Aubrey staggered just a bit, and Thayer asked, "You all right to drive? Maybe you should go back in there and get something to eat."

"Good idea." Aubrey went back to the restaurant.

Thayer watched him go, then took the magnetic disk from his glove compartment and attached it to the Audi's front passenger side-wheel hub.

O'Shea held the Cessna to its heading and altitude. Behind them to the west, the cloud ceiling broke, but to the south another heavy bank rolled up the coast. They flew out over the Chesapeake, away from the major airlines, and reached land again. The Peninsula faded from sight beneath them under the mists rising out of the marshes.

"Where did you learn to fly?" Gould asked.

"Marines."

"This plane yours?"

"No. FBI."

"So, we're on a mission?"

"No. What we're on now is a gold-plated Title 18 felony. But don't worry. I've got friends to cover me."

"Better than mine, I hope."

"Worse. Much worse."

The night closed around them. O'Shea kept his eyes on the instrument panel while Gould stared into the purple vacuum over the plane's nose.

"Fly this thing over to Jersey once or twice a year," O'Shea said. "Gets in my hours. I know the airfield we're going to. Your friends made a smart choice, but we'll get there first." He asked Gould what kinds of weapons were used back at the hangar.

"Pistols. Handguns are all I saw."

"Anything else?"

"Well, automatics."

"How about the shooters?"

"Two of them. I thought just truck drivers."

"Amateurs," O'Shea said. "Should have taken time to make sure they finished you off."

They left land again at Goose Point. The Delaware Bay was a black void pricked only by the running lights of oil tankers and edged by lights along the shorelines. They reached the next landfall at Cape May Point. O'Shea adjusted the bearing and stood out over the Atlantic. When he acquired the Sea Isle City signal, he pulled up the yoke. The Cessna tilted to a 60-degree angle. He leveled off at 5,000 feet. Then he pushed the yoke back in, reduced power, and at 200 feet leveled off again.

The Pomona Air Force base picked it up. The radio in the Cessna squawked out demanding information. O'Shea flipped off the transponder, dropped the airspeed to 100 miles per hour and turned due west.

At Pomona, the unidentified blip went off the screen. The officer on watch processed a request to notify the Coast Guard Base at Cape May.

Gould shifted in his seat as the plane slowed and leveled. "What was that all about?" he asked.

"Just a thought."

"Is that how you land planes down here?"

"No. Just trying to get somebody's attention."

Direct ahead to the west, the last sunlight dropped below the horizon, but the airstrip was still visible.

"How old are you?" O'Shea asked.

"Thirty-eight."

"Well, you'll still be pretty young when you get out of Eglin. Good behavior, I hope."

"Right now, I'm wondering if you actually know how to land this thing."

"Watch and learn."

O'Shea turned the radio back on and clicked it three times. A string of runway lights flashed on. The Cessna fell into line, hit the tarmac and taxied down to the end. He steered it to a string of parked single-prop planes. The engines fluttered to a halt, and the airstrip lights blinked off. The two of them sat for a moment in isolated silence on firm ground.

"Eighteen fucking months to go," O'Shea muttered.

"To what?"

"Retirement."

"Thought I'd retire at forty," Gould said.

"Looks like you'll do a bit better than that. Shit. No more kicking in doors, they told me, when they sent me to white collar crime."

O'Shea unstrapped himself, dropped down on the tarmac, walked around the plane and heaved Gould out. A rolled vellum document fell from Gould's coat onto the tarmac. O'Shea picked it up and scanned the Cyrillic lettering.

"This what you were talking about?"

"That's it."

"So, what the fuck is it?"

"An old bearer bond," Gould said.

"How old?"

"Over a hundred years, I think."

"Connected to this case?" Gould made no reply, and O'Shea said, "I hear you." He threw the vellum back in the plane cabin, muttering, "More fucking paperwork. That's why I hate this white-collar stuff. Why can't you guys just rob banks?"

He re-cuffed Gould to the wing struts and scanned the airfield. The snow from the day before was almost gone, but some of it still evaporated into low-lying mist clinging to the ground. A brittle edge of wind blew off the Atlantic a few miles away.

"You leaving me here like this?" Gould asked.

"For now. Until the posse arrives. Just keep quiet." O'Shea went back to the cockpit, pulled a Kevlar jacket from behind the seats, and checked his service revolver. Then he used the cell phone to call the Professor.

"We're here," he said. "Nothing else is."

"How many calls do you have left?"

"Ten or twelve."

"al-Fasi is on the way."

"I tried something on the landing approach that might get us some help."

The call ended. O'Shea moved out over the tarmac to find a position to rendezvous with al-Fasi, or stop Ingram, whichever came first.

Bryce told Shaw to leave the car under the trees by the chapel a block away from Yale Avenue. He took the deer rifle in one hand and his daughter by the other and began walking to the cottage.

Tess said, "Let's go to the beach, Daddy."

"It's a little cold, Honey."

"But I love the beach at night. We always go there."

"Okay. Let's go."

They passed Yale Avenue, climbed up the wooden walkway over the dunes and down to the beach. The tide had run out and there was a long stretch of hard wet sand. Tess ran ahead of them down along the beach looking for treasure. Bryce told her not to get too close to the waves.

"Can we go out there?" she asked, pointing at the jetty.

"Have to be careful. The rocks are covered with moss. Slippery. Keep your eyes down at your feet."

Shaw started to shake in the cold, so Bryce placed an arm around her shoulder. Small waves lapped against the rocks as the last glow of sunlight fell below the Delaware coast and the full moon emerged behind them in the clearing sky. Bryce used the thumb on his other hand to turn off the safety switch on the rifle.

CHAPTER FOURTEEN

Larson threw another cigarette butt out of the window of the Plymouth and twisted, looking back at the cottage from the corner. He saw them a block away walk past the intersection in the direction of the beach and climb over the dune. When they dropped to the other side, he followed. From the top, he watched Barbara Shaw and Bryce move toward the jetty while the girl ran along the beach at the edge of the waves. Nothing stirred on the street behind him. He took out his Walther and started down on the sand.

Bryce and Shaw stepped carefully halfway out the jetty to where the small waves broke on the rocks. She pulled her shoulder away from Bryce's arm, stooped down, and reached between the rocks for an oyster shell. Standing up again, she turned and stared back at the dune.

"That's the guy," she whispered to Bryce.

Bryce turned with the deer rifle in his hand. "The tail from Washington? My father's killer?"

"Yes."

Larson stopped at the foot of the jetty, aiming his pistol. "Don't move. Drop the rifle."

"Who are you?" Bryce demanded.

"I said drop it."

Bryce laid the gun down on the flat boulder in front of him. Shaw fingered the oyster shell behind her back, moving her thumb and forefinger around the sharp edge. Bryce glanced up the beach. His daughter's back was to them. She poked the sand with a piece of driftwood. The splashing surf smothered other sounds. Larson came closer, scrambling onto the jetty.

"What do you want?" Bryce asked.

"You know. The documents."

"What documents?"

"Pittsburgh."

Bryce lifted his arms from his body. "I don't have any documents."

"Take me to them."

"And if I can't?"

Larson moved onto the next row of rocks. He pointed the barrel of the Walther down the beach.

"That's your daughter, right? You don't need to answer. I got orders."

"Whose orders?"

"The documents."

Bryce stepped back, looking at the moss, and drew Shaw with him. Now, the surf broke in front of them. He knew the water was waist deep at this point. The rifle stock was still within reach, the barrel faced the beach, toward Larson.

"It's Ingram, isn't it," Shaw said. "He sent you. How did you know to come here?" The full moon hung right behind Larson, his face cast in shadow. They could see no expression and he did not reply.

"They're in my car," Bryce said.

"Where's that?"

"There." Bryce pointed up over the dune.

Larson waved the Walther at the dune and said, "Show me." He moved one foot onto the jetty rocks behind him.

"I have to call my daughter," Bryce said. "I can't leave her out here alone."

Shaw kept her attention on Larson. "You think Ingram will let you off?" she shouted over the noise of the surf. "You already know too much, just like I do. Get out while you can. Forget about us."

Larson shook his head. "I know more than you think."

She saw him step on another rock toward the beach. His foot slipped on the moss and his arms stretched out to recover his balance. The pistol barrel pointed down at the sand. She moved her arm holding the oyster shell free of Bryce and whipped it around, snapping her wrist and elbow at the release point.

Larson stumbled and the other foot gave way. The oyster shell struck his face above his nose and lifted a bloody piece of flesh. Blood poured into one eye. He reached up with his left hand and leveled the gun barrel out over the jetty toward Bryce and Shaw.

Bryce flung himself onto the rock in front of him, took up the rifle and let off one round. He thought he hit Larson somewhere in the chest. He bolted in another shell. Larson staggered back and tried to aim the Walther. Bryce fired again, and this time he saw blood spurt off Larson's jaw. Larson discharged his pistol and the bullet hit the jetty rock in front of Bryce. Bryce lunged ahead and tackled Larson at his waist. The Walther flew out of Larson's hand onto the sand. Bryce twisted and launched the two of them into the surf, striking the water with Larson's body under him.

Bryce steadied his feet in the knee-deep water. He grabbed Larson's head under water and slammed the skull against the nearest boulder as the waves broke against it. The body stiffened in his hands and went limp.

A hand touched Bryce's shoulder. He looked up.

"It's over, Harry," Shaw said. She had the Walther. "Let him go."

He released the body and pushed it clear of the rocks. It floated in the surf, bounced on the waves, and drifted away in the rip tide. Finally, Bryce felt the cold water around his legs. He struggled onto the beach. His daughter was standing there, staring. He lifted her, holding her face away from the jetty and started walking to the dune.

"Who was that, Daddy?" she asked.

"A pirate, Honey. Just like in one of our stories."

"Where's he going?"

"Back out to sea where he came from."

Barbara took the rifle off the rocks and followed them. When she got beside Bryce he said, "Nice throw. I forgot you played ball. What's your position on your softball team?"

"Third base."

"Five-four, pick off the lead runner."

"By the way, nice shooting on your part."

"All those hunting trips. First time I ever hit anything. It was all about beer anyway, back then."

Karev stopped in front of the service bay under the canopy. Vrenc's directions led him here through a maze of two-lane, pine-bordered roads. The station looked closed. Except for the light sea breeze, the only sound was Country and Western music thumping from the bar across the street. A pick-up truck screeched out of the bar's parking lot and disappeared down the road into the woods. He tried the station door and it opened. A voice from inside the service bay called him in.

A man in a turban and oil-stained denims stood next to a Ford Galaxy up on a lift. The man reached into the engine bay and drew out a Colt government model automatic. He handed it to Karev.

"How many rounds?" Karev asked.

"Eight. Here is a spare magazine." The man took it out of his denims.

"I am not familiar with this." Karev tucked the pistol and the magazine under this coat.

"Take some practice shots in the woods down the road. Nobody will hear you," the man said. "That model is common around here. It is not traceable to us. Discard it at your discretion when you are finished."

The man showed no interest in Karev, and no anxiety about handing him the weapon. Karev wondered if he had coverage in the shadows in the back of the bay, but heard nothing.

"Which way to the airport from here?" he asked.

The man pointed to his right, down the road and through the pines. "That way," he said. "You will see some signs after a mile or so."

"What about the police?"

The man nodded his head at the bar across the road. "They'll be too busy dealing with drunk drivers and bar fights to worry about you."

"Good."

"You must go now," he said. "I will let Milos know."

Karev bowed and left.

When they were in the cottage, Bryce put Tess down and went back to a bedroom to change his clothes.

"Do you have anything to drink here?" Shaw called from the living room.

"Corner cabinet."

Bryce listened to the clinking of glass as he took off his suit and put on a pair of denim jeans, a sweatshirt and leather boots. When he came out, Shaw and Tess were sitting at the dining table, Tess with a Coke and Shaw with a tumbler, straight with no ice. His father's bottle of Jameson's sat beside the rifle and the pistol, and a second empty tumbler sat across the table, next to Tess.

Bryce took his daughter in his lap and sat down.

"Join me?" Shaw asked.

He looked at the bottle. "Not now."

She took a long sip. "It just feels right after that."

"Maybe later." He pushed the empty tumbler aside.

"There might not be a 'later,' Harry."

He watched her for a moment.

"Oh, there will be a 'later,'" he said. "We don't know when it will be, though. Anything more you want to tell me about Gideon?"

"Most of his clients are small business government contractors. He's made a specialty out of all the regulations. Some were probably at that party."

"Like Ingram?"

"Yeah."

"I think Aubrey was involved somehow in two attacks yesterday, Pittsburgh and Maryland. I can turn him, Barbara, but only with your help."

She took another sip. "I know. I knew that when I called your father."

"He'd be the perfect witness. Law firm records and all."

"'He'd be the perfect witness,'" she repeated. "Sure he would. Everybody knows that. And they know I can help you turn him." She lifted the tumbler to her lips again and put it down. "Everything I know about this comes from Gideon. It's all hearsay. If he does turn, you don't need me. And if he does, or is off the board some other way, I'm useless to everybody—you and them."

"So you think..."

"Yes. Gideon's a target, too."

"You think he knows?"

"He acted that way the last time I saw him, the day after the party, with Ingram. He seemed as scared as I was. Harry, I never thought anything like this would happen. I don't think Gideon did either, but I do think he put me at risk in that meeting on Christmas Day to reduce the danger to himself."

Bryce paused a moment to rub his daughter's hair, then took her across to the living room and found a cartoon show on the television. Coming back to the table, he said, "There's something else, Barbara— Professor Kauffman. Seemed like my father didn't quite trust him, but he never told me why, exactly. The thing is, the Professor is the only one I notified about the informant contact, and he reported it to Thayer, the Deputy AAG."

"You told me, the night of the party"

"But not the details, like I gave him."

"So you think the rat is either Kauffman or Thayer. Besides me." She reached for the bottle and refilled her tumbler. "I told you Gideon called me that day and asked me to find out what I could about the informant. So one of them had to tip him off."

"No clue which one?"

"Nope."

"How about that guy on the beach?"

"He was trying to get your notes out of your car that night at the party. Then, there was some hint Ingram was sending him up to Philly to try and intercept you again. That's one reason I called your father."

Bryce moved his eyes to the untouched tumbler in front of him. He reached for it, but squeezed his hand shut. "So, Gideon passed on the information, to Ingram probably, and he sent the shooters to Pittsburgh and Maryland. Plus the one out on the beach. Which means they know about this place. We have to get out of here."

He went into the living room and got his daughter's coat. Barbara took her own coat off the chair.

"Any ideas where?"

"The only direction from here is north. Follow me. I'll lead you to the Atlantic City Airport."

"I'll bring my car around," Shaw said. As she opened the front door, the growl of a heavy car engine moved across the front of the cottage, headlights off. It kept going slowly down the street. She closed the door.

"Somebody's out there," she whispered. "Get down."

Bryce reached for the wall switch and most of the inside lights went off. He picked up the guns, called for his daughter and took her under the dining room table.

There was a knock on the door and a male voice said, "Mr. Bryce?"

Bryce could see him under the porch light, holding a pistol with the barrel pointed up.

"I know you're in there, Mr. Bryce. I saw Mr. Whitten's van down the street."

Bryce finally asked, "Who are you?"

"Dr. Kauffman sent me."

"Not the right answer."

"I understand. I have someone else with me."

A female figure came up under the porch light. Bryce recognized her.

"Come on in," he said.

They stepped through the door, and stopped just inside the open frame. Bryce crawled out from under the table with his daughter.

"Barbara," he said. "This is the informant, Allison Caldwell."

The wrecker's truck arrived under flashing yellow lights and pulled over hundreds of yards ahead of them. The crew hooked up the crane and slowly started righting the tanker truck. When it was back on its wheels, they hauled it over onto the grass between the north and southbound lanes. The fire crew, surrounded by their own red trucks and flashing lights, hosed off the spill. An ambulance lit up its flashers and sped off in a low wail.

After waiting for nearly an hour, things started to move as State troopers waved vehicles around orange cones onto the shoulder. With the panel truck behind him, Ingram lurched forward in the middle of miles of backed-up traffic. Once past the accident scene, they accelerated.

Ingram fumed alone in the Cadillac, but the tension drained as he gathered speed. He checked the time on the dashboard clock, and the panel truck in the rear view. They would get to the airport much later than he planned, but still be there when the plane arrived.

"We need help," al-Fasi said.

"You need help? Show me some ID."

al-Fasi took out his badge and tossed it on the floor at Bryce's feet. He looked down and kicked it back.

"So, what's the Professor want from me now?"

"How much do you know?" al-Fasi asked.

"I know at least four goons tried to kill me in the last day and a half. One of them just now out there on the beach."

al-Fasi spun around to the street and raised up his pistol. "Don't worry, he's gone," Bryce said. "Rip tide has him. Maybe some fishermen'll find him in a few days out in the ocean."

"Anything else?" al-Fasi asked.

"That's the guy that killed my father, so I'm told. Another one got my best friend." He pointed at Caldwell. "Because of her, I know about Miltech, Ingram and Blue Mountain. I have the documents she gave me. And because of her," he pointed at Barbara Shaw, "I know about Gideon Aubrey. You guys know about him?"

al-Fasi stared without answering.

"Yeah. Just what I thought. But my daughter's more important than any of that. The one thing I don't know is who set all this up? The Professor?"

"I was in Pittsburgh. You know that," al-Fasi said. "Dr. Kauffman sent me and my partner out there to protect you. We were late. My partner got killed trying."

"You're the one who told us to get out of town. Protect me from what? What was the danger nobody told me about?"

Caldwell interrupted. "They killed Harlan Moan, Harry."

Bryce looked at her, and back at al-Fasi. "You were late for that, too?" Bryce said.

"I picked her up in Morgantown. But now, we need to make contact with Agent O'Shea."

"Why?"

"He's at a general aviation airport near here called Cold Spring. It's the location for final delivery. Tonight."

Bryce kept his hand on his daughter. "That's not my problem.

Or, if it was, I should have been told before all this started. Not anymore."

Caldwell broke in again. "This agent, O'Shea, has custody of Tom Gould, Harry. Tom Gould. Like Jack said, he connects the documents I gave you."

"You should talk to Dr. Kauffman," al-Fasi said.

"Why? You and Pete are the guys trained to deal with what ever's happening at the airport. I'm just a lawyer. The last thing you guys need right now is somebody like me in your way."

"Dr. Kauffman wants you to bring Mr. Gould and the documents back to Washington. Pete flew with him down here from Baltimore. They tried to kill Gould, too, up there."

Bryce retreated behind the dining table with Tess and laid down the rifle. Everybody remained standing. "So, the Professor's thinking, I've got the documents. Pete's got the witness. And she," indicating Shaw, "can nail the lawyer, and that wraps the case. Whatever the case really is. Which means the Professor is the only one living who knows what this is all about. Right now, we have to get out of here because this place is not safe. And I am not putting my daughter in any more danger. So, Special Agent, if that's what you really are, the hell with the Professor, Tom Gould, the documents, the delivery, the case. The whole shooting match."

"The guidance systems they're shipping out are for drones, missiles," Caldwell said. "I told you that."

"And like I said, that's their problem. Pete O'Shea and this guy."

"There's something else" al-Fasi said. "Ingram, the head of Miltech, will be there. You know who he is?" Bryce said nothing.

"I thought so. Two more things. First that airport may be the safest spot for the next few hours because it's the last place in the world they'll be looking for you. Second, there's a bulletin out for a white Cherokee with Maryland plates like the one parked down the street. Not in New Jersey, yet, but in Pennsylvania and Maryland." al-Fasi pointed at the guns Bryce left on the dining table. "You have any weapons besides those?"

"There's a shotgun out in the Cherokee."

"Let me make another point," al-Fasi said. "There is reason to believe the shooters were foreign nationals from the Caucasus."

"You people know a lot more than you say, Special Agent, at least to me. All right, I'll talk to the Professor. So, how do you want to do that? Phones in here are shut off for the winter."

"Can't use cell phones," al-Fasi said.

"Right. Too bad, then." Bryce started for the door with his daughter. "We're going, Honey."

"Okay," al-Fasi said. "Come with me, outside." They went down the street to the black sedan. "You recognize it?"

"Dual exhaust pipes, extra wide tires. Yeah. The Professor's."

"You'll need to take this back to Washington."

They climbed into the front seats, with Bryce still holding Tess. al-Fasi punched the numbers on the car phone. The Professor's voice came up.

"Harry? Keep it short."

"'Keep it short,'" Bryce repeated. "Okay. This guy claims to be a Special Agent working for you. He says he wants me to meet Pete O'Shea at a nearby airport. He says a man named Ingram will be there, too. You know who he is and what he did?"

"Some of it now. I'm sorry, Harry."

"And these agents, Pete and the other guy, want me to pick up a witness, bring him up there to you, and close the case."

"You put it quite succinctly."

"We haven't talked for a few days now, Professor."

"I cannot explain any of it over this line. All I can say now is that circumstances forced me to improvise. You realize what the shipment is?"

"Now I do."

"Then you understand why this is urgent. I had to by-pass some channels."

"Who is the stuff for, really?

Kauffman did not answer. The car phone remained silent. Finally, he said, "This line may not be secure, Harry. I will tell you more in person."

Bryce waited. "It's the worm, isn't it?"

"You know about that? "

"My friend, Jack, figured it out. He's dead, too."

"So I was advised, by agent al-Fasi. Because of that, the worm,

I must ask you to bring the documents and Mr. Gould to my townhouse first. Not to Main Justice."

Bryce waited again, then asked, "Who do you really work for, Professor? Anybody?" There was no answer. He looked over at al-Fasi who averted his eyes.

"Was my father involved in this case, Professor?"

"I can't go into that over this line, Harry."

"Okay. If I do what you ask," Bryce said, "will that put an end to this for me and my family?"

"Yes."

"And one more thing. Were you informed about Barbara Shaw and Gideon Aubrey?"

"Yes."

"But she's clear if I do what you ask, right? Nothing more with her?"

"Yes."

Bryce waited for some conditions, but none came.

"I don't trust you, Professor. But there is one person I do trust," Bryce said. "Only one, the informant. You met her, I gather."

"Yes."

"Then we agree," Bryce said. "Pete and this guy stop the delivery. I bring you the evidence and write the closing memo. I'm clear. My daughter's clear. Barbara Shaw's clear. The informant, Ms Caldwell, is clear. That's it."

"Yes." The line went dead.

They walked back to the cottage. Bryce took an overcoat out of a closet for himself and wrapped Tess in one of his mother's coats. He told Shaw to take the Walther from the dining table, and headed outside with Tess, holding the deer rifle in his hand.

"We'll go through the pines, local roads, so we don't have to worry about State police and that bulletin," he said to al-Fasi and Caldwell. He looked back at Shaw. She stood in the doorway with the Walther and reached over to switch off the cottage lights.

"Like you said, I'm going to Atlantic City," she said. "I'll get my car and follow you out."

"Caymans, right?" Bryce asked.

"Yeah."

"You still think that's a good idea, Barbara?"

"You have a better one?"

Bryce shook his head and put his daughter in the Cherokee.

She asked, "Where are we going, Daddy?"

"To Washington. It'll be a long drive, Honey. Try to make yourself comfortable."

"Who were you talking to in that black car?"

"I thought it was my boss. Right now, Sweetheart, I honestly don't know."

He started the engine and the Interceptor came up behind him. They went around the block to Barbara Shaw's Cavalier. Then they moved in a train, north to the mainland.

Karev circled the airport and identified the isolated hangar by the flaking paint that read "Techair Maintenance." He spotted a two-engine Cessna parked in line with single engine planes, and as he continued past he saw a man sitting against the landing gear. He drove to the far end of the landing strip, and found a break in the fence. He drove the Peugeot into the woods walked back through the break.

He walked around the perimeter, watching the hangar. Halfway to the signal tower, a black sedan with a heavy sounding engine pulled into the parking lot, followed by a white Jeep Cherokee. As he stopped, a man appeared out of a shadow behind the hangar wall.

Barbara Shaw passed the other two cars when they made the turn into the airport and continued north following signs to the Parkway. She came to a crossroad with an open bar on one corner and a gas station on another. The neon lights in the bar and the sound of country music reminded her that she needed another drink. She made her way inside through the smoke and ordered a draft. The television screen played extreme skiing in deep powder. At the back, young men hung around a pool table. One of them came over and tried to start a conversation, but she pushed him off and signaled the bartender for a second round. Nothing in there, not the skiing on the screen, the music in the air, the men playing pool or the second glass of beer could get Harry and Tess out of her mind. She dropped some cash on the bar and left.

The Cavalier kicked up a spray of cinders and she steered it back down the road she'd come.

CHAPTER FIFTEEN

Bryce left the Cherokee's headlights and the engine running while al-Fasi and O'Shea conferred in front of the Interceptor. They pointed to the hangar, at the row of single engine planes, and came over to him.

"Saad tells me you have some rifles," O'Shea said.

"In the back seat—there's a shotgun with a box of slug shot and a deer rifle."

"We'll need them. Turn off those headlights and come with me." Bryce got out, telling his daughter to stay. O'Shea handed the shotgun and the slugs to al-Fasi. "How about ammo for the rifle?"

"Here's what I have." Bryce emptied his pocket and handed over five shells.

"Shit. Okay, let's go."

"Where?"

"Out there."

"Why?"

"You need to take custody of somebody."

"Tom Gould?"

"Yeah. Haul his ass out of here. Take him to the Professor."

"I have to talk to her"—Bryce pointed over at Caldwell—"and my daughter first." Bryce asked Caldwell to stay with Tess, but instead she spoke to O'Shea, "Let me help. Give me the shotgun again."

al-Fasi said, "There's another Kevlar in the Interceptor, Pete."

"Maybe you'd better get it," O'Shea said. He handed Caldwell the shotgun. "Stay here with the girl until Harry returns with the witness and takes off. Then put that jacket on and join me." He started out to the parked planes with al-Fasi and Bryce.

"How many do you expect?" al-Fasi asked

"At least three from Baltimore. Plus whoever flies in. Try to take out the plane first. We'll worry about the truck last."

"Ingram will be with them?" Bryce asked.

"I'm sure he will."

"And you'll take care of him, too?"

"Priority is to stop the smuggling, Harry. That guy's just collateral."

They stopped near the hangar. O'Shea pointed toward the signal tower. al-Fasi gave Bryce the keys to the Interceptor. "Take that to Washington. Police won't stop you." He jogged across the front of the hangar and disappeared in the grass and shadows off the tarmac.

O'Shea led Bryce to the Cessna. He released Gould from the landing gear, lifted him up and recuffed him. He reached into the plane cabin, took out the vellum he had confiscated from Gould and handed it to Bryce.

"What's this?" Bryce asked.

"More for the Professor. They're your problem now, Harry. Now, get out of here." He walked back into the shadows near the row of Piper Cubs.

The DHC Caribou flew ten miles off the coast, well away from other air traffic. When it intercepted the Sea Isle City beacon, the pilot turned inland. Pomona Air Force Base called for identification and he ignored it.

The airfield lay in darkness edged with scattered house lights. The pilot dropped down to 1,000 feet. The runway lights blinked on. He came around to the north and brought the plane in.

O'Shea yanked Bryce and Gould down to the tarmac behind the Cessna as the Caribou raced by sucking the night air into the feathered engines. After it passed, they watched it taxi to the hangar and stop.

O'Shea held them still for a moment. "Okay, the others aren't here yet. You showed up just in time, Harry. Now get going, fast."

Bryce pushed Gould ahead of him by the shoulders. "Let's move, pal. Whatever happens next is for the pros."

They moved across the still lighted runway toward the parking lot. Caldwell came up to them with the shotgun. She reached toward Gould, but pulled back when she saw the handcuffs. He said nothing.

"Which way to your Special Agent?" she asked.

Bryce said. "Over there," and pointed at the Cessna and Piper Cubs. "Do what he tells you. Nothing more. And be careful."

She trotted off, across the tarmac. The runway lights snapped on and she picked up her speed.

O'Shea watched Bryce and Gould as they reached the Interceptor. He crouched down, holding the deer rifle, and slipped behind the line of planes while the Caribou's propellers fluttered to a stop. The cargo ramp hissed down. Landing lights still flooded the area in front of the hangar's bay, but the runway lights popped off.

It took Caldwell more time than she expected to find him.

O'Shea jerked around when she touched his shoulder from behind.

"You got that Kevlar on?" he asked.

"Yes. Under my coat."

"Okay. Cover the rear of the hangar. Stop anybody you see coming out the back door."

She crouched down and darted into the shadows behind the building.

Karev waited at the base of the signal tower. He saw three men move from the parking lot to the hangar and one of them vanish into the grass off the runway in front of him. He watched the other two, one with a rifle, disappear on the other side. He only had the Colt. He needed to get closer, but before he started, two more figures hurried across the tarmac to the parking lot, one in handcuffs. They did not look armed. Another came up to them carrying a long gun, and started out toward the hangar. The runway lights came on. The last figure ran past the side of the hangar and vanished. The Caribou landed, taxied and stopped. He started toward the plane, circling the dark beyond the runway lights.

The pilot came down the cargo ramp, looked around and couldn't find anyone there, but he did see a fuel truck next to the signal tower. He walked toward it, coming out of the cone cast by the Caribou landing lights. He stepped off onto the grass and started to light a Marlboro.

The runway lights went off, and the pilot now stood in the dark. al-Fasi saw his chance. He rose up from the grass hollow and jammed the pistol into the pilot's side. The pilot dropped his pack of Marlboros and raised his hands. al-Fasi forced him around and did a quick pat.

"You fly solo?" he asked.

"Yes."

"Armed?"

"No."

al-Fasi took out his handcuffs, yanked down the pilot's hands, bound him and frisked more thoroughly than before. He told the truth. No weapons. "Quiet and come with me," he said.

They went to the back wall of the hangar. Caldwell stepped up to them.

"Pete stationed you here?" he asked. She nodded yes.

al-Fasi cuffed the pilot to a vent pipe. "Well, then, keep an eye on him, too. I'm going to disable the plane." He went to the Caribou and looked into the cargo bay for any more flight crew. He started to climb the ramp and stopped. Two pairs of headlights came across the airfield toward him and the plane. He ducked under the fuselage and tried to make it to the grass hollow, but the headlights shifted and caught him.

The Colt fired three times. al-Fasi lifted off the edge of the tarmac and dropped on the grass in the dark. Karev came over, took the handcuff keys off the agent's belt and the pistol from his hand.

The panel truck and the Cadillac stopped in front of the hangar. A man got out of the truck and pulled open the bay door. Both vehicles moved inside. Karev sprinted to the open bay and shouted a warning. The truck drivers reached for their weapons at the voice, but stopped when they saw him. He handed Ingram the handcuff keys and the gun.

Caldwell saw al-Fasi go down. After the shooter went into the hangar, she ran to him on the grass. He started to regain consciousness.

"Get to Peter," he said. "Tell him to take out the plane."

She looked for his wounds, but he told her to go. She glanced at the hangar bay. The shooter was pointing at the row of Piper Cubs, then beyond them to the perimeter fence and the parking lot. She slipped behind the hanger, and did not see the shooter start out toward the parking lot, Harry Bryce and his daughter.

O'Shea stopped next to a cinder block storage shed and watched the truck and the Cadillac move into the hangar. He brought the rifle up to his shoulder and fingered the five extra rounds Harry had given him. al-Fasi understood the strategy, but with no direct way to coordinate with him, no sight and only solid rounds, he had to be careful. Four men disappeared into the shadows beyond the plane. He lowered the rifle and decided to wait until they started loading.

Karev almost caught them before they reached the lot. For the first time, he noticed one wore handcuffs. He moved up another few yards, stopped, spread his legs, and lifted the Colt up at arms' length with both hands. The one without handcuffs had to go first. He fixed his right eye down the barrel. Then the headlights blinded him.

Shaw flipped on the high beams as she came through the pines. The Cavalier made a hard right on the access road, and the rear end skidded out, but she kept her control and speed. The car steadied again on the paved surface. Her headlights revealed Bryce and another man in front of the Cherokee. As she turned into the space next to them, the lights illuminated somebody else a few yards back toward the runway on the grass, up to his ankles in fog, his arms holding a pistol aimed at Bryce.

The man shifted to her direction and fired two shots toward her headlights. One round blasted through her windshield on the passenger side. She did not know where the other shot went, but she flinched and dropped her head below the dashboard, still holding the steering wheel. She pressed the accelerator to the floor. The Cavalier leaped over the concrete car stop. She heard the muffler tear off, but the car maintained its momentum. One more shot, and then the Cavalier struck him. He disappeared with a thud. The Cavalier stopped, the engine still running and the radiator hissing steam.

She groped for her seat belt, yanked it off and jerked open the door. A pair of hands touched her and helped her out. She pressed against Bryce's chest. For several minutes, they said nothing. Finally, she pulled away, leaned back against the car door and wiped a sleeve across her face.

"Did you see that guy?" she asked.

"I sure did. Just as you picked him out in your lights. I heard the shots, too."

"Where is he?"

Bryce pointed to the ground. "Under your left front tire."

"He was aiming at you."

"Well, thanks again, Barbara." He took her in his arms. "Why did you come back?" he whispered to her.

"I owed it to you." She gave a dry laugh. "Account paid, now?"

"Just one thing."

"Only one?"

"Well, two. You have that Walther from the beach?'

"In the glove compartment."

He took her by the shoulder and led her over to the Cherokee. "What's the other thing?" she said.

He handed her the ignition keys to the truck. "Take Tess back to Winchester," he said. "She knows you. I should never have come out here with her. Goddamn that Professor."

Shaw took the keys. Bryce embraced his daughter and told her to go with Miss Shaw, in the Cherokee, that he would see her back at her grandparents'.

"What are you planning to do?" Shaw asked him from the driver' seat as she inserted the key.

Bryce nodded at the hangar. "It's time to end all this crazy shit."

He waited until the Cherokee started for the airport exit. He pushed Gould down on the concrete stop and told him to wait. In the grass, the Cavalier idled, steam still blowing out with the headlights on. He checked to make sure the gunman under the front tire had not moved, then turned off the ignition. He reached into the glove compartment, found the Walther, and jogged across the runway.

One of the truck drivers raised the loading door of the panel truck, climbed inside and dropped down the ramp. He carried the first carton to the concrete floor.

Ingram and the other driver walked around the outside. They spotted a woman in the back, moving away from them and holding a rifle.

"Drop it," Ingram said. "You're covered."

Caldwell let the shotgun fall to the ground and turned around.

"You FBI, too?"

She didn't answer.

"Where's the other guy?" he asked. No answer. "Okay, we got two of you. We'll deal with any others out there."

They released the pilot from the vent pipe and told him to get the Caribou ready for immediate take-off. Ingram cuffed Caldwell's hands in front and led her back along the steel wall. He told the driver to start loading the plane. He kept Caldwell close by his side. In front of the hangar bay he turned her around, first toward the signal tower, then to the line of Piper Cubs. He held the barrel of the service revolver against Caldwell's temple.

From the cinder block shed, O'Shea saw one driver go back into the hangar. The pilot ran out and vanished into the Caribou. A man held a woman next to him. O'Shea muttered a curse. He watched the man wave a pistol in the air and look almost directly at him behind the shed. The other men started moving cartons up the cargo ramp.

He picked up the deer rifle and rubbed his right eye. He could only get off one shot, and Caldwell would be killed if he missed. He might disable the plane, but the truck was inside. They would still have the goods and Caldwell would be dead. Where was al-Fasi? He had to assume Saad was off the board. He edged between two Piper Cubs, staying out of the light. Then he saw another movement in the perimeter of the runway in front of the Caribou's nose. It disappeared in the shadows again, but he recognized something. The coat. It was Harry Bryce.

"Jesus H. Christ," he muttered. "First a bookkeeper. Now a lawyer."

He kept moving closer.

Pomona radioed the second call to the Coast Guard: another unidentified aircraft turning inland at low speed, transponder off. The Coast Guard Officer on Duty knew their response to the first call had found no wreckage offshore. He scrolled down the computer screen until he found the reference he wanted. He went out to the helipad, signaled to the crew, and boarded. The Vertol helicopter lifted off the pad and swung north this time, over the mainland.

O'Shea crouched under the wing of the last Piper Cub and looked across the open, dark space between himself and the hangar. Still no sign of al-Fasi. He could not risk a shot even from here at the man holding Caldwell, but he hoped al-Fasi could. Then Bryce reappeared, in front of the Caribou, aiming a pistol at the truck drivers. The drivers dropped the cartons and fell behind them. It looked to O'Shea as if Bryce and the truck drivers all let off shots that went wild. Bryce darted behind the other side of the hangar.

"Jesus Christ," he thought again and brought up the rifle to give Bryce some cover. He fired at the nearest truck driver, wounding him in the thigh. He ducked under the cargo ramp. The other ran inside the hangar. O'Shea got off another shot and hit the steel wall. He dashed across the open space toward the hangar. As he did, he heard helicopter engines over the Pine Barrens, and when he turned, he saw searchlights stabbing at the ground off in the distance. The man holding Caldwell looked that way, too. O'Shea kept going until he reached the corrugated steel wall.

At the sound of the shots, Ingram pulled Caldwell with him in the direction of the cargo ramp.

"Take off," he shouted up at the pilot. "You've got enough."

He motioned to the truck driver behind the ramp and waved at the other driver inside the hangar.

"Take the truck," he said. "Get the rest of it out of here." He pointed out across the airfield to the perimeter. "That way. Pick me up behind the hangar."

He threw Caldwell down and made it into the hangar but not before another shot tore through the flap of his jacket. The truck backed out as the Caribou jolted ahead toward the runway.

Bryce stepped around the steel wall and fired at the man who was running to get inside the hangar. He must have missed; the man did not stop. He saw Caldwell down on the landing surface, but starting to her feet. The hydraulic ramp started humming as it lifted to the Caribou's fuselage. The propellers turned over, moving the plane forward. He saw the truck backing out of the hangar and made a decision. He broke into a run and leaped on the rising metal ramp. It closed behind him while he scrambled forward on his hands and knees to the cockpit.

"Cut the engines," he yelled through the racket.

The Vertol blew across the Caribou's nose with a roar, its searchlights flooding the area and its rotors churning up the few patches of snow that remained. It settled on the tarmac, the blades still moving. The Caribou's propellers shuttered down.

O'Shea stepped from behind the hangar wall just as the truck pulled out, shifted gears and turned down the opposite wall before he could get off another shot. The Caribou was moving forward to taxi as the cargo ramp rose under the roar of the helicopters. He aimed his rifle at one of the landing tires, but Bryce shot across from the other side in front of him and grabbed onto the ramp. O'Shea ran that way, too, and then the Vertol dropped down and the Caribou stopped. He pivoted to get a shot at the truck, but it turned behind the back hangar wall.

Caldwell pointed to the hangar and yelled. "He went in there."

O'Shea laid the rifle down on the tarmac and took out his service pistol. He heard no sound inside but his own footsteps. The passenger door of the empty Cadillac stood open. He saw the double-hinged door on the back wall standing ajar. He moved to it and saw the truck across the field pull through the break in the perimeter fence and turn onto a local road. He looked more carefully over the ground fog. A man ran across the same field toward the fence break. O'Shea started out, got to the fence and stopped, looking into the pine barrens across the road. He saw movement in the trees, the back of a large man who was holding a parcel in his left hand and a cell phone in his right, against his ear. O'Shea crossed the road and just inside the tree line aimed his pistol at the large man.

"Drop it," he said.

The man froze and held out his arms.

"Drop both of them." The parcel and the phone fell down on the dark pine roots. The man turned around.

"You're not FBI, are you," he said. It was not a question.

"Not in this fucking mess."

"So, you're not arresting me." O'Shea said nothing. "And you know what that is, don't you?" He gestured down at the parcel. O'Shea still said nothing. "Then you know they won't let you take it."

The man reached behind his back and leaped toward one of the trees. O'Shea fired three rounds. The man stumbled deeper into the woods and dropped. O'Shea walked to the body, picked up the pistol and threw it into a dark pool of water.

"That's for Harry and his father," he muttered. He took the parcel and cell phone and jogged back to the hub of sound and light in front of the hangar.

Bryce clambered out of the Caribou behind the pilot. Two armed Coast Guardsmen ordered them to place their hands over their heads. Bryce surrendered the Walther and started to identify himself, but they told him to keep quiet. The Commander approached with Caldwell.

"Who and what are you?" he asked.

"I don't expect you to believe this," Bryce said. "I'm a Federal prosecutor."

"Sure you are. Any ID?"

"Not on me."

"Anybody else?"

"Me." O'Shea walked into the lighted area. The Guardsmen swung their weapons around. He held up his hands with the diplomatic package in one and his service revolver in the other. He kicked his gun along the tarmac toward them. "It's all right," he said. "I've got this."

He took his FBI badge from his pocket and handed it over to the Commander who examined the photograph, gave it back, and pointed suspiciously at the envelope.

"Evidence," O'Shea said. "Those two are good guys." He indicated Bryce, still with his hands on his head, and Caldwell.

"And them?" The Commander gestured at the pilot and the injured truck driver. "Plus we've got someone wounded."

"Bad guys. Maybe illegals," O'Shea said. "You said something about wounded?"

"Another guy shot, but lucky he was wearing Kevlar. Just a patch up."

They walked out into the dark together, down into the dip in the grass and found al-Fasi back on his feet with the assistance of a Guardsman.

"Yeah. That's my partner," O'Shea said. "Show them your ID, Saad. Come with us if you can walk. We'll talk about what happened later."

"I need to contact your superior," the Commander said. "Confirm this is an FBI matter."

"Can you call Washington from in there?" O'Shea pointed into the Vertol. The Commander confirmed he could. O'Shea gave him Kauffman's number. In a few minutes, the Commander came back out.

"Okay," he said. "Your boss will fax a written confirmation to the base."

"Hoped you guys would get here sooner," O'Shea told the Commander. "But glad you made it."

"We monitored the call from Pomona. Two of them actually," the Commander told him. "We thought the first was a crash at sea, but didn't find any wreckage."

"That was me." O'Shea pointed back at the FBI Cessna and explained he had flown in from Baltimore to intercept the transfer.

"I figured that now. So, what's it all about?" the Commander asked.

"National security. Trying to smuggle out some high-tech Pentagon stuff. Most of it should be in the plane, I hope. I'll need to use your radio to alert the local police to nab the truck that took off as you got here. It might have some stuff, too. Definitely a couple more bad guys."

They glanced over at Bryce and Caldwell. "And who are they?" the Commander said.

"Innocents. A prosecutor and his witness who dropped into the middle of this by mistake. My boss's fault, Commander. Did he tell you that? Both dumb. Both innocent. No business either of them being here."

Two more Guardsmen approached escorting a man in handcuffs, a woman and a small girl. One of the Guardsmen reported they found a body out near the parking lot.

"Probably another illegal," O'Shea said.

"And these people?"

"More witnesses. We have to get them all back to Washington. I'll take the guy in the cuffs."

"Then they better get going. Local police will be here any minute. You'll have to stay. Take care of all the official business and cover my ass."

They walked over to the Caribou where Bryce and Caldwell joined Tess, Shaw and Gould. O'Shea took Gould by the arm and handed the parcel to Bryce.

"That's for the Professor," he said.

"What is it?"

"The Professor will know. He'll tell you what he wants about it. Don't ask me any questions, counselor." O'Shea looked down at Tess, clinging to her father's knee.

Bryce stroked her and brought her up into his arms. "You took care of him, Pete?"

"Get out of here, Harry. Saad, you okay to drive?"

al-Fasi said he was.

"Then you take off, too. Use the Cherokee. See if you can track down that truck. I think it'll stay on local roads."

O'Shea and the Commander watched them walk to the parking lot. "I'll stay here with you guys as long as it takes," O'Shea said. "Let me use that radio of yours, again. Got to check in with my boss."

Bryce belted his daughter into the rear seat. Caldwell got into the passenger side and Shaw sat beside Tess. He took the files and the brief case out of the Cherokee and dropped them in the trunk along with the envelope from O'Shea. They headed out the access road and onto the two-lane road through the pines. Police car sirens wailed behind them then faded.

"I watched you and Tess leave. How did you end up back here?" he asked Shaw.

"I saw the helicopters and decided to stay."

"Are you coming to Washington or do you want to be dropped off somewhere? Atlantic City?"

She said nothing for a while, staring out into the passing woods.

"Barbara?" Bryce asked again.

"I heard you, Harry. I've been thinking. Drop me off at Atlantic City. Thanks."

CHAPTER SIXTEEN

It was nearly five in the morning when the Interceptor pulled up to the house in Georgetown. Leah Kauffman escorted them into the study wearing her bed robe. In one arm, Bryce carried his sleepy daughter who lay quietly against his chest, and in the other, the briefcase filled with Caldwell's documents along with his own papers. The Professor rose to greet them, still in his three-piece suit from the evening before.

"Ms. Caldwell and I have met," he said. "And this is your daughter, Harry?"

Bryce placed Tess on the leather sofa by a wall filled floor to ceiling with cherry wood bookshelves. Caldwell hesitated and then took a seat on the sofa next to Tess. Bryce sat on the stiff antique chair in front of the Professor's desk. He set the brief case on the desktop, opened it and removed the files and a cell phone, and set the closed case down on the floor by his knee. He pointed to the cell.

"That's from Savage River," he said. "You'll probably find some useful numbers in there. A call came in but I don't know who from. So, it's all yours now."

Kauffman scanned the papers quickly. "Thank you, Harry. It took you a while to get here. Where is Barbara Shaw?"

"You promised me she was clear."

"She will be."

"Well, she asked to be dropped off at the Atlantic City airport and it took a while to be sure she was rebooked on a new flight."

"Where is she going?"

"Her flight was to Miami. She had plans before all this to go to the Caymans, but I don't know if that is still her intent." It was not exactly true. It had taken Shaw extra time to book the connecting flight from Miami and Bryce knew that.

"What about that company executive?"

"Tom Gould," Caldwell interrupted.

"Pete's got him," Bryce said. "The other agent you sent down there is with him, too, cleaning things up."

Kauffman took off his half-rim glasses, rubbed his eyes. He looked at Bryce again. "What else do you have to report, Harry?"

"The Coast Guard has custody of the pilot, along with the goods in the hangar and the plane, but the truck got away. There was a dead man—one of the ones sent to kill us—under Barbara's car, and another guy that a fishing boat might find out in Delaware Bay in a few days. Your body count is getting pretty high, Professor."

Kauffman handed across a folded section of the Washington Post. "There's another casualty."

Bryce read the headline and scanned down a couple of paragraphs. A local attorney, Gideon Aubrey, died in an automobile accident on the Beltway. The police ruled he was under the influence. It quoted a spokesperson for the Herrick firm saying Aubrey had recently resigned. The story almost made him angry. Another target he could not prosecute. He handed the paper back.

"You know his involvement in this, don't you? Murdered, you think?"

"I don't know, of course. Suspicious, yes."

"But Barbara is clear," Bryce said. "Aubrey's the only one she could really implicate or could implicate her."

Kauffman put his glasses back on and turned to Caldwell. "Your daughter is expecting you. When I confirmed you were on your way with Harry, I made flight arrangements for you to San Francisco. If you are ready, I'll ask my wife to call a taxi."

She rose from the sofa. "Yes, please. I appreciate you doing this."

Kauffman went around the desk and pulled open the pocket doors. Leah was on the other side, waiting with the portable phone in her hand. "Taxi for the airport," he told her. She made the call and then asked Tess if she could get her anything.

"Ice cream?" Tess said.

"How about some strawberries with that?"

"Oh, yes."

Bryce walked over to Caldwell and offered her his hand. "I'm sorry about this. Thank you for everything," he said. "Take care of yourself. And your daughter."

"Will you be talking to me again?" she asked.

"I hope I don't need to."

"Me, too." She said goodbye to Tess, and left the room with Leah. Kauffman pulled the doors shut behind them and motioned Bryce back to the chair, but Bryce ignored him and sat next to his daughter with his arm over her.

"We have a bit more business," Kauffman said. He returned to his desk, pulled open a drawer, removed some papers and began sorting through them.

Leah returned with a bowl of ice cream and placed it on the coffee table in front of Tess.

"Harry," Kauffman said, "here are some other documents you need to see."

"Why? The case is closed. And I'm resigning, anyway. You must have figured that."

"I will not accept your resignation until you draft the closing memo."

Bryce looked at his daughter who was concentrating on her ice cream. He went back to the antique chair. "You have the floor. Shoot."

Kauffman pointed first at the papers he took from the drawer. "Saad al-Fasi, that agent you spoke of with Peter, found these."

"Where?"

"Mr. Gould's apartment in Pittsburgh and a trash bin in Virginia. I assume you know about Miltech."

"I do now, no thanks to you."

"Well, with these, and what Caldwell produced," he indicated the pile from Bryce's brief case, "and Mr. Gould's testimony, of course, and," he held up the diplomatic pouch, "that stuff Peter gave you, there should be a case."

"What case? Against whom? The principals are all gone. Caldwell says the corporations are just shells. No assets."

"That's not the case I mean."

Bryce shifted uncomfortably in the hard chair seat and felt the vellum document in his jacket pocket. He took it out. "I forgot about this. Pete gave it to me at the airport."

The Professor unfolded the stiff, translucent calfskin and laid it out on the desk.

Bryce saw for the first time that it was printed in Cyrillic script. "You can read that?" he asked.

"Yes. Did Peter say where he got it?"

"From Gould."

"This looks like the last piece in the puzzle," the Professor said. "It's a security instrument of an entity known informally as the Trust and traded in something called a 'dark pool' so there is no record of who buys, sells or owns it. Essentially, it is a bearer bond."

"What was Tom Gould doing with that?"

"He must have some unusual contacts." Kauffman pushed it aside and put his finger on another document in the pile from his desk drawer. "Then, there is this."

Bryce picked it up and scanned it. "Pickering Thayer," he whispered. "Where's this from?"

"Miltech internal communication."

"Who is this Milos Vrenc?" Bryce pointed to a name on the memo.

"Publicly, a prominent antique oriental carpet dealer in Manhattan. Privately, an investment banker."

"One of Gould's contacts?"

"Probably."

"And you knew about him, before assigning me this case?"

The Professor broke off eye contact for a moment. "Yes."

"And the diplomatic envelope from O'Shea?" Bryce asked.

"That should trace the money," Kauffman said. "Let's take a look." It was in Latin script.

"Mozambique," Bryce said. "Caldwell produced a travel document to there."

"So, you begin to see," Kauffman started, but Bryce stopped him.

"No, I don't see. I never knew what the target of this investigation really was. Why didn't you tell me? What did you keep back? What did my father have to do with it?"

Kauffman tilted back and looked up at the ceiling. "A few years ago, long after we all left the Department and I was teaching at Penn, the Administration asked me to review some closed case files as a consultant."

"What kind of cases?"

"Defense contract fraud, they said. I examined them, and

suspected there was something else lurking behind the surface. I contacted your father and Harlan for their input, even though that was technically wrong."

"Illegal, you mean."

"Well, let that go for now. We started meeting several times a year at my townhouse in Philadelphia. None of us wanted any direct contact with Washington. I had the files."

"And you thought you detected this Trust?"

"Yes."

"And something inside Justice."

Kauffman put his glasses back on and leaned over the desk. "We tried to keep everything off-record as far as the Department was concerned. Your father and Harlan filed a couple of court petitions in their own names. I took a sabbatical from the University and accepted an offer to return to Washington. I brought in Peter O'Shea from the FBI. I had him set up computers in his home, still keeping it out of the Department. Then, about a year later, Peter detected the worm, or virus, whatever he calls it, in the Department's computer system. Some if it sneaked into Peter's system, too. Official attempts to block it were not successful. It kept mutating. So, we, your father, Harlan and I, broke off contact."

"Worm," Bryce said. "From the Caucasus, right? So, the Tuscarora complaint came in and you thought it might lead you to the Trust."

"Yes."

"But you did not tell me."

"Security. You might have entered reports in the computer system that would expose the real nature of the investigation. Durham must have figured something out when you told him about this case. I thought having you followed would be enough. It never occurred to me he might be at risk, too."

"It wasn't just me. My father, my daughter, my friend." Bryce went to sit by his daughter on the sofa. More questions, he thought, but not ones to ask now. Maybe never.

The telephone rang.

"Barbara. Where are you?" the Professor said. "I'll ask him."

Kauffman looked at up Bryce. "It's Barbara Shaw. She wants you to pick her up at 30th Street Station in Philadelphia on your way home."

Bryce nodded, and Kauffman returned to the receiver. "Okay. He will. And I'd like to talk with you in a couple of days." He listened some more and turned back to Bryce. "Can she stay with you? I'd rather see her in Philadelphia first than in Washington."

Before Bryce could agree, Kauffman told her it was arranged and hung up. He started to gather the documents off the desk. He folded two into his jacket, rose, came around, and put the rest into Bryce's brief case.

"Now we have a meeting to go to. You and I," he said.

"Meeting? Where?"

"Main Justice."

"It's barely six."

"I know." He called his wife. Leah came in and they exchanged looks. She went to Tess.

"Would you like a tour of the house, dear?" she said. She picked up the half-finished ice cream bowl. "Let me show you the kitchen first."

"She'll be fine with Leah," Kauffman said to Bryce, and to his wife, "We won't be long."

Tess looked at her father, and he told her to go ahead. She followed the older woman through the doors. The men went out to the street. Kauffman told Bryce to put the brief case in the Interceptor's trunk and drove.

They walked down the marble half-lit corridor. The corner office at the end was the only one showing any light. They entered and closed the door behind them. Pickering Thayer did not look surprised. He invited them to take seats without rising from his chair. He picked up his pen and began marking on a legal pad, a maze of intersecting triangles without words or numbers.

"This is awfully early for a meeting, Winston," he said. "What's up?"

"The Tuscarora matter, Pick," Kauffman said.

"Oh, yes. And this is Harry Bryce? The lead counsel?" Bryce nodded. "So, you have something new?"

"I believe you already heard of the latest development. But this is not about that. It is about your resignation."

Thayer looked up from his pad, smiled, and put down his pen.

Kauffman waited, and then added, "We now have evidence implicating you. Through the Trust."

"The Trust?"

"We can document it. Here's one sample." Kauffman handed across two folded papers from his jacket. Thayer examined the documents briefly and handed them back.

"That's all?"

"There's more. In a safe place. As I think you know, the delivery was aborted last night. Harry was there. There is a witness in custody who can authenticate these." Kauffman put them in his jacket.

Thayer darted a glance at Bryce, then returned to Kauffman. "What are you talking about, Winston? Mail fraud? Wire fraud? That's not enough to win at trial."

"It's enough for an indictment, and that's all we'll need. You can't go to trial. The Trust won't let you."

Thayer swiveled in his chair and looked absentmindedly out the window.

"I drafted a resignation letter for you last night. Here." Kauffman removed a piece of legal paper, yellow and lined, from his jacket. Thayer took it.

"Your handwriting is hard to read. But I get the gist. Thank you, at least, for not entering this draft in the system." He put it down. "And what happens with the case files? The originals. All that stuff you say is in a safe place?"

"Harry will write the closing memo."

Thayer turned slowly around and stared at the Mall through the wrought iron bars framing the flood lit Capitol Dome.

"I will sign off on it. You have my word," Kauffman said. They waited, looking at the back of Thayer's head.

Kauffman added, "Then it all gets sealed up and sent to the vault in Quantico."

Neither Bryce nor the Professor spoke until they entered the townhouse and stood together in the foyer. Bryce dropped the brief case on the oak floor. The Professor told him he could take Leah's

Audi home with his daughter and reminded him to pick up Barbara Shaw on the way.

"I'll get my wife a rental car until you return to Washington. Take a month off. See to your family. The funeral. Then come back and draft that closing memo."

"You better tell me something about the Trust, then," Bryce said.

"Leave that out of it."

"I will, but tell me anyway."

"It is an entity created in Russia in the late 18th Century to compete with the British East India Company. Old Silk Road. Tea, spice, Persian carpets."

"That guy in Manhattan…?"

"Yes. And illegal trade, too. Slaves, opium. Somehow it survived all the revolutions and wars. No tangible assets that the Tsars or the Communists could confiscate. Then, when the Soviet Union broke up, it found new opportunities."

"Strategic arms."

"Yes."

"And what about you, Professor? What about you, my father and Harlan Moan? Not to mention Pete O'Shea and that other agent down there? I could draft indictments on all of you—start with conspiracy and work my way down through how many federal statutes you've violated. What in God's name did you think you were doing? And why, if you were doing all this crap, did you get me into the middle of it without some inkling of what the case really involved? All those lives lost."

"I said I am sorry. My thought at the time was that it was better for your father to tell you first. I can only ask you to accept that."

"And what about Thayer? You just let him off."

"Another jurisdiction has venue over him, Harry."

Tess came into the foyer pulling Leah Kauffman behind her. Bryce picked her up and gave her a kiss. He waited until Mrs. Kauffman retreated back into the house.

"Who actually asked you to review those closed case files? Was someone in Justice?" The Professor did not answer. "What did my father really know? Or Mr. Moan? How much does O'Shea know?"

A discrete silence lapsed without response. Bryce kicked the brief case across the floor away from himself and his daughter. "All right. I'll write the closing memo. Then I'm gone, taking over my father's law practice. I'll leave it to you to clean up the rest of this mess."

Kauffman picked up the brief case. "Have a safe drive, Harry," he said. "Now, I've got other business to attend to."

The Ossete pressed the button on the keyboard, and visualized the petrodollars flying up into the ether in binary code and then down the other leg of the triangle to Peshawar. The screen went dark, and he shut off the power. There was nothing more to do.

He walked out into the courtyard and up the stone steps inside the walls of the Portuguese fort. At the top, he laid his hand on one of the antique iron cannons pointing west, inland, toward the native settlements, the setting sun and the reddening sky. He stared at his private helicopter under a column of greasy smoke, just outside the stone walls, holed by a single 20-millimeter cannon round. The local warlord must have just gotten another paymaster.

He looked past the wreck to the steaming huts and listened to the falsetto cries rising above the crack of rifle fire and the throb of drums. The sky was darkening, and they would come after last light. He was alone.

Earlier in the day, the mercenaries left without explanation, but he did not need one. They saw the cross, too. He dismissed the young Egyptian computer genius and transmitted the algorithms he created to Peshawar, but he sent the funds themselves to his clan in Baku and confirmed they were secure. There was nothing of importance left in the old fort, only himself, the only tangible target the enemy could reach now.

He walked back down into the courtyard and squatted beside the trickling fountain beneath the fig trees. Outside the walls, the din grew louder. The electric lights along the walls flickered, and then all power vanished.

He listened to the mob banging against the heavy wooden fortress door. The banging stopped. He took a deep breath. Honor. And family. The only assets he would leave behind. He recited aloud what he could remember of the Psalm, waiting for the explosion. It came, and fragments of the door burst in, seeming to float, musically, around him. He breathed deeply, slowly, and drew up memories of the distant snow-capped mountains he knew from childhood.

They poured through the opening blasted into the wall, all eyes, hands and teeth, a single bellowing monster. He kept his own eyes closed.

The voices screamed louder, driving off all sensation but the skull-splitting sound itself. In a final spasm, a hundred hands tore away the pieces of his body and flung them over the fig trees, allowing the still-warm blood to rain down into the fountain. Then the mob grew silent.

They spoke little on the drive into Center City Philadelphia. Shaw had the address, but Bryce knew where it was and found a parking space in front of the Kauffman's brownstone on Spruce Street. Shaw gave a conspiratorial wink to Tess and stepped out. Bryce got out, too. They embraced on the sidewalk, shared a proper kiss and held hands for a final few seconds.

"Do you really want to go in there?" Bryce asked her.

"He holds all the cards, Harry." She broke away, walked up the marble steps and pressed the bell.

Leah Kauffman led her through the foyer over a blue Ishafan carpet and then out into the glass-walled addition in the back. Winston Churchill Kauffman, the Professor, replaced his telephone receiver on its rotary cradle and waved her in. He sat on one of the four canvas deck chairs. An easel next to him held an unfinished painting of a square-rigged frigate. On the other side a crystal decanter on a silver tray sat on a chipped escritoire. The Professor offered Shaw some brandy. She accepted, and he filled a silver sneaker for her. He motioned to a chair between Peter O'Shea and Saad al-Fasi. They acknowledged each other without speaking.

She looked out through the glass walls and ceiling. There was little to see—a cloud-covered sky, the backs of houses on the next street, and over their walls the cables of a suspension bridge. She sat down and took a sip.

"I am so glad you agreed to meet with us, Barbara," Kauffman said. "You know Peter and you met Saad the other day. We all are pleased that you agreed to remain in the Division."

"Little choice in the matter, Professor." She scanned the room "Nice place," she said. "And what is it?"

"A solarium. I had it built when I started painting." He gestured at the frigate.

"That's not what I meant. I meant this. The three of you."

"I'll cover that later. Right now, we have some business to discuss. Peter?"

O'Shea went over to the escritoire for a refill and returned to his chair. He had no notes.

"The plant in Corinth, Mississippi, is still in operation," he said.

"No change in ownership? Nothing like that?"

"Nothing in the public record."

"What about the truck at the airport?"

"Disappeared. The local and state police found nothing."

"So, they must have other resources down there. What else?"

"Aubrey and Thayer, of course."

Shaw interrupted. "Just a minute. Gideon Aubrey? What about him."

Kauffman answered. "Give her the news about Mr. Aubrey, Peter."

"Fatal accident on the Beltway a few days ago. Ruled DUI. So, the only live witness left is Mr. Gould. I assume everybody saw the media reports about Thayer."

"Thayer?" Shaw said. "I heard he committed suicide."

"So it was reported," Kauffman said. "He submitted his resignation two days ago. Gould is in protective custody for the time being. He is now the only live witness, but he is of no value after Harry submits his closing memorandum."

She took another long sip of the brandy. "Closing memo," she said. It was not a question. She was not surprised to hear it, and no one in the room offered a response.

O'Shea passed over to Kauffman a folded Arts Section of the New York Times. "Another thing—Milos Vrenc closed his store in Manhattan. He's quoted as claiming that he is relocating to Pakistan to operate a Persian carpet factory."

Kauffman dropped the paper on the floor. "I saw that."

Shaw spoke up again. "The last time I saw Aubrey, in Ingram's office, he said Ingram was talking to an angel, an investment banker, in New York. Is Vrenc that guy?"

"The money man, yes," Kauffman said.

"Does all this mean I'm free?" Shaw finally asked.

"It means you're free of prosecution," Kauffman said, "but no, not free. You did violate quite a few criminal statutes. So have Peter, Saad and myself, but all in a higher cause."

"And that cause is?"

"Law enforcement. Of course."

"So, you can always get me." Shaw sipped her brandy again and smiled. "But then, I can..."

"Yes," Kauffman said. "That is why we can trust each other." He turned to O'Shea and al-Fasi. "So, back to those new computers. They should be secure from that worm for a few months at least. Did you confirm where that last mutation came from, Peter?"

"Mozambique, like you thought. They tried to make it look like Manhattan."

"Worm?" Shaw asked.

"Sorry. It will take a bit of time to bring you up to date," Kauffman said. "Something or somebody penetrated the Justice Department computers and even threatened ours. Peter tried to block it, but it constantly mutates and gets back in. We've had to stay out of the system. Even now, I'll have to edit Harry's closing memo very carefully. At least the Ossete is gone now. Killed in a riot this morning, our time, in East Africa, or so it was reported."

"And who or what is the 'Ossete'?" Shaw said.

"He created the worm, or caused it to be created," al-Fasi said. "There was no choice but to take him out."

"However, he managed to save their money," O'Shea said. "I did scan that."

"It will take them some time to find a successor," Kauffman added.

"Anybody higher up know of our role in all of this?" O'Shea gestured at al-Fassi.

"My role, and in those old petitions, Durham Bryce and Harlan

Moan. They may speculate about Harry's involvement, but you are all out of the official records on this one." Kauffman turned toward Shaw. "When you get back to Washington, Barbara, I want you to go through that case file before we bury it in Quantico. Make note of all the contractors and subcontractors."

"Harry?" she said. "He might still be in danger? You have to warn him, then."

"I will," the Professor said. "Warn him."

"And warn him about what? What are you guys dealing with?"

Kauffman finished his brandy, stood up, and took the silver sneaker from Barbara's hand. "Our business here is concluded."

While they moved through the house to the front door, Shaw said, "You're the ones with that telescope across from my apartment, aren't you."

He escorted the three of them to the front door. He took Shaw by her arm as she stood on the marble step.

"They will drive you back to Washington," he said. "They will answer your questions in the car."

"What about my account in the Caymans?" she asked. "And my father?"

"Case closed, Barbara. Case closed."

After they crossed the bridge and were in New Jersey, Harry told his daughter about his plans to move to Winchester.

"So, I'll be able to see you every week-end," he said.

"When, Daddy?"

"In a few weeks. I have to go to Washington and clean up a few things down there."

"Will you and Mommy get back together, then?"

"I don't know, Honey."

"I miss you, Daddy."

"I miss you too."

After a few minutes, she asked, "Are you going to marry Barbara instead, Daddy?"

He laughed. "We're a long way from that."

"But you hugged and kissed her back there."

"I do that with you and your grandmother and your aunt."

"Well, she's a nice lady."

"Yes, she is."

They made a few turns and settled on the State highway north toward his old home and his ex-wife, Maureen.

"How about you tell me a story, Daddy?" Tess asked after a while.

"Okay, Honey. Which one this time?"

"Pirates. The pirate story."

"Pirates," Harry said. "Well, once upon a time, a long, long, long time ago, Lady Tess and her Daddy were walking on the beach after dinner. And it was cold and dark and windy. And out on the ocean, they saw a big sailing ship. And then, when they looked down the beach, they saw a bunch of pirates rowing a boat out of the waves onto the beach. They watched the pirates get out of the boat and start digging a big hole in the sand."

"For treasure," Tess said.

"Yes, for treasure."

"Just like this Christmas," she said.

"Well, this was a long, long, long time ago."

EPILOGUE

One Month Later

Bryce parked as he was directed in the courtyard inside Main Justice. He cleared security and went up to Professor Kauffman's office. Mrs. Williams led him in and closed the door. He dropped three pages on the desk.

"The closing memo," Bryce said. "And my letter of resignation."

The Professor left them undisturbed. "How was the funeral?" he asked.

"I thought you might be there."

"It seemed best not to go." He picked up Bryce's documents and scanned them quickly.

"How about Mr. Moan's services?" Bryce asked. "Did you go to that?"

"They didn't have one." The Professor put the papers down. "You kept it very brief. That's good. I'll have Barbara Shaw review it for accuracy. Check the corporate documents. I might add a few details."

"You noticed I recommended leaving the civil side open, in case there are damages?"

"I saw that."

"You agree?"

"I have to think about it."

"And I left out Thayer and Milos Vrenc and the Trust."

Bryce waited but when he got no response he got up to leave. The Professor motioned him back. "You said you were taking over your father's practice," he said. "How is that going?"

"I sent out letters to all his clients. I went through the files quickly to see if anything needed my immediate attention. Nothing urgent. His secretary agreed to stay on for a while."

They looked at each other until Bryce broke the silence. "I haven't gone into his vault yet, if that's what you're asking. You know my father's offices, in that old bank building?"

"The walk-in vault. I am familiar with it, yes. Very secure."

"I haven't gone in there," Bryce repeated.

The Professor said, "Keep the files intact, Harry. The vault's a good place for them."

Another brief silence separated them. Bryce asked, "Is Barbara okay? All that cleared up and everything?"

"Yes. Will you be going over to your old office? You'll need to clear out your desk anyway. She should be over there."

"What about her father?"

"Taken care of."

"And the others? Ms. Caldwell, Tom Gould?"

"They're all in witness protection for the time being."

"And after the case is closed?"

The Professor said nothing. Bryce got up to leave again. Kauffman let him stand this time, but asked, "Did you see that piece in the news about the drone missile in the Caucasus?"

"No," Bryce said. "I haven't been following the news. Been busy with other things." It was a lie. He had read about it, but he did not want to learn more, at least until the closing memo was officially approved.

The Professor came around his desk to see Bryce out. "It failed after launch and dropped in the Caspian Sea."

"And?"

"Some of those guidance devices got delivered."

"The ones from that truck that left the airport at the Cold Spring? Pete O'Shea said he would alert the State police about it."

"It disappeared. However, we learned that Dennis Fancher, from Corinth, Mississippi, the former Air Force engineer, arranged for the shipment to be nothing but off-line defects. I never thought of that. But thank God for him."

"They were all rejects?"

"Yes."

"How do you know the missile had one of those devices?"

The Professor smiled.

"So this was all about nothing, wasn't it? My father, my friend Jack. All the others." Bryce placed his hand on the doorknob. "What about the Trust," he asked. "Thayer? Is all that still around?"

The Professor moved Bryce aside and opened the door. They walked into the hallway. "Forget it. Go clear out your desk and say hello to Ms. Shaw for me."

Bryce rode down the elevator and paused on the ground level.

He expected to leave Washington as soon as he turned the memo over to the Professor. His desk, Barbara, all that could wait until his resignation was official and the case was closed—well, couldn't it? He took a moment to decide, then left his car in the Courtyard and walked outside across Pennsylvania Avenue.

THE END

Scott Griffith retired from a career as a Senior Trial Attorney, Antitrust Division, U.S. Dept. of Justice in the Philadelphia Field Office and lives in Cape May, NJ.

Made in the USA
Middletown, DE
19 March 2022

62620756R00135